WITH LOVE FROM THE PAST

ALSO BY LAUREN SMYTH

LAUREN SMYTH

WITH LOVE FROM THE PAST

A NOVEL

AMBASSADOR INTERNATIONAL
GREENVILLE, SOUTH CAROLINA & BELFAST, NORTHERN IRELAND

www.ambassador-international.com

WITH LOVE FROM THE PAST

©2022 by Lauren Smyth

ISBN: 978-1-64960-137-7
eISBN: 978-1-64960-187-2
Library of Congress Control Number: 2022930543

Cover Design by Hannah Linder Designs
Interior Typesetting by Dentelle Design
Edited by Megan Gerig

AMBASSADOR INTERNATIONAL
Emerald House
411 University Ridge, Suite B14
Greenville, SC 29601, USA
www.ambassador-international.com

AMBASSADOR BOOKS
The Mount
2 Woodstock Link
Belfast, BT6 8DD, Northern Ireland, UK
www.ambassadormedia.co.uk

The colophon is a trademark of Ambassador, a Christian publishing company.

To Mom and Dad, who helped me overcome the injury that inspired this book, and to my physical therapist, who motivated me to turn a tough situation into a story to inspire others.

I want to be in control of everyone so I can know how you felt. I want to be the author of your story.

Writing was my favorite—my only—pastime. I wrote on the walls and on the floor because nobody would give me a sheet of paper. That's when I first started thinking about writing for *you*.

Ari sat up and rubbed her eyes, dazed from sleep. What was that noise?

The high-pitched ringing made her ears ache. She rolled out of bed and onto the floor, crawling slowly toward the source of the sound. Since when had her apartment gotten so dark?

Her hands scraped across the carpet, and the crumbs stung her palms. Maybe getting up wasn't worth it after all, not if it meant leaving the warm solitude of her bed for the dingy nightmare that was her apartment. And the sound—it was just her phone, after all. It was plugged in on the kitchen counter, and she couldn't remember the last time she'd touched it. Why was it ringing now?

She pulled it out from under a pile of trash, dragged herself back to the bed, and pulled the blanket up over her face.

"Hello?" she murmured.

"Hello!" A playful voice screeched so loudly that it disintegrated into static. "It's Lia!"

"Why are you calling so early in the morning?"

"You haven't forgotten, have you?"

Ari clenched her fists around the blanket. *The wedding.* "No, I haven't. Of course not."

"Aww, I knew you wouldn't. You'd never do something like that." Lia laughed. "You're such a tease. Can I throw you the flowers? I really want you to have them. They would look so pretty in your apartment."

"I don't want you to waste the bouquet." Ari let her phone slip through her fingers to the floor. She could hear Lia's voice faintly: "Hello? Hello? Ari, are you okay? Are you there?" She reached down and hung up. *Bad service. That's a good enough excuse.*

She peeled away the covers and swung her legs off the side of the bed. The air in her apartment was stale and chilly, like an icy blanket against her skin. She pulled a brush through her hair, avoiding her own eyes in the mirror, then dug through the wad of wrinkled clothes in the corner of her bathroom floor and pulled on a sweatshirt.

She went to the kitchen and opened all the cabinets one by one. Empty. She tried the fridge next. It was empty, too, and it reeked of stale cheese. Ari slammed the door shut before the smell could leak into the room.

A sense of unrealism hit her. The clothes piled on the floor, the food wrappers scattered on the table, the unwashed dishes piled on the sink. The musty scent of the carpet, the thick coating of dust everywhere, the mold thriving near the trash can. She slid down to the floor with her back against the fridge, pressing her freezing hands to her hot cheeks, wondering if she was awake or if this was all just a horrible dream.

This is what you've been doing this whole time.

Did you think it would all just go away after you forgot?

CHAPTER 2

The grocery store had always been the bane of Ari's existence. It was her only unavoidable chore, and it meant going out into the world and facing strangers—strangers who could see the reflection of her dirty apartment in her eyes. They could read her pale skin and know she hadn't been outside in weeks. They couldn't hide the sneering flicker of judgment on their faces before they looked away, too preoccupied to spare her a kind thought.

From the moment she left her apartment, she kept her gaze fixed firmly to the ground. The street noises faded away into a dismal hum at the back of her mind, and it was easy to drown them behind the whispering voices in her head.

As she reached the grocery store, she felt a wet drop on her shoulder, then another and another. The drizzle soon turned into tiny pellets of hail which clicked loudly against the roof. Ari avoided the windows, filling her basket with groceries, trying not to stray too far from the aisle with the fewest people. In one of the freezer doors, she accidentally caught a glimpse of her reflection. Stained sweatshirt, several sizes too big because it was the only one she had left. Messy hair bunched up on one side. Dazed eyes that were barely visible in the glass, sunk like holes into her face.

You're disgusting.

She wanted to escape the endless rows of glass freezers, but she couldn't walk home in a hailstorm. So she slipped into the checkout line and paid for her groceries. Her wallet was almost empty. It reminded her that her rent payments were on auto-deposit, and she didn't know if there was anything left in her bank account to withdraw. Well, there was nothing she could do about it. Maybe she would become homeless. Maybe she would just have to get used to being outside in bad weather.

She plopped down on a wheelchair, surrounded by brown paper bags, and let her head fall back and her eyes drift shut.

"Jules?"

Ari jumped to her feet so quickly that the bag on her lap slipped and sent cans rolling across the floor.

"G-Grey!" she stammered, scrambling to clean up the mess. "What are you doing here? Where's Lia?"

"I think she's getting ready for the ceremony." Grey shot her a friendly smile and picked up a stray can that had stopped against his shoe. "I'm supposed to pick up some snacks, but I saw you here and figured you could use an umbrella. Want me to help you get these bags home?"

Can I say I've been sick? Out partying? How do I explain why I look like this?

Grey bent down and picked up the rest of the cans. "You coming?"

Ari hesitated. But since he had her groceries hostage, she couldn't refuse.

They walked along in silence for almost a block, their conversation drowned out by the hail pattering on the umbrella, the chatter of people around them, and the traffic noise. Ari was glad Grey couldn't ask any questions. She avoided looking at him, stifling her curiosity to see what he looked like. It'd been so long.

They turned down a side street, and the noise around them faded to a gentle hum.

"How are you doing?" Grey asked. "Have you heard from any of your friends? Found a new job?"

Ari shook her head, and a few drops of melted ice fell onto her face from her hair. "I don't keep in contact with anyone," she answered.

Grey cleared his throat. "Have you thought about a government career? The NDEB, maybe?"

"I wouldn't know how to apply." Ari flushed. Just as she'd suspected, he saw right through her excuses. He always did.

"That's where I work. I'm sure they'd be happy to take another veteran."

She forced a smile and clenched her fists around the handles of her sacks. "I don't know if it's worth it. I'm sure I could find work at one of the stores near here if I needed to."

"You might as well try it out." Grey sounded pitying—not at all the reaction Ari was hoping for. "You really should be doing something productive, Jules. I'll submit all your details to the chief. Promise me you'll consider it if they ask you to come for an interview?"

"Sure." She stopped abruptly in front of a row of apartment buildings—much nicer ones than hers. For a moment she felt almost envious. "This is my place. You can just hand me the groceries. I'll take them up."

Grey helped her gather all the paper bags into her arms, then stepped back. "You sure you've got that?"

"Yeah." She paused, took a deep breath, and added, "And please stop calling me Jules."

"Sorry . . . " Grey dragged the word out like he wanted to say something else, but Ari turned away without giving him the chance.

Once she safely rounded the corner, she slid down against the wall, her arms burning from the constricting paper handles. She was still half a mile away from her apartment, but she couldn't stand another second of Grey's well-meaning condescension. Better to carry the eight paper bags herself than listen to him talk about how much better his life was now that he'd found work, a wife, and a reason to stop and help someone he hadn't spoken to in years.

You're sad you can't be like him?

Poor you!

She shook her head, trying to dispel the voices. The worst thing was that they never lied to her—whenever they accused her, their words rang true. She hated how they always harshly dragged her out of her self-pity, and she didn't want to listen. The longer she sat still, the louder they'd get.

She peeked around the corner, half-hoping Grey would still be there, worrying about her, waiting to see if she'd gotten inside safely. But he was gone.

Ari turned her back to the mirror and glanced over her shoulder to see her reflection. Her long, navy blue dress brushed the floor with a soft rustle. It was wide open in the back, and Ari felt uncomfortably exposed. Somebody was sure to ask about her scars, but this was the only formal dress she had. She couldn't show up at Grey and Lia's wedding in uniform.

She took her keys from the hook beside the door, looking closely at the key fob. It had been so long since she had driven that she had forgotten which button unlocked the car. And when she went outside, she realized that she had also forgotten where she parked her car. She paused at the bottom of the steps and looked around uncertainly.

Far corner, of course. Where I always park it.

But when she got in the car and felt the cold leather against her bare back, the draft against her face where the windshield had cracked and never been fixed, and the grime on the steering wheel that she hadn't bothered to clean, her resolve weakened. She knew she wasn't the person Lia wanted at her wedding. Lia was looking forward to seeing the Ari she remembered from the army days—the composed, disciplined, self-motivated Ari. The one who knew how to clean a saber and march in line and salute her superiors, not the one who hadn't left her apartment in months and didn't look anyone in the eyes. Despite all the time she'd spent in front of her mirror, Ari hadn't managed to change back into her old self. Whatever she'd done since the army wasn't reversible, and Lia would know it the moment she saw her.

Ari turned her key in the ignition, guiltily suppressing her excuses. She *had* to be there for Lia, just like Lia had always been there for her.

But the engine didn't start.

Ari's frustration got the better of her, and instead of investigating, she climbed out of the car and bolted back inside. She had a real excuse now—if her car wouldn't start, she couldn't get to the wedding. End of story. That was all she had to tell Lia, and she'd be free from all her obligations. If there was any money left in her bank account, maybe she could even have a late wedding gift delivered. By mail, not in person, of course.

She changed back into a sweatshirt and jeans and tucked her face securely under her hood. There was a bar just down the street from her apartment, a sleazy place where she wouldn't be an eyesore. Maybe, after a few drinks, she could work up the courage to call a taxi and go to Lia's wedding.

She left the apartment and hurried along the sidewalk, nearly slipping in the puddles left from the hailstorm. Her phone was ringing in her pocket, but this time she ignored it.

She'd never been to this particular bar before, but she'd been watching it from her window, keeping tabs on who went in and out. She knew how long they stayed and who the designated drivers were, who left drunk and who left only a little tipsy. They all looked just like her—*lowlifes*, she told herself. She could tell from the way people walked in front of the lights on dark nights that the counter was in the back. That was where she'd feel the safest. She walked inside, perched herself on a stool, and ordered a shot of straight vodka from the bartender. He slammed the glass on the counter without sparing her a second glance.

One tentative sip. Then another. Then the glass was empty. Ari's eyes glazed over. People mingled and flowed around the room, their movements dizzying. Now she remembered why she hated crowds. There was too much to take in, and she felt totally out of control. She ordered another drink and rested her elbows on the counter.

A strong hand clamped down on her shoulder. "Miss Ari?"

She glanced up, startled and ready to fight, and found herself staring into a pair of unfamiliar blue eyes framed by whitish blond hair. His pupils were dilated, and it was obvious he'd been drinking. Not much of a threat.

"Relax, we're all here to have fun." The man sat down and offered her his hand to shake, which she ignored. "Well, it's nice to meet you. Or see you again, rather." The man took a swig from a glass the bartender handed him.

"I don't know what you mean." Ari shot a quick glance across the room to see if anyone was within earshot. But the music was loud, and nobody had been paying attention to the silent girl who looked like she wanted to be left alone. "Do you know me?"

"From the army. How could you have forgotten?"

Ari shifted uncomfortably. Strange man, strange drink, strange environment. Her eyes were crossing. There were two columns, one, then two. How had she gotten drunk so fast? She put a finger in her drink and stirred. Maybe . . . there was something powdery in the texture. Or maybe there wasn't. Her finger trembled against the glass.

The man's friendly smile changed to a pitying smirk. "You're exactly what I thought you'd be—a hopeless, lazy shut-in. I was going to help you, but now I'm not sure there's much left to be helped."

Ari staggered unsteadily to her feet, realizing that she ought to feel offended. The room blurred around her. Voices swirled into an indiscernible medley of empty noise.

Now she was on the floor, staring blankly up at a woman's face. She seemed scared. Ari wondered what she was worried about.

How did I get here?

He was balanced on the edge of the roof, swaying back and forth, his heels barely touching the edge. A few more seconds and he'd fall.

She tried to take a step forward. Her legs were heavy and stuck to the ground. She couldn't lift her feet. She opened her mouth to scream. No sound came out. Her throat was hoarse with yelling, yet she couldn't even hear her own voice. She reached out her hands, praying he'd somehow hear her movement and turn around, yet even the soft rustling of her clothes as she moved was inaudible.

He was going to fall, and she couldn't stop him.

"Kira!" she screamed.

His name echoed, and Ari took a deep, ragged breath.

Where am I? What was that?

"Kira?" Lia's twittery voice sounded sharp. "Did you have a nightmare?"

Ari managed to focus her eyes on Lia's face. She had changed out of her dress and was wearing a sweatshirt over leggings, but her bridal makeup was still intact. Rhinestones that looked like tears sparkled under her eyes, and they made Ari dizzy.

"What happened?" She tried to sit up, but a sharp pain in the front of her head forced her to lie back down. She closed her eyes and shivered. "How did you get here?"

"Apparently, I'm the emergency contact in your phone," Lia said. A dry edge to her voice suggested the discovery wasn't welcome. "I got a call from your number and thought you might be explaining where you were. But instead, a paramedic said you needed somebody to drive you home or you'd have to spend the night in the hospital. You've been here for hours already."

"I could've called a taxi." Ari tried again, successfully this time, to sit up and take a deep, comforting breath. Her tongue was dry, and her head was throbbing. *Where have I felt like this before?* She shook her head gently, trying to clear her thoughts. That feeling . . . something about it was painfully familiar, but she couldn't quite place it.

"I was worried when you didn't show up." Lia leaned back in her chair and clasped her hands together. "I was afraid . . . " Her voice trailed off.

"Afraid?"

"That maybe you'd done it yourself." Lia sighed. "The doctor said your drink might have been spiked, but when they saw your psych record, they started testing you for an overdose."

"Not this time," Ari snapped. She couldn't help feeling guilty that she'd given Lia reason to be worried.

After a strained pause, she added, "I'm sorry."

"We can leave when you feel better," Lia said with forced cheerfulness. "I've got your car, so I can drive you home and get you to bed."

Ari rubbed her eyes. "What time is it?"

"I think it's only nine or ten. At night, of course."

"Lia, don't you need to get back? I can drive myself home." Ari's face was burning red with shame. Of all the ways to make a nuisance of herself, this was just the worst—caught skipping out on her promise, passing out half-drunk at a bar, and finally making Lia think she'd tried to kill herself. She just wanted to get away from it all as soon as possible. "It's not a big deal. You don't need to stay."

"No, no, no!" Lia shook her head obstinately. "I'm not letting you do that. The doctors said it wasn't safe, and besides, what kind of a friend would I be if I wasn't there when you needed me?"

Lia's words cut like a knife. If only Ari had been that kind of friend, maybe accepting Lia's help wouldn't be so hard.

"Okay." She slid off the bed and tried to steady herself. "Let's go."

Lia gave Ari her arm. "Are you sure you can make it down the hallway?"

Ari nodded stiffly.

With several rest breaks, they made their way down the sterile hallway. The smell of hospital cleaning chemicals made Ari want to gag. What interest could anyone have in drugging her? Her throbbing headache . . . she'd felt this same pain somewhere before.

"Did they catch who did it?" she mumbled.

"What?"

"The guy next to me. The strange guy."

"Did you meet someone at the bar?"

"He was—" Ari searched her memory, but her mind went blank. "I don't remember," she finished uncertainly.

Lia shook her head. "I don't know anything about it."

Ari sighed. "He said he was from the army, and now I feel like . . . The serum we made. It feels like I've taken it. Remember how we used to get a small dose so we'd have a resistance to it?"

"Whatever happened tonight must've messed with you a lot!" Lia laughed.

"It's not that strange of an idea." Or maybe it was. Ari's head hurt too much for her to be sure of anything. "Did the doctors figure out what was in my drink?"

"I don't know anything. I just told you that. Did you forget already?"

"I'm probably wrong." Ari tried to pull the front door open, but it was heavy as a wall, and her muscles wouldn't obey her. Lia held it open, and the cold night air hit Ari in the face like a slap.

"You're definitely wrong," Lia continued. "Get a good night's sleep before you worry about anything else."

"But I'll forget what I'm feeling like," insisted Ari, rubbing her fingers across her aching forehead. "Surely you know something about that serum. Do you remember the name? What it was made of? We could have the doctors check for it."

Lia raised an eyebrow. "You're really sold on this idea, aren't you? Why is it so hard to believe that somebody spiked your drink with pure alcohol, and you're just really hungover?"

"Because . . ." Ari was beginning to feel groggy. "I don't know. I'm just curious, that's all."

"Well, if it was a chemical we made, the doctor wouldn't be able to sequence it anyway." Lia opened the car door for Ari and helped her inside.

"But all that information is declassified now. We could give someone the exact formula, and they might be able to find something."

"You think a regular hospital has time to search your drink for assassination drugs?" Lia burst out laughing until her eyes teared up. "You have a serious case of main character syndrome, Ari. I'll tell you what. I'm not going to give those poor doctors any more work, and I'm not going to do the research for you. But I will tell you that the chemical was called oxyarcyan. You look it up yourself and tell me if you think there's any way someone tried to assassinate you with it." She wiped the tears from her cheeks and sniffled, unable to stop laughing. "If you can even remember this conversation in the morning, that is."

"Oxy-ar-cyan?" Ari repeated, slightly chagrined.

"Right." Lia glanced anxiously back at her from the driver's seat. "What you need is a good night's sleep. You can lie down if you want."

Ari stretched out across the seats, cushioning her face on her sweater. "I'm really sorry for making you come all the way out here."

"It's no problem!" Lia was wide awake and cheerful now that they were out of the hospital.

The rest of the ride was quiet. Ari closed her eyes and tried not to move. Lia hummed softly to herself in her childish voice, and the sound was comfortingly familiar to Ari, though she didn't recognize any of the tunes. Slowly, she drifted off to an incoherent sleep.

"Hey, wake up," hissed Lia in her ear. "We're at your apartment."

Ari sat up quickly. "I didn't give you the address."

"You're kidding," Lia scoffed. "I know where you live."

"Does Grey know, too?"

"Yes, he does."

Ari flushed again. He wasn't fooled at all.

Lia supported her on the way up the stairs and unlocked the front door with Ari's key. "Just go to sleep for now. I promise you'll feel better in the morning." She paused. "And maybe don't go to bars anymore, Ari. You're too convenient of a target."

CHAPTER 3

"This is Yuno from the National Drug Enforcement Bureau."

Ari's drowsy eyes widened.

"I wanted to follow up on the application one of our employees submitted on your behalf. I'm pleased to say you've been selected for an interview. Will you be available this afternoon?"

"An application?" Ari tried to sound as professional as the caller, but she was scrambling out of bed and searching frantically through her closet, trying to find something businesslike to wear. Her head was still throbbing, and her painkillers weren't in the medicine cabinet where she thought she'd left them. "Sorry. I'm surprised you called so soon. Yes, I'm available today. Where should I go?"

"Do you know where the NDEB headquarters is?"

Ari typed the name into her phone. "Downtown, right?"

"Can you be there by two o'clock this afternoon?"

Ari glanced at the microwave clock, wondering how much she had overslept. It was ten o'clock already, and she hadn't had a chance to get her car fixed. She'd have to get a taxi, which meant she'd need to leave plenty of extra time. Being late to an interview was unthinkable—at least she remembered that much from her army days.

"I can make it," she said.

"Great." Ari could hear the businesslike smile in Yuno's voice. "We'll be expecting you."

"Do you mind if I ask a question before you go?" asked Ari. "When did you receive my application?"

"We require a minimum of two weeks to determine each candidate's suitability," answered Yuno. "So probably between two weeks and a month ago."

"Thanks," answered Ari politely and hung up.

She was mystified. There was no point in calling Grey—Ari was sure he'd be busy with Lia. But she couldn't help wondering why he would've submitted her application without asking her first. After all, he'd just mentioned the idea to her yesterday. Grey was impulsive, but that seemed a little over the top, even for him.

But if he hadn't done it, who had?

Ari reverse searched the phone number. Sure enough, it belonged to the NDEB. And when she searched Yuno's unusual name, the very first result was his LinkedIn page, which said he was the head of the NDEB's special agent division. If anyone was trying to scam her, they had gone to a lot of unnecessary effort to make the hoax realistic. And besides, if she went straight to the NDEB headquarters, the worst thing that could happen was that the receptionist gave her a funny look and refused to let her in. She had seen the NDEB building before—it was near a busy street surrounded by off-duty NDEB officers eating lunch in their cars. If she was careful, nobody could hurt her there, even if the phone call *was* a fake.

Ari stumbled into the bathroom and opened her closet. Her closet was full of old military uniforms, pajamas, and casual everyday clothes that were mostly unwashed. She glanced at the old uniforms. Maybe she could recycle them as business wear if she plucked off the nametag and epaulets.

She modeled for herself in the mirror, wondering if anyone would notice where the clothes were from. The dark blue material and sharp cuts made her straight figure look even skinnier, but she had no other options. She took it off and put on a bathrobe to make breakfast.

Her phone vibrated in her pocket, and this time she checked the caller ID before she answered.

Lia. Perfect chance to ask why Grey's application got through so fast.

"Welcome back to the real world!" Lia screeched. Ari pulled the phone away from her ear and rolled her eyes. "Feeling any better today?"

"Yeah, thanks. I have a question for Grey," Ari said quickly, her face burning with embarrassment. She still hadn't figured out how to explain to Lia why she was at a bar instead of at her wedding. "Is he there?"

"Sure," chirped Lia. She seemed to be in a good mood today. Any other time, she wouldn't have let Ari slip away without an explanation. Then she yelled into the phone: "Grey!"

Ari winced. Lia hadn't changed a bit. She was still the same happy nuisance she had always been. And come to think of it, Ari hadn't changed much either—she was still jealous.

"What's up, Jul—Ari?"

"I got a call from the NDEB this morning," she said. "Did you submit the application yesterday after we talked? I didn't expect to hear from them so soon."

Grey yawned into the phone. "I haven't submitted it yet. A scam, maybe?"

"I don't think so," said Ari. "They invited me to an interview at their headquarters. There's no reason for a con artist to send me straight to law enforcement."

"Really? Then where'd they get your information?" Grey pulled the phone away from his mouth and yelled to Lia. "Did you send Ari's application in to the NDEB?"

"Be careful what you say on the phone!" Lia scolded him. Ari could hear them arguing for a moment, then Lia emerged victorious with the phone. "No, Ari, I didn't do that," she said. "Did the caller say he'd gotten your information or your application?"

"He specifically called it an application," Ari answered.

"Are you sure you didn't send it in right after the army kicked us out?"

"I didn't. But nobody else knows me well enough to fill out all the information they'd ask for."

"Well, at least you got the interview," Lia said. "Maybe they found your information in an old file or something. There's some leftover cake if you want to come over later, by the way."

"No, thanks."

"I want you to come over," said Lia shortly. Her voice was pinched and sharp. "We need to talk."

Ari winced. So she hadn't forgotten yet. "We . . . we do?"

"You missed the ceremony, and besides, I haven't seen you in months. I miss us being friends, Ari."

"I can't come," said Ari flatly. *Not until I figure out what I'm going to say.*

"You could make time if you wanted to!" cried Lia. There was a hysterical edge to her voice that made Ari wonder if she was about to cry. "You could just say you don't want to be friends anymore. I'd understand if you said it has something to do with the army. You're not obligated to come see me, but don't leave me hanging."

"Okay," Ari murmured. She twisted the tie of her bathrobe through her fingers. "I'm sorry."

"That's all you have to say? You apologized yesterday, but you're not doing anything different." There was a long pause. "I'm not going to call back anymore."

Ari put the phone in her pocket. She didn't even want to see the screen. Lia might call her back and say exactly what she deserved to hear: that she was a failure of a friend.

I shouldn't care. Nobody's making me care. I don't have to care if I don't want to. But for once—for the first time in a long time—her recycled, old excuses weren't very convincing.

The stiff, white interview room brought back vivid memories for Ari. Right after the army, she had been a young, inexperienced, scared girl trying to get a job to save herself from starving. Her talents, varied though they were, weren't marketable. Interpersonal skills, which she discovered was the most highly sought-after skill in entry-level work, were never a priority in her army unit. There, negotiations had already failed, and there was no choice left but to kill. And nobody yet had approached her with a request to kill off their customers, so there wasn't much she could offer.

She'd specifically tried to pick a job where she could work in a cubicle, far away from the windows she hated. But she'd ended up as a cashier in a gas station. She'd visualized the windows across the front of the store shattering until she'd grown too scared to go back.

This isn't going to be like that.

"There isn't too much I need to ask," Yuno said. His formality made Ari feel even more like she was back in the army. The only thing that shattered the illusion was the thick smell of the gel he'd used to smooth his hair. That scent was too identifiable—nobody would've been allowed to use hair gel in the army.

"We've seen your record from the military," he continued, "so we know a little about your strengths. But we do ask all our applicants from the military about their interpersonal skills since that's not something they teach you much about. What have you been doing since you left the military, and how would you say that has helped you develop those skills?"

Ari clenched her hand over her knee, wondering what she was supposed to say. *He might as well ask me how staying in my apartment for weeks on end has helped me make friends. I don't know. I don't care. He's right—that's not something I needed to worry about in the military.*

Not that she could answer honestly even if she wanted to. She simply didn't remember enough to say for sure. Even two days ago was little more than a hazy blur. Shadows from her apartment windows mixed with the soft haze of her blanket against her face and a gnawing feeling of hunger. She had been too lazy to go to the store, so she stayed in bed instead, wondering if she'd get hungry enough to go or if she'd just let herself starve. That was her everyday life.

Interpersonal skills? *Ha.* Ari couldn't even take care of herself.

"I don't know if this will exactly answer your question," she began uncertainly, "but when I was in the military, I did have one close friend. We worked together on a couple of missions, even though we weren't on the same team. They were always very kind to me, even when I couldn't reciprocate. But unfortunately. . ." She blinked, feeling suddenly sleepy. *Why can't I talk about this?* "Unfortunately, they were killed in action shortly before my unit disbanded." *No, that's not right. But it's good enough for now.* "I admit, since then I've had a hard time making new friends. I keep in contact with a few people from the army, but I'm still learning how to connect with people on the same level we did when we were all—well, when we were all getting shot at together." She managed a half smile, which Yuno reciprocated. "However, I went to a friend's wedding last night." *Would have, probably . . . if I hadn't gotten roofied.* "That was a great opportunity for me to talk to people. It's definitely a long process, but I'd say the army taught me to make extremely strong connections in short amounts of time. Especially with coworkers—teammates." She studied Yuno's face, wondering if he had noticed that she had skirted his question. Hopefully, she'd put enough filler into her answer that he had gotten lost in the process.

He tapped his pencil against his notebook and said, "You know, at the NDEB, it's extremely important to forge strong friendships even with people who aren't your teammates. You might need a civilian's help to solve a case, and you'd have to be on good terms with them. Since you can't tell me how you've already done that, why don't you tell me about how you *would* do that?"

Another extremely vague question. Ari took her time to think before replying.

"I became friends with that person from the army because they were always there for me when I most needed help," she said at last. "They brought me bandages when I was injured in training and talked to me when I was depressed. And they had no reason to do it. They didn't want anything from me—they just wanted to be nice. So, if I was going to form a close relationship with someone who wasn't my teammate, I'd try to be sincere with them. I'd push all my personal goals to the back of my mind and focus on simply being a nice person first. I wouldn't want to form a fake friendship just to get what I want."

You sound like what you are—a manipulative little liar. The voice was so loud and close that Ari started.

"Good, good." Yuno scribbled something on his notepad, and Ari was thankful he didn't seem to notice her reaction. "I'm sure you were expecting more, but those are the only scripted questions I have for you. Again, we've seen your records, so we don't really need you to demonstrate any further qualifications. Is there anything else you think we should know about you?"

Ari had already rehearsed her mini speech. The army had even asked her this when they were preparing to send her out into the civilian world. "Be a good reflection on your unit," they had said. "Show them we're not what they say." She couldn't fail this question if she was going to reflect positively on them.

Them. They. Who were they, again?

"There was a lot of negative publicity about our unit," she began. The newspaper clippings she'd kept taped to her wall since who-knew-when said as much. "The media made it seem like we were all angels trapped in the underworld, forced to do things we hated. But that's a bad representation. We were all there because we wanted to serve each other. We didn't have any esoteric goals. We just wanted to make sure that we had a country to come home to and that the people there never had to go through what we did. I'll do anything to make that happen. That's what the army taught me."

Yuno nodded slowly, then wrote in his notebook.

"Well, Ari," he said after a long pause. "You're exactly the kind of person we're looking for. We don't generally offer positions on the spot, but I can see from your records and your answers to my questions that there's no need for me to consult the other team leaders. You'd be a welcome addition to the team. What do you think?"

Ari blinked. "You're offering me a job?"

A quick smile crossed Yuno's face. "That's right."

"Of—of course I'd like to do it," stammered Ari. "When can I start?"

"Tomorrow." Yuno snapped his notebook shut. "I'll email you some paperwork to sign tonight. Bring it with you when you come in." He stood up and held out his hand. "Welcome to the team, Ari."

Ari shook it, trying not to show her confusion. Everything was happening too fast. "Thank you."

"Just one more thing." Yuno held the door open for her. "You don't remember your army days very well, do you?"

Ari paused and frowned at him. "No. But how did you know?"

"Nobody does," he said. "We've never had a former army applicant who was able to tell us much about what they did while they were there. That's why the records are so important for us."

She pasted on a smile. *Then why ask?*

"Well, no, I don't remember much. That's probably why my answers were a little vague. Sorry about that."

"No, no, it's fine. I'm surprised you were able to tell me as much as you did." He nodded. "Thanks for your time, Ari. I look forward to seeing you tomorrow."

That night, Ari collapsed onto her bed, sore and exhausted. Her phone felt warm in her hands. She'd been turning the screen on and off for half an hour now, fidgeting restlessly and trying to decide whether she should call Lia and grovel. Had she been serious about never calling back?

Her fingers navigated to her contacts. They unconsciously pressed Lia's name, then the call button.

Ten seconds, then twenty, and the ringer still hadn't cut off.

"Who's this?" Lia's voice was curt.

"It's Ari."

Pause.

"I deleted your contact. I didn't think I'd be hearing from you."

Ari fidgeted. "Sorry for calling."

"Did you get the job?"

"What's that?"

"You had an interview with the NDEB today. Did you get the job?"

"Oh." Ari relaxed. "Yeah. I start training tomorrow morning."

"Okay. Anything else you want to say?"

"I—" She choked on her words. "That's it."

"Goodnight."

Click.

CHAPTER 4

I told them. I told them who did it. I have a right to be mad, don't I?

"This is your new desk. I've printed a copy of today's schedule. We can't have you officially begin work until you've completed your training."

"Is it just one day of training?" asked Ari absently. Her mind was occupied with plans, speculations, and a touch of self-congratulation. True, she hadn't even technically applied for the job, but she had passed the interview, and she was starting to feel more like a responsible twenty-one-year-old adult. In a matter of days, she'd gotten a chance at patching her life back together.

"It'll last for two weeks. After that, you'll have a physical exam. If you pass, you will be officially hired. If you don't pass, we will have to let you go."

"Is the training here at the office?"

"The skills part is here. The physical training will take place at the gym down the street. We'll rent out a room in the back, and you'll be training with your partner. You already know how to shoot, but of course, you'll need a refresher. Plus, you'll be learning the basics of knife combat and self-defense without a weapon. These are all skills you'll need for this job. You'll also be building your strength with stamina exercises." He adjusted his glasses. "But you have to learn some things here at the office. Protocol, of course. You'll be taught about common drugs, their components, their effects, how to recognize them, and how to reverse an overdose. Simple things. You have about an hour before training starts."

He snapped his mouth shut and stared disapprovingly at her. The years of military training kicked in, and she straightened up and looked him in the eyes without a smile. "Yes, sir."

"Have an excellent first day, Ms. Ari."

Ari waited until, from the corner of her eye, she saw him disappear into the adjoining hallway. Then she let out a deep breath and collapsed into her desk chair, spinning around and around and letting her shoes kick against the filing cabinets.

She couldn't see anyone else from her cubicle. It was tucked in a corner, small, and enclosed, an uncomfortable reminder of the weeks she'd spent locked indoors. Ari pushed herself to her feet and stepped out into the hallway.

As she walked down the hallway, eyes drifting away from everyone she passed and hands tucked in her pockets, she noticed there was a row of pictures of people who must have been NDEB officials. They all looked severe and serious, like they were having their mugshots taken. Ari made note of the fact she hadn't yet seen anyone smile. They seemed to take their dedication to their work a little too far, she thought. Not that many people smiled back where she had worked before, but at least the ones who were supposed to did. Like Lia.

A girl in a pencil skirt and low heels came the opposite way down the hallway. Ari looked every direction except at the newcomer, hoping she'd be ignored, but the girl stopped right in front of her.

"Are you Ari?"

"How do you know who I am?" Ari finally looked at the girl. Small, graceful, and pale were the first adjectives that popped into her head. And delicate. Breakable.

"I think you and I are working together." The girl extended her hand with a friendly smile. "Nika. Pleasure to meet you."

Ari shook her hand. "Working together?"

"When you're done with training. Or they might even make me go through training with you."

Ari looked Nika up and down. She looked too fragile to be a special agent.

"Were you in the military?" she asked.

Nika chuckled. "No. But I heard you came from there. What *was* your job?"

"It was . . . " Ari's mind blanked. "I don't know how to describe it."

"Don't worry," Nika said. There was a flash of seriousness in her eyes, quickly replaced with a smile. "Do you want to see my file? You can find it in the library, so you'll know what questions to ask next time we see each other. It's a good way to get to know your teammates."

"Sure."

"I've already seen your file," continued Nika. "If you go to the bottom floor, you'll see signs for the library. It's not really a library— it's a categorical record of all the agents who work here. Like the Book of Life, if you know what that is. Anyway, you can find my file under Nika Coulter." She raised her hand in a friendly wave and continued down the hallway.

Curious, Ari went to the elevator and pushed the button for the basement.

It looked like a warehouse with rows upon rows of metal shelves, which creaked as she walked by. The only light came from the blindingly white LEDs on the ceiling, which made the shadows only darker. She couldn't believe the NDEB had this many records stored here where anyone could read them. What information about herself, she wondered, was public?

She found the section for last names beginning with *C* in the far back right corner. Nika Coulter. Ari couldn't forget an unusual name like that. There was her file, sandwiched between a Costner and a Dubois. Ari pulled it off the shelf, sat down on the floor with her back to the shelf, and opened it.

Basic information was listed at the top. Ari skipped the mundane details—birthday and parents' names—and found what she was looking for.

```
NAME: Nika Coulter
MISSIONS TO DATE: Seven: KK, LK, MK, NK, SK, TK.
```

The space under "specialty" was blank, and Ari had no idea what the abbreviations under "missions to date" meant. They were classified, apparently.

```
BACKGROUND: Graduated from Georgetown with a degree
in economics. Worked in fraud investigation with the
FBI as an intern. Transferred to NDEB six years ago.
```

What was an Ivy League graduate with an economics degree doing in the NDEB? Something must have gone wrong with Nika's previous job in the FBI. Ari couldn't imagine giving up an analyst position to be a special agent. Who'd want to be shot at and screamed at all day when there were other options available?

She stood up on her tiptoes and replaced the file in its place on the shelf. She hadn't learned anything of value except that, despite appearances, Nika had plenty of experience with the NDEB and had been a member of the agency for a while.

Her own file was only a little further down the row. Much to her relief, it was listed under her real name—Ari—not the name she'd used when she was in the military. She flipped it open, curious to see what Nika already knew about her besides her name.

There was a picture of her in uniform clipped to the top of the folder. She examined it closely, looking for any hints about was happening to her when the picture was taken. But her face registered nothing—no smile, no frown, only tightly pinched lips and blank, gray eyes. She couldn't even read her own expression, let alone remember what she'd been thinking about.

MISSIONS TO DATE: N/A
BACKGROUND: Achieved rank of lieutenant in the U.S. Army.

That's it? She breathed a deep sigh of relief, but it was tinged with disappointment. If she ever wanted to remember what had happened to her in the army, she'd have to check her military files. And those wouldn't be easy to find.

She walked heavily, and the shelves rattled as she passed them.

"Please be quiet."

Ari started. She hadn't realized anyone was there.

"Behind you."

She spun around so quickly that her hair caught over her shoulder and covered her eyes. When she shook it loose, she saw a man sitting on the floor, slumped against the tallest shelf, his face buried in a file. He didn't look up, but there was nobody else nearby who could've spoken to her.

"Sorry." Ari wasn't sure how to respond.

"Ari, right?"

She wondered how everyone already knew who she was. "Yes."

"We've met." He closed the file and stood up. "My name's Mikael. Do you remember me?"

She stared blankly at his face. He did look a little familiar, but she couldn't place him.

He smiled slowly. "It's nice to see you again."

"It's nice to see you, too," Ari echoed warily.

"You and I will be working together," continued Mikael. "I'll also be your teacher for the next two weeks. Since we were in the army together, I think I know what we'll need to work on."

Ari stayed silent. She didn't want him to know that she had no idea who he was.

Yuno did say there were other applicants from the army. I wonder if that's why he decided to pair me with Mikael?

"We might as well start your training today. I'll meet you at the fitness center down the road in fifteen minutes. Don't be late."

She smiled and clenched her fists behind her back. Pulling rank—that was the thing she hated most about being a subordinate. There was nothing she could say except: "Yes, sir."

"I look forward to working with you." Mikael sat back on the floor and pulled out his phone.

A wave of discouragement and exhaustion washed over her. The ride up the elevator felt like the floor was oscillating under her feet, and in the bright sunlight of the parking lot, her eyes crossed and blurred.

Not this again.

She blinked, trying to wake herself up. The heat from the pavement burned her face, and she could feel her cheeks reddening. The first thing she did when she got in her car was turn the air conditioner on, but that didn't seem to help. The cold air felt like needles.

The fitness center was much further away than she'd expected. Did she really have to drive this far every day? Or was she just too exhausted that it felt further away than it really was? She found a parking spot, pulled in, and turned her car off.

As her engine died, everything went silent, except for the voices. No, they weren't voices—they were just noises. Mumbles, whispers. The incoherence hurt her ears. Ari opened her door and stepped out into the parking lot.

The level ground shifted again under her feet, and she crashed into the pavement.

His face was all smiles. She couldn't hear his voice, but she knew what he was saying without having to hear.

Did you like the music?

Ari nodded. His excitement was rare but contagious, and it was spreading fast.

I can send more if you want. It helps take the edge off the training.

A chill shot up her spine. "Training . . . ?" she mumbled, looking down at the ground.

Are you handling it okay?

She knew Kira would listen. "Depends on how you define 'okay.'"

He nodded sympathetically and held out his hands to hug her.

"No!" she shrieked, pulling away. "No, Kira, stop!"

She tried to scramble from the bench, but he forced her back down. His fist was clenched around a knife. It crept closer to her face, brushed her throat. She couldn't even lift a finger to push him away. Her muscles were so tight that she could barely manage a shaky breath. Her throat was dry as sandpaper, and her tongue refused to let her squeeze out a word.

He smiled gently, his expression twice as cruel because it was deliberate, passionless. Ari shrank away.

"You did this to me, so why shouldn't I do it to you?" he asked, somehow in Ari's voice.

Then she realized he was just standing there, looking down at her in total bewilderment. No knife. No smirk. Just confusion about why she was screaming. Where had the knife come from?

She woke up a second later gasping for air.

"Lay down," said a familiar voice.

Ari opened her eyes. Between the flashes of light exploding at the edges of her vision, she distinguished a face. Nika, the girl she'd met earlier. She had changed out of the pencil skirt and into athletic clothes.

"Do you have a headache?" Nika asked.

Ari shook her head. No, that wasn't right. Now that she was moving, her head did hurt. She changed her response to a nod.

Nika laughed. "Don't worry. My sister used to pass out like this all the time. Chances are that this is from standing up too quickly or not drinking enough water. Your blood pressure is sky-high, but everything else seems okay."

"He told me something important." Ari wasn't sure who she was talking to, or even who "he" was. The mumbled words came out of her mouth by themselves.

"What are you talking about?" Nika asked.

"Never mind." She propped herself up on her elbows and looked around, trying to think of something to say before Nika could ask any more questions. After all, how was she going to answer without sounding crazy? But there was nothing to see except rows and rows of green metal lockers and plain tile floors.

"Where am I?" she said at last.

"You're at the gym. The General found you in the parking lot and carried you to the locker room. Hey, maybe you should lie back down."

"Don't worry about it." Ari smiled as best she could and managed a stretch and yawn to convince Nika she was relaxed. "I'm ready to start if you are."

"You can't do any training today!"

Ari swung her legs off the bench and rubbed her eyes. "I'm fine."

Nika put a hand to her forehead. "You're really cold."

"Cold?" Ari could feel sweat dripping down her back, and she wondered if she looked as drained as she felt. "Well, I guess it's chilly in here," she said weakly.

"I thought it was hot."

Ari stood up. Her knees wobbled, but she straightened and tightened her muscles. No more shaking. In fact, she felt better now than she had before she passed out. Maybe all she needed was a reset—though she wished that reset could just be a good night's sleep.

"I'm fine, see? I'll have to thank—who'd you say found me?" Making small talk was the perfect distraction.

"The General."

"Who's that?"

Nika looked momentarily surprised. "I thought Mikael said you guys had met before."

Ari sighed. What a great impression she'd made.

"Have you guys actually met? Everybody calls him the General because he's so uptight. I figured you'd know about that."

"We didn't get into details. Does he know everything about me, too?"

"What?"

"Never mind. I've already made us late." She could hear movement nearby, and there was nobody in the locker room but them. At least her training hadn't worn off yet. She could still tell when someone was looking for her.

"Are you sure?" asked Nika, but Ari was already at the door, looking out into the hallway.

"Miss Ari, you're late," a terse voice said from around the corner.

Mikael had also changed into sweats and a black sweatshirt. Ari wondered how he wasn't overheating, because Nika was right—the room was painfully hot.

He held a clipboard in his left hand and a grocery bag in his right. "Take this." He handed her the bag. "Get changed. You'll be doing extra work to make up for the delay."

Ari changed in the bathroom and scurried upstairs, biting back a sarcastic reply about how the delay wasn't her fault. Her downfall had always been her unwillingness to keep her personal opinions to herself, and she wasn't going to let it take over now.

Nika was waiting for her at the top of the staircase. "Sorry about him," she whispered, guiding her through the workout machines to a private room in the back. "I'm sure he's never passed out in his life, so he has no idea how it feels. Look at him, wearing that fleece in this weather. His nervous system is perfect." She held the door open for Ari.

"You'll begin with fifty pushups as a punishment for being late," Mikael said as soon as she walked in the door. He tapped his pen against his clipboard.

Ari obediently dropped to her hands, confident in her strength. But after months without training, that confidence was misplaced. A sharp ache shot through her shoulders.

Mikael watched her critically from the front of the room, lounging against the row of polished mirrors. "You used to be one of the strongest trainees."

She paused and looked up at him. "Were you the military shooting instructor?" That was the only face she had seen every day that she couldn't remember clearly anymore.

"Don't stop."

She returned to her workout, breathing heavily. *That could've been a yes, but if it was, why didn't he just admit it? All that information is declassified now.*

A few seconds later, she finished and stood up, stretching her wrists until they clicked. Her head throbbed painfully, reminding her that she'd forgotten how much water she needed to train effectively. That was something she'd learned on the first day—how much else would she have to relearn? A wave of fatigue washed over her, and she sucked in a deep gulp of air. She didn't want Mikael to see how tired she was, but if training was always this intense, she couldn't hide it for long.

"Miss Nika, go outside and run on the treadmill for the next thirty minutes. Two minutes on, thirty seconds off, and continuously for the last ten minutes. Miss Ari, you'll stay here with me."

Nika snapped to attention. "Yes, sir!"

He nodded and handed Ari a gray plastic knife with a flexible rubber blade. "Take this."

"Are you sure this is a good idea?" She didn't remember much about hand-to-hand combat training, and she didn't want to get hurt on the first day. Her arms were still shaking from the pushups.

But if Mikael heard, he ignored her. "The basic rules of knife combat are similar to those of the martial arts you learned in the army. Keep your hands in front of you and close to your body. Keep your feet moving, and keep that blade pointed up. If you tilt it too far down, you've given me the chance I need to get it out of your hands. Pay special attention to your neck. A cut across your chest won't hurt you—the chances of it landing through your ribs are relatively small, especially with a good defense. But if the blade brushes either side of your neck, you'll bleed to death." Mikael's voice was flat and emotionless as if he was reciting a math lesson. "Also pay attention to your legs, particularly your knees. If someone kicks you there, you've lost."

Ari nodded absently. She had heard all this before, and she was more worried about how she was going to put it into practice.

"Show me."

"What?"

"Back up until you're against the wall."

She obeyed. Mikael stopped about five feet in front of her. She searched vainly for his weak points, but it'd been months since she'd put any of her army skills into practice. His eyes never wavered for a second. His expression never changed. There was nothing obvious to exploit.

"Show me what you'd do." Mikael raised his matching rubber knife.

She had a split second to think before he slipped toward her with the agility and speed of a cat. She ducked out of the way just in time to avoid being pinned, but not quickly enough to escape. He reached down and wrapped his hand around her throat. Her knife was knocked out of her hand. Something spun her around and collided with the back of her knees. They crumpled in response.

Mikael's elbow twisted around her heck, choking her. She struggled desperately to free herself, but his grip was like a bar pinning her to the wall. If they had really been fighting, she realized suddenly, she'd be dead. She stopped resisting and tapped Mikael's shoulder.

"You need more practice." He released her, and she stumbled back against the wall, rubbing her throat and coughing. "You did all right for a first try," he continued, a little less harshly. "But you weren't quick enough. And you should've ducked toward my left hand because you know I'm right-handed. If you didn't know, you should've been paying closer attention."

Ari nodded and wiped the sweat from her chin. She hated feeling so vulnerable.

"We'll be doing drills like this for the next week. For now, until Nika gets back, I'd like to try something a little different." He went to the closet in the corner of the room and brought back a stack of long, flat platforms, which he stacked on top of each other to make a wall that was over Ari's head. "This time, I'll be coming from around the corner. The key in this case is to aim for my side since that will be the most exposed at this angle. Just don't forget that it won't be immediately lethal. If this was a real attack, you'd need to strike again somewhere else."

Ari hid herself behind the wall, flattening herself against the boards like she had been taught. Her heart raced as she waited. The handle of her knife, gripped between both hands, was damp with sweat. She wouldn't get much warning. Mikael would take only one step before he came around the corner because he knew she was there and could reach further than she could.

Though that step was quiet, it was all she needed. A thrill of satisfaction rushed through her whole body as the rubber blade made contact, not with her instructor's side, but with his throat.

"Well d—" he began, but she cut him off with a sharp elbow jab to the neck. He put his hands to his throat to keep her away, and she seized the chance to turn his knife blade inward.

"Stop," he shouted hoarsely. "What are you doing?"

She kicked him sharply in the side of the knee and lunged at his shoulders. He was barely able to stop himself from falling, and in the split second it took him to regain his balance, Ari smacked his wrist. His knife clattered to the floor.

"Stop," he repeated, raising his arm to shield his face. "I said stop."

Ari blinked. Her muscles had moved on autopilot, and she hadn't heard a word he said.

He took one shaky step back, then paused. "That was a nice kick, but if I'd known you were planning to do that, I would've worn a brace."

"Are you all right?" Ari asked. She wondered why she hadn't been able to stop herself, but it was a sign her apathy was wearing off, and she was proud.

"Yes." He walked to the front of the room with a barely noticeable limp and sat on the floor, his back against the wall, both legs extended in front of him. "Go outside and join Nika until the thirty minutes are over."

Ari glanced back at him, her hand on the doorknob. His head was tilted back against the mirror, and he looked like he was mumbling something to the ceiling. A quick smile crossed his face, and Ari ducked out of the room before he could look back at her and see that she had noticed.

"If he can already laugh about it, did it really hurt that much?" she mumbled, shutting the door softly behind her. *Maybe he's just glad I'm not really as useless as I looked this morning.*

Nika sat on a bench, sipping from her water bottle. She raised an eyebrow. "You're done already?"

"Aren't you supposed to be running?"

Nika shrugged. "Running isn't useful in my specialty. If you have to run, it's already a bit late, so why bother?"

Ari saw her chance. "What's your specialty?"

Nika smiled slyly and put a finger to her lips. "Where's the General?"

Ari winced. "I think I might've done some damage."

Nika shrugged. "I'm sure he's fine. Are you actually going to work out, or would you rather sit here with me?"

Ari wavered, wishing she could find an excuse to leave early. But she did need to rebuild her strength. It had been too long since she'd put this much effort into anything, let alone physical training. "I should probably work out," she concluded after a pause. "I'd rather not, but Mikael—I mean, the General—thinks it's important."

"Responsible and very correct of you, but boring."

CHAPTER 5

I found the evidence. It'll ruin him, but I don't care because it's just payback for what he did to me.

The next day, Ari asked Nika for a tour of the building.

"You won't get your clearance card until you're done with training, so you can't really go anywhere. Although . . . " Nika smiled slyly. "You could buy me lunch."

"Lunch . . . ?"

"Don't you ever let yourself take a break, Ari?"

"I took a break all afternoon yesterday." She couldn't say that she was too scared to take breaks because she might lose her motivation. "Sure, let's get lunch. I have a lot of questions to ask you anyway."

"Then let's go somewhere safe."

They drove to a small café near the office building, which to Ari looked like the most stereotypical coffee shop she'd ever seen. It was a small brick house, with wide open windows and light green shutters. The inside was painted mostly white with inspirational quotes on the walls. There was even a glass case full of pastries, which smelled sugary and made Ari's mouth water.

The waiter seated them outside in the warm summer sunshine and left them with tea and a basket of bread. Ari tore her eyes away from the pastries.

"This place claims to be French," said Nika, sipping her tea. "I've never been to France, but it feels French to me."

This looks like someplace Lia would like, Ari thought absentmindedly. Hadn't they once held a secret meeting in a place like this? It was the perfect cover—nobody would think twice about a pair of chattering girls in a coffee shop, no matter what they were talking about.

"So, what do you want to ask me?"

"I guess I'm just curious about what you do," Ari said slowly. There was so much she didn't understand that she didn't know what to ask first. "The NDEB, publicly, enforces the country's rules about regulated drugs. That's a vague mission statement, and they didn't tell me anything else during the interview. Can you clarify?"

"You mean you didn't ask before you took the job?" Nika mocked. "Well, I can fill you in. You and I are special agents. We mingle and collect information without attracting any attention. Then, once we've found everything we can, we arrest everyone we have evidence against."

"So basically, we pretend to be addicts?" Ari was amused.

"We're not allowed to use drugs. Usually, you'll be given some specific role to act for cover, and that won't change no matter what missions you're doing, for consistency's sake in case anyone tried to trace you. You're being trained for combat, so I assume you'll be going to the depths of the slums for whatever you do. Have fun." Nika snickered. "I live in the high places of the world."

Ari tried again. "What do you do?"

"We aren't supposed to share information like that in public," said Nika dismissively. "But I will say, I think this next mission—the one we're training for—is going to be different than the ones I've done before. Did you know that the General just showed up at the NDEB a month ago? I should be higher ranking than him, but he started at the top. And he was specific about wanting you on his team."

"How do you know?"

"I was sitting in on a conversation between him and Yuno—that's the department head, the guy we all report to—and they argued about it for half an hour. Yuno didn't want you because he preferred to use someone he's familiar with, but the General convinced him that you would be better than any agents we have. He said a lot about your level of expertise, so he must've seen you train."

"Wait," interrupted Ari, curious. "How did Mikael—the General— get a job in the first place?"

"That has to do with your old team and their division," answered Nika. "At least, that's what I heard. When it was disbanded, the NDEB snapped up all the recruits they could get, especially high-ranking officers like the General."

"But you said he was hired this month. Our team disbanded a year ago, so what happened in between?"

"I don't really understand that either," said Nika. "It probably has to do with how long the application process takes."

"Mine took only a few days."

She shrugged. "I don't know all the details, and to be honest, I don't really care. I do what's expected of me and leave it at that."

"All right," conceded Ari reluctantly. "But there's still a lot that doesn't make sense."

"There's a lot that doesn't make sense to me either. It seems like you don't really know who Mikael is, or at least that you haven't seen him in a long time. Why's that, if you don't mind me asking? I thought you guys worked together."

Ari paused. "I just don't remember what he did in the army. And he doesn't seem very happy that I don't remember," she added ruefully.

The waiter brought their meals and replenished their tea, interrupting the conversation.

"So," said Nika, her mouth full of sandwich, "what were things like in the army? I was planning to enlist before I heard about the NDEB."

Ari choked on her drink, distracted.

"You okay?" Nika handed her a napkin.

Ari looked down at her sandwich and pretended to be choosing a fry, which bought her enough time to think of a reply. "I don't really remember," she said vaguely. After all, there was nothing else she could say, even if she had wanted to talk about it.

"You don't remember?" Nika looked puzzled. "You were just there a year ago, right?"

"I don't remember," repeated Ari. "I mean, I remember some things, like our uniforms and the names of the people who were on my team. And some faces. But that's it. I don't remember much about what we did."

"Sounds dramatic," said Nika. "Like they wiped your memory or something. You sure you're not some kind of bionic superhuman?"

Ari shrugged halfheartedly. That wasn't something she even wanted to joke about.

"Didn't your code name used to be Jules or something?"

"Not you, too," snapped Ari, slamming her teacup on the table so hard that the breadbasket rattled. The words tumbled out before she could stop herself. "You might as well just call me by my employee number. I don't even get to keep my own name. Is that all I am?"

"Oh, I'm sorry!" cried Nika. "I didn't mean to—"

Ari took a deep gulp of air. "No, I'm sorry. It's fine." She cursed her own frustration. How could Nika have known not to call her that? "I just don't like hearing that. It's not my name."

"Okay." Nika returned to her sandwich, and there were a few minutes of tense, gloomy silence.

"Sorry." Ari was getting too good at apologizing.

"Oh, no, it's fine," said Nika. "I guess you didn't really like it. That's understandable."

"I didn't not like it, I just—" Ari struggled for words.

Every time I try to tell someone . . . this. This stupid mental block.

"You don't have to tell me," said Nika kindly. "But either way, maybe we should talk about what we're doing now. What other questions do you have for me?"

Ari shook her head. She couldn't think of anything but the mumble and jumble of voices that were telling her to run, to get away from her interrogator no matter how ridiculous she looked.

"I don't know anything else about the General," said Nika, obviously trying to change the subject. "Are you ready to go back?"

"Here's a list of common abbreviations." The instructor pointed to the projection screen.

Ari yawned in boredom, hiding her mouth behind her hand. She wanted to close her eyes and rest her head on the desk, but it would've been too obvious since she and Nika were the only students in a tiny classroom. She forced herself to focus on the board, but she saw only a maze of letters and numbers and subscripts.

"Each drug is made differently, of course, but common components of meth, as an example, include drain cleaner, battery acid, antifreeze, and fuel. Especially meth—it's relatively easy to find the ingredients needed to make it. I hope after knowing this that you won't try anything."

Ari clicked her pen. How much of a temptation did the instructor think modified battery acid was?

"Don't forget to look online for copies of the slides. You'll be expected to know it all by the end of the week. That's it for today."

Ari stood and pushed her chair under the desk out of sheer habit. It felt like being back in the third grade. Even the army classes hadn't been this boring. She held the door for Nika as they escaped the classroom then followed her into the hallway. The door clicked shut behind them.

Nika giggled. "I've been in that class three times," she said. "It doesn't get any better."

"How come you've repeated this class?"

"They keep re-assigning me the class every time I get a new partner."

"Why do you keep changing partners? Wouldn't it be easier for everyone to keep the same partners for every mission? That's how we did it in the army . . . " Her voice trailed off. She studied the sharp curve of Nika's shoulders: tense and uncomfortable. "I mean, I never switched partners when I was in the army," she added hastily. "I guess that's more normal here."

"For now, we just need to make sure we're ready for the quiz," said Nika abruptly. "I'll help you study if you want, but I have to file some paperwork first. Call me when you're ready." She clicked past Ari and disappeared around the corner.

Ari paused in the middle of the hallway, disappointed and confused. She'd never been partnered with someone she didn't know intimately, and it was jarring to realize that her safety might depend on someone she couldn't even have a normal conversation with.

"Hey, hey, hey! It's the new recruit!"

Ari recognized the voice. "Hello, Grey."

Somehow Grey managed to make even his suit look casual, with his hands stuffed in his pockets and his coat slouched off one shoulder. Ari thought he looked exactly like a classic spy from the old movies. All he needed was a pair of dark sunglasses, and the picture would be complete.

"I wish I could take responsibility for getting you here, but since I can't, I'll just wish you all the best." He leaned against the wall and smiled. "You're partnered with Nika?"

Ari nodded, unsure what she was allowed to tell him.

"You guys will make a good team."

"I hope so. I haven't known her for very long. It's not like when you and Lia and Kira and I all trained together for months at a time."

"I bet I know exactly what you're worried about," said Grey teasingly. "I bet you're thinking, why doesn't she ever tell me anything?"

"Right," answered Ari, raising an eyebrow. "Let me guess. Lia knows about Nika, and she told you that's how I'd react to having her as a partner. That's the only way you could've known."

"Spot on!" He clapped. "Well, mostly. Lia met Nika when we first started working here, and they know each other pretty well—for casual friends, at least. It's not like they're besties. But apparently Lia tried asking Nika some questions and got vague answers, and she thought that would bother you, so she mentioned it to me."

"She's too sharp to be a psychologist." Ari smiled. "She should go into the detective business. She could be the next Sherlock Holmes."

Grey laughed. "I hope not. I'm fine with her being a practicing psychologist, and I don't mind that she works here, but I don't want her doing field work anymore. The special agent division was . . ."

"Too much," finished Ari. "I agree. I'm glad Lia has you to rely on."

"Me, too!" Grey gave her a thumbs up. "All right, I'll get back to work. Good luck with Nika and Mikael. They're characters, all right. And if you ever . . . " He hesitated. "I know you and Lia aren't on good terms, but if you ever need a psychologist, or just want to talk, Lia's two floors down."

"Thanks." *Of course Grey would want us to start talking again. I bet Lia's been venting to him about it.* She mock saluted, drawing her heels together and straightening up. "Before you go, what department are you working in? I might have more questions for you later."

Grey laughed, and Ari thought he sounded a little embarrassed. "Well, originally, I wanted to be a special agent. But Lia didn't like that idea, so I went into chemical synthesis. If we find a drug we don't know, I plug it into the computer to see what it's made of. If there isn't any real work to do, they put me in paperwork."

"Thanks, Grey."

She hurried down the hallway in the opposite direction to see if she could find Nika, but nobody was in sight above the cubicle walls, so she sat down in her desk chair and spun around thoughtfully. She couldn't shake a vague feeling of guilt. So far, she'd been as useful as a roadblock. She was just another new face to train.

At least Lia and Grey know what they want from life. Why can't I be more like them?

CHAPTER 6

They said it was him. I said it couldn't have been. They said they'd get me the proof I need. I don't want proof. If Kira did something like that, I don't want to know.

Ari made a conscientious effort to succeed at training. She memorized pages of facts, sniffed chemicals until she could identify them all without a second thought, and practiced administering overdose reversal. She and Nika stayed in the office late at night, quizzing each other.

She took the final exam at the end of the week and passed with flying colors, exhausted and proud of herself. How long had it been since she'd tried this hard at anything?

"We have the rest of the day off." Nika tucked her pencil behind her ear and yawned. "We should go get coffee to celebrate."

"I have some errands I need to run—you know, groceries and stuff," Ari said. "Can we skip the coffee for today?"

"Oh, sure, that's fine with me!" Nika agreed. "I should probably stop by the store, too. Where do you live?"

Ari gave her the wrong address, feeling like a hypocrite for thinking Nika wasn't transparent enough with her. "I'll see you tomorrow."

Ari drove to the grocery store, filled up her basket with frozen vegetables and microwaveable dinners, and brought them back to her apartment.

The room was dark, and she opened all the windows to let in the fading sunlight. Someday she'd make up for lying to Nika by inviting her over. But today wasn't that day.

She flicked on her light switch. Nothing happened. She flicked it again, and again. Then she tried another one across the room. Still nothing. She peeked out the window and saw that the porch lights, which came on at the same time every evening, were shining brightly. Why would her lights be off if those were on? A sneaking, sick feeling in the pit of her stomach warned her that it wasn't simply routine maintenance, but she checked her circuit breaker anyway. Nothing was wrong.

She flipped through her mail, piled high on the counter. Auto-pay, auto-pay, auto-pay. Was her credit card working?

She dropped onto her bed and opened her laptop. There should've been enough left from her pension to pay the electricity bill for another month at least.

Then she saw the balance. $10.54.

For a moment she was startled, then she remembered. The rest of the account balance had gone to pay her hospital bills the night of Lia's wedding.

With a frustrated sigh, she slammed her computer shut. She hadn't been paid yet for her work at the NDEB—she still had a week to wait. That meant a week without lights, and she had a feeling that electricity wasn't the only thing missing. She turned on her sink. Full flow . . . a little less . . . drip, drip. The water trickled to a stop.

"A nice mess I've made," she mumbled. "What am I supposed to do, shower with bottled water? And how am I supposed to buy the bottled water? And how am I going to cook all this microwaveable food?"

Slowly she put it all back in the grocery bags and slung them over her shoulder. Because she couldn't afford to waste gas by driving, she walked the two miles back to the grocery store, cursing both her bad luck and her bad decisions.

She returned all the groceries and bought canned food instead. It was heavier to carry, but Ari tried to cheer herself up by thinking that this exempted her from the day's workout.

Two miles back. Every step felt heavy and full of shame, no matter how she tried to distract herself. She'd have to find someplace to fill her water bottle . . . a drinking fountain, maybe? She hadn't seen a single one on her way to the store. There was a park nearby—maybe there was one there. But still, even if she had groceries and water, she wouldn't be able to use her bathroom.

A wave of frustration swept over her, and she stopped in the middle of the sidewalk. There was no point in trying to make the best of it when the best looked like this.

She pulled out her phone. For a moment, she was afraid it wouldn't work, but when she saw the reassuring four bars in the upper right corner of the screen, she dialed Nika's number.

"Hey," she said, as confidently as she could manage. "They're doing some work on my apartment, and I can't stay there next week. Is it all right if I come stay with you?"

"Sure!" Nika said. Ari sighed with relief. "Now I have two people to cook for!"

"I can bring my own food if you'd—"

"No, no, I'm happy about it. I love cooking!"

Feeling a little less hopeless, Ari hurried back to her apartment and packed a duffel bag with enough clothes for the week. She wished she had something to give Nika as a polite hostess gift, but she couldn't find anything except what she had in her pantry—cans upon cans of refried beans. So, she gave up the idea, put her suitcase in the car, and drove to Nika's apartment. When she arrived, she still had half a tank of gas. Maybe enough for the week if she was stingy.

"Sorry." She excused herself over and over as Nika helped her unpack. "This was sudden. I promise I won't be too much of a nuisance."

"It's fine!" Nika reassured her. "Seriously. I'm happy to help."

Ari nodded.

How lucky am I to have a friend like this. Even if there are some things we can't talk about.

"There's no training this week." Mikael flipped through the papers on his desk.

"Why not?" Nika leaned forward and tried to peek over the papers.

Mikael flicked them out of sight. "Ari trained with the army special agents division, and you took this class seven times, so it seems superfluous to do it again." He paused. "We'll give you a mission instead."

Nika's mouth dropped open.

"It goes against protocol, but some things are more important than rules."

"Like what?" Ari asked.

"Like Vita."

"What's Vita?"

"I don't have all the details, either." He shifted in his chair, and a quick flash of frustration crossed his face. "There's a lot you'll need to know before you can take this mission. It's best if your teammates brief you because they all have prior experience with Vita. One of them even met him in person. Isn't that right, Nika?"

"That's right," Nika said slowly. Her face looked slightly gray.

"Hopefully, you'll both be leaving Tuesday or Wednesday of next week," Mikael continued. "Travel, room, and board will be covered by the NDEB, so you don't need to worry about that. Your only job is to blend in as much as possible. I'm sure you both know that doesn't extend to using drugs. But they'll cover all the rules."

Ari glanced at Nika from the corner of her eyes. She looked nervous. All the muscles in her arms were tight.

"Thank you." Ari stood up, promising herself she'd buy Nika a coffee later as slight repayment for her hospitality. Maybe that would calm her down. "Where should we go for the briefing?"

"To the conference room down the hall."

The room was bright and airy, surrounded by clear, reflectionless windows on three sides. In its center was a long conference table surrounded by soft, luxurious office chairs. Ari pinched herself, trying not to think about how much fun it would be to sit in one and spin round and round. When she'd been briefed in the military, they'd usually been in an underground, windowless bunker with hard plastic chairs—if they got chairs at all. Perhaps she was working her way up in the world, after all.

At the opposite end of the table from the door, two agents were setting up a whiteboard. One of them was short, dark-haired, and tight-lipped. He curtly introduced himself as Yuri. Ari couldn't quite put her finger on any defining feature of the other agent. She could've walked out on the street anywhere in the city and seen a dozen people who looked like him. But when he raised his arm to clean the whiteboard, she noticed a deep, white burn scar peeking out from under his sleeve. That kind of mark she could recognize anywhere. He introduced himself as Calvin.

"Sorry for the delay," said Calvin. "There was a mix-up with some of the files. Yuno was supposed to give them to me an hour ago, but he says he was never told about it. They're classified, so it might take him a while to fill out all the paperwork he needs."

Nika squinted. "Yuno never forgets anything. Are you sure he was in charge of this?"

Calvin shrugged. "Mikael told me he'd give me all the information we need."

"Maybe there was some information they wanted to add or take out first," suggested Yuri, without looking up.

Ari was quick to guess the relationships in the room. Calvin and Yuri clearly already knew Nika—their introduction had been specifically directed at Ari. Though Yuri, with his drooping eyes and pinched lips looked too uninterested to be close friends with either Calvin or Nika. Well, regardless, that made Ari the only outsider. Why hadn't she been introduced to Calvin and Yuri earlier? Had that been yet another oversight on Yuno's part?

And why, come to think of it, is Yuno directly overseeing this mission? Isn't he the head of the whole department?

"What did Mikael tell you?" Calvin swiveled his chair to face Ari.

Maybe Calvin already knew what Mikael had said, or maybe he didn't, but he obviously wanted to see if Ari could repeat it clearly.

"He told us only that we're going to Seattle and that our mission has something to do with Vita."

"Vika, not Vita," corrected Yuri from the corner.

"Right," said Calvin. "You must've heard the name wrong."

From the corner of her eye Ari could see Nika shaking her head slightly.

"That was a typo on the paperwork," she said. "You guys spelled his name wrong. It's Vita."

"Vika," said Yuri.

"Vita."

"Look, I've met him. Among his agents, he's known as Vita. But his real name is Vika." Yuri crossed his arms irritably.

Nika conceded with a curt nod. "Well, fine, but nobody knows him as that. Do you know his last name?"

"No."

"Then how do you know his first name?"

Yuri was about to give an annoyed response, but Calvin cut him off. "You'll both have access to what we know about him, which isn't much, but the first thing you need to know is what you'll be doing."

Nika sat back in her chair, and Yuri turned to face the window.

"Ari is correct that you'll be traveling to Seattle. That's where Vita lives. And you can find out a lot about him by going online." He fiddled with his laptop and turned it around so that Ari and Nika could see it.

"Online?" Ari blinked and stared at the Instagram account.

Calvin looked down at the keyboard, obviously trying not to laugh. "He's a celebrity."

"Ninety thousand followers?" Nika shook her head. "That's more than he had when I was there last year. He must be making a killing."

"Hold on," Ari stammered. "Isn't this one of those geeky health nut profiles? The guy on here … he can't be into drugs. It looks like he eats only … carrots and healthy smoothies and stuff. Maybe marijuana, but even that seems like a stretch. Are we sure this is in the NDEB's jurisdiction?"

"He's not into drugs," Yuri said.

Calvin pushed his laptop toward Ari, and she scrolled through the profile. Vegetables. Endless rows of carrots. Muscular men in the gym, selfies with organic advertisements. She had never seen anything so painfully stereotypical. Vita, whatever else he might be, was obviously a walking smoothie brand.

Calvin pulled the laptop back over in front of him. "Nika, tell her what you know."

"It's complicated," Nika said. "I'll leave out some details to make the story shorter. Basically, we've seen an influx of Class I drugs smuggled up to the Northern states, especially as high-class drugs are becoming recreationally legal. We know they're there because the hospitals are crammed full of people who've OD'd."

"Straightforward so far. But what does this have to do with Vita?"

"I was in Seattle last year investigating. I convinced some patients in the hospital that they wouldn't get into legal trouble if they told me everything they knew about where they got the drugs. Everything they told us traced back to a guy they called Vita."

"I went to clean up after that mission," Yuri interrupted. Nika rolled her eyes. "I met him, and he told me himself."

"Hold on." Ari held up her hands. "You talked to this Vita person, and he straight up told you he sells drugs?"

Yuri nodded.

"So why didn't you arrest him on the spot?"

"Because we have no solid proof."

"What? How can you not have proof if he told you? You didn't record it?"

"No. I wasn't expecting him to say that." Yuri looked sullen. "It's my word against everybody's. There's nothing that would hold up in a court of law, and, as I said before, he's popular. If we tried to do anything underhanded, the story would be all over social media in a matter of hours. And we'd be the ones in trouble, not Vika."

"How do you know he wasn't joking?"

"Because he gave me this." Yuri held up a tiny plastic bag full of white powder.

Nika nodded. "Meth."

"Right. I had the lab sequence it to make sure."

Ari blinked. "Are you serious? Why didn't you just check the fingerprints on that plastic bag? There's no way he could've handled it without leaving something behind."

"You think we didn't try that?" Yuri began, but Calvin cut him off.

"That just speaks to Vita's skill," he said. "There wasn't a trace of DNA on the bag. He must have cleaned it thoroughly before he gave it to Yuri, and even then, we're not sure how he managed to avoid touching it at all. Even a single hair would've been enough, but there's nothing."

"He even had gloves on when he handed it to me," added Yuri. "Special gloves. He must have known ordinary ones wouldn't be sufficient."

"Then how are we going to catch him?"

"Oh, you three get the best job!" Calvin turned to the whiteboard and began writing.

Ari leaned over to Nika and whispered. "Three?"

She nodded, keeping her eyes fixed to the whiteboard. "Yuri," she mouthed.

Ari typed a note on her phone under the table where Nika could see it. "What about Mikael?"

Nika glanced down. "He stays here," she whispered. "Mission heads don't leave the office."

"Here's what you're going to do." Calvin held his dry erase marker to the board next to the number one, followed by Ari's name. "Ari, you and Yuri will have pretty much the same job. You'll be blending in with the people who are buying these smuggled drugs so we can find out who their dealers are. Hopefully, if you're lucky, you'll be able to join one of their cliques—"

"We call them syndicates," Yuri interjected.

"—and rise up in the ranks until you start hearing about Vita. If you do well, it might take a year. If you're careful and don't rush, two years. This is going to be a long mission."

Ari pinched her arm to make sure she was awake. So far, not a single detail of the story she'd been told made any sense at all.

"Nika will be—"

"I'll get my marching orders later," she interrupted with a cheerful smile. "I don't want anyone getting confused. I know Ari got a lot of information thrown at her all at once."

"Let me get this straight," Ari said slowly. "You want me to travel to a city I've never been in, start buying drugs in hopes of joining an actual gang—syndicate—and then try to become one of the leaders?"

Calvin nodded. "Basically."

"Will Yuri and I be working together?"

Yuri shook his head in undisguised annoyance. "Of course not. Special agents almost always work alone. That way, if one gets caught, the other can keep on with the mission."

"What happens if you *do* get caught?"

"Well, guns aren't technically allowed in Seattle, which means that you won't be defending yourself if you're stupid enough to let anyone find out who you work for." Yuri shrugged.

Wonderful.

But she didn't have much of a choice.

"So when do we leave?"

Calvin winked at Yuri. "I told you she'd go for it."

Ari narrowed her eyes and crossed her arms. "Is this some kind of joke?"

"Of course not." Calvin pushed a pen and stack of papers toward her. "Can you sign these pages at the bottom, please? It basically says we aren't responsible if you die and who to send your paycheck to if you go missing."

"This is ridiculous." Ari glanced over the first page. She felt the same familiar adrenaline rush she remembered from the first time she'd signed up for the army. "You can't possibly be chasing a criminal Instagram celebrity and not know how to arrest him. You should be able to trace his internet records or something. You can't be at a complete loss."

"I like that attitude," said Calvin. "You should be skeptical, but not of us. As your teammates, we wouldn't lie to you."

"You would say this," mumbled Ari indecisively, scanning the documents as quickly as she could. They all looked official. If this was a prank, everyone seemed to be taking it seriously.

Now they were staring at her, waiting expectantly for her to say something.

"I'm not going to sign my name to this until I'm sure you're not messing with me."

"We're not," said Nika. "As crazy as this sounds, it's all real."

Ari paused. *Surely Nika couldn't have faked her reaction when Mikael first told us about the mission.* The clenched fists, the pale face, the unsuccessful attempts to hide her nervousness—they hadn't seemed staged. And if this really was a prank, Nika was obviously in the know, so she should've been excited or amused, not frightened.

She glanced at Yuri and Calvin. There wasn't a trace of a smile on their faces. In fact, if anything, they looked anxious.

"All right, what gives?" she said at last, scribbling her signature on the last page. "If you're messing with me, I'll just sue *you*."

"Great!" Calvin organized the pages into a neat stack and tucked them into a yellow folder. "Mikael said you'd be happy to take the mission."

Ari didn't reply. She was too busy wondering what would happen on the off chance that the mission wasn't a prank, and she was really moving to Seattle.

"We'll email your plane tickets tomorrow," Calvin shut the folder and stood. "All three of you will be taking different flights so you can't be traced."

"Do we need fake identities?" Ari asked.

"We don't do that here," Yuri answered.

"Why not? Wouldn't it be odd if our stories contradicted each other?"

"You have a lot left to learn," he scoffed. "Having fake identities is what causes contradictions in the first place. If we all use our real identities, there won't be anything to worry about. Of course, we'll leave out the part about working at the NDEB."

Stifling her irritation, she walked up to him and held out a hand. "It was nice to meet you, Yuri." They'd have to get along if they were working together, and she might as well start trying early.

He looked up at her from his chair for a long five seconds before standing up and shaking her hand. His dark brown eyes crinkled in the best smile he could manage.

"I look forward to working together." He sounded as pleased as if he'd bitten into a lemon.

"Not super happy to be working with you again, Yuri." Nika brushed past him.

"Same to you."

"Ah, I'm just kidding." Nika shrugged.

"I wasn't, but thank you for clarifying."

Nika stuck her tongue out at him, and Calvin sighed. "I'm sorry for putting you with these two, Ari. They've known each other since forever. That's why the NDEB always puts them on the same team."

"It's all in good fun," said Nika. "We don't get along, but that's expected given Yuri's personality, or lack thereof. Don't you think we should go pack now, Ari?"

"Sure, if you're ready. Do we need anything else?" She looked at Calvin, giving him a last chance to tell her it was all a prank and she wasn't really going to chase a kale-crazed social media influencer.

"No, you're good to go."

What kinds of clothes do I need to bring if I'm going to blend in with criminals? Do I look like a criminal?

Ari studied herself in the mirror. Dark hair and dark eyes—that was all right. She didn't have any piercings—not even in her ears—and definitely no tattoos. But, she mused, wasn't street fashion characterized by boisterous, cheap jewelry? She felt uncomfortably unprepared. If this was the army, she would've been given a uniform and told to wear it, no questions asked.

She stuffed the few clothes she'd brought from her apartment back into her suitcase—t-shirts, ripped jeans, and sweatshirts and a few spare uniforms. She could buy more clothes in Seattle now that she didn't have to worry about her electric or water bills for a while. Then she sat on the suitcase, zipped it up, and pulled a strap around it. *Ready to go.*

She opened her email on her laptop and printed her boarding passes. Then she checked her bank account. Five dollars and thirty-six cents. Enough for a coffee in the morning. Then, she'd just have to hope she didn't encounter any more serious expenses until she received her first paycheck.

Nika was waiting for her when she got back to the apartment. Ari could smell eggs and bacon, and she sniffed hungrily.

"Plenty for all." Nika waved her spatula invitingly toward Ari.

"Thank you." Ari fought off a sudden urge to cry and give Nika a bear hug. Food was the fastest way to her heart. "It smells amazing."

"Of course!" Nika took the pan off the stove and divided the eggs and bacon between two plates, one of which she set in front of Ari. "I like to cook for someone who likes to eat." She went back into the kitchen, poked around in one of the cabinets, and produced a bottle of white wine. "Want some?"

Ari was suddenly and bitterly reminded of Lia's wedding night. She hadn't touched alcohol since. "No thanks."

"Aww, too bad. I hate drinking alone." Nika replaced the bottle. "We'll save it for a good party time."

Ari nodded, her thoughts elsewhere. The scent of alcohol made her feel as if she was still lying on the floor in the bar. And that reminded her: in the rush of training and excitement of getting her first mission, she'd forgotten that she wanted to find out what she had been drugged with. The hospital report, still sitting on her counter at home, was inconclusive. That was unfinished business she didn't want to let slide.

Didn't Grey say he works in the chemical synthesis division? He might be able to figure it out.

"You just reminded me of something." Ari stood up and brushed the bacon crumbs off her shirt. "I'll be right back. I need to run to the office."

"Run to the office? Wait, you're going back to work?"

"I'll be quick." Ari felt a sudden stab of anxiety. This was her last chance to figure out what had happened. There was no time to waste—their plane took off early the next morning. She hoped Grey was still at the office.

It felt like ages to Ari before she pulled into the parking lot, swiped her key card at the front door, and ran up the steps two at a time to the laboratory. Third floor—or was it fourth? No, it was third. The door was locked. Impatiently, she swiped her card again and burst inside. The office was quiet.

She glanced around. Where would Grey's desk be?

"Are you looking for someone?"

Ari jumped, and the shy chemist started back and stumbled into the wall.

I'm looking for Grey," Ari stammered.

"I think he's in the laboratory." He gestured toward the glass-enclosed space at the center of the room. "You'll need to suit up if you want to go inside. Swipe your badge at the door."

"Thanks." Ari borrowed a white suit from the rack near the door of the glass room, slipped it on as quickly as she could, and let herself inside.

"Is that who I think it is?" One of the three people in the room squinted at her from behind a pair of safety goggles. "Ari?"

"Grey?"

"What in the world are you doing in here?" He dropped the safety goggles, and Ari could read surprise on his face. "Were you looking for me?"

"I told you I might have some questions."

He nodded. "Go on."

"So I'm leaving tomorrow for a mission—"

"Good for you! You must've done well with their training if you're out so fast."

"Yes, well. Do you remember what happened to me on your wedding night?"

"Yes," said Grey warily. "You're not going to ask me to talk to Lia about it, are you? She's still pretty upset."

"No." Ari bit her lip. "I'll talk to her myself. There's a lot we need to work through. But meanwhile, I need you to figure out what I was drugged with."

"No can do. I don't have any of that drink left."

"I can give you a hint. I think it might have been oxyarcyan."

Grey raised an eyebrow. "Do you mean oxycodone? Nobody outside of our army division would know about oxyarcyan."

"Not oxycodone. I'm sure it was oxyarcyan."

"Why?"

"Because the man I met with right before I started getting dizzy was from the special agent division, and he's the only one besides the bartender who could've spiked my drink. And you remember how they made us read up on all the effects of the drugs they created? We had to take a whole course on it. What I felt exactly matched the sensations they described from the oxyarcyan."

"From what I heard, you had a pretty generic reaction." Grey shrugged. "The drug really could've been anything. Or you could've just been drunk. Besides, oxyarcyan is an assassination drug, and you should've died if that's really what you took."

"I didn't die because the dosage was small," Ari insisted. "And I was on only my second drink, so I wasn't drunk yet. I'm serious about this, Grey. I can't prove who drugged me or why. But I want to find out."

"Nobody's supposed to know the formula. It's classified." Grey sighed. "Why are you so insistent on figuring it out? It's not going to help you. Even if we still had a sample of the drink, it would be difficult to compare the formula to whatever drug was in it. I'm not supposed to use this equipment for personal reasons like that."

She paused, tapping her fingers against the table. Any explanation would only make Grey more reluctant to help her.

"Please," she said at last. "I have a plan. It's not an official plan. I know it must sound like I'm crazy, but I can't just accept that it was all a coincidence that someone from the army showed up on the same night I got sick."

"But how is the formula going to help?"

"I really need you to stop asking questions, Grey. Trust me on this."

He frowned. "I'm not going to risk losing my clearance over a hunch."

"Think about it," Ari pleaded. "Someone from the army has tracked me down after years of no communication with anyone from the unit. They refused to tell me who they were or how they knew me. They obviously spiked my drink. Maybe they were even trying to kill me. Don't you think we need to look into that?"

"If it was so important, someone else would be looking into it."

"No, they wouldn't. Nobody even wants to talk about us anymore, and they're certainly not going to protect us. We have to keep ourselves safe now. Me, you, Lia—we could all be in danger and not even know it."

The moment the words were out of her mouth, Ari knew she'd hit on the only possibility of convincing Grey to help. His one weakness, no matter the situation, was Lia. But she felt like she was abusing Lia's name. She didn't deserve to be dragged into this, and Ari felt a brief flash of guilt.

Still, it couldn't be helped. And there was always the possibility that she was right, and Lia really was in danger.

"I guess I can try to get it for you," Grey said reluctantly. " Do you know what the components are?"

Ari shook her head.

"Mostly a modified arsenic compound and cyanide. Technically, in some forms, it's explosive, too."

"I'm glad I made it through that," she said. "Not many people can say they've drunk cyanide and survived."

"That's why I don't think you did," Grey said. "Remember, I can't prove anything. But if you think it'll help, I can get the formula."

"That's not all I want," Ari said. "I need you to reproduce the drug."

Grey crossed his arms. "Ari, didn't you hear me say that it's an assassination drug? You're not supposed to have it. I'm not supposed to have it. If we're caught with it, we'll be in huge trouble. I'll get you the formula, but that's it."

Ari hesitated. "Okay," she said. "That's enough."

"What are you trying to do?"

Ari gave him a huge smile. "Nothing! I just was curious to know if we could make it again, that's all. I know the file was destroyed when our team was disbanded."

"Whatever you say."

She nodded. "Thanks for clearing this up for me. Oh, and . . . " Ari paused. "Can I visit Lia tonight? Or is it too late? It's already after seven."

"Sure! She's missing you a lot, and I think she really wants to make up with you before you leave." Ari could sense his tension dissipating.

"You're sure she won't mind?"

"'Course not," Grey assured her. "She won't want you to leave without talking to her. And you'll be gone—next week, did you say? For how long?" He wrote down their address on a sticky note and handed it to her.

"I'll be gone for a while," Ari answered. The paperwork she'd signed earlier barred her from saying anything more. "Thanks, Grey. I'll go visit her."

Ari left the building satisfied. She hadn't gotten everything she wanted, but at least she had Grey's promise that he'd find the formula. With that, all she needed to prove her theory correct was the drug itself. Surely among the people she'd meet in Seattle, someone would know how to make it.

It was a ridiculous, dangerous idea that could get her killed. *But it's not like I have much to lose.*

What do you have to gain?

She knew the answer, though she didn't want to admit it. It wasn't just that she enjoyed the feeling of being in danger or that she wanted to prosecute whoever had drugged her. All she wanted was to show that someone *had* used oxyarcyan because if they had, it would prove someone had targeted her specifically. And she couldn't get rid of the feeling that it might have had something to do with the past she couldn't remember—the same past that the tormenting voices in her head constantly teased her with. If she could remember, maybe she could finally come to peace with what had happened, and the voices would be silenced once and for all.

Key word: "maybe." But is this worth dying for if something goes wrong?

"Anything to shut you up." Ari always tried to avoid answering the voices aloud, terrified of mixing the fantasy in her mind with reality. But today, finally, they felt so distant that she could risk it.

She hummed along with the radio on the way to Grey and Lia's apartment, feeling better than she had in a long time. This was her last night to relax. And it was also her chance to make things right with Lia before she left.

Lia opened the door before she even knocked. "Ari!" She enveloped her in a bear hug. "I've missed you!"

"Me, too!" Ari disentangled herself and wrapped her arms around Lia's thin shoulders, breathing a sigh of relief. Lia wasn't angry with her. "I'm so sorry I haven't come to visit sooner. I really did mean to. It's just that I've been busy, and stuff hasn't really been working out, so . . ."

"Don't worry about it! You're here now," Lia chirped with her usual bright, artificial cheerfulness. "Want some coffee?"

"This late at night?" Ari smiled to herself. Lia hadn't changed at all.

"Yes, of course!" Lia dragged her into the kitchen and handed her a steaming mug. Ari sniffed it and lost all power to refuse. "This is the time of night when you start needing coffee. What have you been up to? Sit down over here and tell me."

I guess we're not going to talk about that last phone call?

Ari curled up on the edge of Lia's white sofa against a sheepskin pillow and put her coffee on the table beside her. The whole apartment, she noticed, was furnished much more maturely than she expected. White sofa and colorful accent pillows, minimalist lamps, and tiny succulent plants scattered around any flat surface in the room. There wasn't a trace of the pink and glitter she associated with Lia's personality. Grey must have taken a hand in the decorating, thought Ari, though she was surprised he didn't like pink and glitter, too.

"Well," she began, "I guess the first thing I should tell you is that I'm leaving tomorrow. The NDEB is sending me to Seattle for a mission."

Lia's face became serious. "Seattle? Some of the agents who come see me have mentioned that. It's where the drugs are being crossed into Canada, isn't it?"

"Right," said Ari. "Apparently . . . " She stopped herself.

"Don't worry, I already know about Vita. I follow him on social media." Lia put her phone in Ari's face, and she leaned back to see the screen clearly. "@LifeStyleByVita is his username everywhere. I was surprised when I heard what he really does for a living. One of my clients told me, and I had to go check the library to make sure he wasn't psychotic. I couldn't believe my eyes."

"Me neither," agreed Ari. "Though I hadn't heard of him before today."

"Today? You're leaving tomorrow, and they just told you about it today? Sounds like the army all over again."

"It is. In fact, the team leader—I guess that's what we call him—reminds me of Kira."

"Mikael? Is that who you're talking about?" She laughed. "I suppose he is a lot like Kira—snobby and dramatic."

That wasn't how Ari thought of Kira, but she didn't remember enough to argue. She smiled uncertainly.

"Speaking of Kira," continued Lia, "he was executed exactly a year ago today. Did you know that?"

Ari searched herself for any shred of emotion one way or the other, but the news affected her about as much as if Lia was talking about a total stranger. She couldn't even picture his face anymore.

"Do you ever find it hard to remember what happened at the army?" she asked suddenly. "Like it was all a dream, or something?"

"I don't remember the details."

"Of course you don't." Ari forced a smile. "I'm sorry. That was part of your training, wasn't it?"

"Training?" Lia tilted her head. "What training?"

"Well, I guess not calling it training was part of your . . . training, too." Ari couldn't help laughing. "We don't need to talk about this right now. I'm just glad you're doing better, Lia. You and Grey take good care of each other. I'm happy for you. I really am." And for the first time in a long time, she sincerely meant it.

"I should head out," she added. "I have to finish some packing, and the flight leaves early tomorrow . . . so I need to get some sleep."

"Aww, it was too short," protested Lia. "But I get it. Call me occasionally, please? I want to hear how you're doing."

"Sure."

She paused at the door, trying to decide if she should run while she had the chance. She'd been expecting Lia to nag her about their argument, even if she put it off to the last minute, but so far, Lia hadn't said a word about it. And Ari couldn't leave without apologizing.

"Lia," she began uncertainly. "About your wedding . . . "

"That was such a lovely evening!" Lia gasped, folding her hands together and smiling brightly. "Everything about it was perfect. I'm so glad you got to see it."

"So glad I got to see . . . what?"

"I guess you'd better find someone to marry soon." Lia giggled. "Since you caught the bouquet. It's tradition, you know."

Ari was mystified. "What bouquet? What are you talking about?"

Lia paused, and her forehead creased. "You don't remember? Man, I thought it was going to be the most memorable evening of my whole life." She looked a little hurt.

Ari laughed uncomfortably. "Earth to Lia. I don't know what you're thinking of, but I didn't go to your wedding. Is this something that happened in the military?"

"The military?" Lia's head tilted to the side, and she looked puzzled. "No, my wedding was a few months ago. I know time goes by fast, but you're not usually this forgetful."

Ari had seen that look somewhere before, and after a few seconds of confused silence, she realized. Lia really hadn't changed in all the years they'd known each other. How could she? The training they'd been forced to endure wouldn't just wear off like that.

"Please let me apologize." Ari stared at her, searching for words. "I don't like that you're still using this technique to cope. I'd rather you remember the truth, even if it makes me look like a terrible friend. I know you don't remember much about what happened in the military, but I don't like that you don't remember what's happening now."

"Technique?"

How could she explain it? Ari opened her mouth to say something, but no sound came out. She couldn't bring herself to shatter Lia's happy illusion. Traumatic events were the trigger for Lia's altered memories—that was how she'd been taught to cope, and that was why nothing and nobody could ever make her unhappy. Not even Ari missing the most important night of her life.

Why did that have to be the only part of your memory that changed?

"I'm sorry," was all she said. She could feel tears brimming in her eyes. Impulsively, she pulled Lia into a hug. After a slight pause, Lia squeezed back, patting her comfortingly on the back. A flood of guilt overwhelmed Ari, and she couldn't bring herself to let go.

"I promise to be a better friend," she sobbed. "I won't let you do this again."

CHAPTER 7

So, that's it? It's just over because somebody leaked to the press? It's not fair. It's not. I wanted out, but not like this.

So, this is the coffee capital of the world.

Ari sniffed wistfully. She hadn't been able to afford coffee for weeks, and she missed the smell. It made the air around her seem warmer, especially when combined with the sweet smell of the vanilla creamer bottle on the counter next to her.

Seattle, the land of coffee and Ferris wheels and, apparently, illegal drug trafficking.

But before she had the chance to process her thoughts, Yuri appeared out of nowhere and whisked her out into the street in front of the airport. Puzzled, Ari tried to ask him why he'd been waiting for her when they weren't supposed to be together, but his only answer was: "I'm taking you to your apartment." He hailed a taxi and put a stern finger to his lips to warn her not to discuss anything further.

They drove deeper and deeper into the city, and Ari craned her neck out the window to see the sights she'd read about online. The Space Needle, Pike Place Market, the Seattle Aquarium—that was what she expected to see, but what she saw instead were dirty streets and dark alleys disappearing like holes between the buildings. A sharp smell of cigarettes and car fumes drifted through her window, and she rolled it up, her throat aching.

Eventually, the taxi stopped in front of a dim, dusty side street, littered with trash. An ancient plastic bag floated up from the ground and smacked Ari's window, and she was too disgusted to move it, so she slithered out Yuri's side.

"Welcome home," said Yuri curtly. A slight grin crossed his face as he watched Ari's expression. "Sorry, you don't exactly get to live high-class here. It's expensive. Not to mention pretentious." He picked up her suitcase, paid the taxi fare—much to Ari's relief—and disappeared between the sagging buildings.

She trotted after him, picking her steps carefully between the piled garbage. The buildings weren't tall, but she could tell from the windows that they had many stories with low ceilings. The windows felt like eyes, staring at her through the darkness.

Yuri stopped in front of a peeling, brown door and fished in his pocket for a key. "Number seven." He handed her the key and set down her suitcase. "See you later."

Ari watched him disbelievingly. Was this really where she was going to spend a whole year of her life—in a dark, musty alley without a trace of sunlight?

The apartment's total furniture included a sofa, a bed, and a pole lamp with a dead light bulb. Its former owner had apparently kept pets and smoked because the whole place reeked of fumes and cleaning chemicals. At least somebody had tried to tidy up—but how long ago, Ari couldn't guess. Everything was covered in a thick layer of dust.

Her first order of business, with the last five dollars in her bank account, was to combat the smelliness of her apartment with a warm cup of coffee. But the moment she went outside in search of a coffee shop, her skin prickled with a latent sense of danger. All the sidewalks were blocked by tents or shacks made of garbage bags and cardboard, and she hated not being able to see what was behind them.

"Can you spare some change?" asked a cracked voice from behind her.

Ari started and stumbled back against the wall. The old, tottering man didn't seem much of a threat. But Ari was suspicious. She should've known he was approaching, but she hadn't been able to sense his presence at all. Come to think of it, she hadn't heard footsteps, either.

"Sorry," she said and tried to walk away. He pinched her sleeve, trying to keep her back, but Ari broke free and fled.

The next alley she passed, she ducked behind a dumpster. Carefully, she peeked around the corner to look behind her. From there, she saw that the old man was still following her—and not just the old man, but several other younger men. He seemed to be giving them directions, pointing to where she'd gone and gesturing for them to move forward.

Amateurs. Ari scoffed. But if they did manage to corner her, it would be five against one, and she had no way of knowing what they'd want from her. She couldn't take the risk, though she couldn't help feeling that getting into an altercation might relieve her nervousness. She ran down the alley, ducking carefully through the shadows, and emerged on a brightly lit street.

After a few more twists and turns, Ari found a cozy coffee shop and sat down on a barstool in front of the window, glad to take a break. She made use of the free internet to figure out where she was relative to the coast. Not close, according to her map. And this was one of those missions where she didn't get scheduled days off—she had to be available whenever she was needed. She hoped she'd have a chance to visit before the mission was over, but who knew what would happen next?

Pocketing a few creamers in the hope that she'd get more coffee later, Ari cupped her drink in her chilled hands and stepped back into the street. The weather was depressingly rainy—not real rain, but a soft drizzle that never got anything wet. Ari didn't like the cold. She pulled up her hood and hurried back to her apartment.

In ten minutes, she was at a street corner she didn't recognize. She gulped the last of her coffee in a futile attempt to cheer herself up. This city was too unpredictable. Right around the corner from the beautiful neighborhoods were the unhealthy slums filled with people Ari didn't want to meet.

She hesitated, looking up and down the street. Cars whizzed past her without a second thought. They wouldn't stop for her, and it was probably dangerous to ask for a ride.

Maybe someone would know if I can think of a nearby landmark. I passed a theater on my way here.

On her right was a tattoo parlor that looked at least slightly cleaner than the surrounding buildings. She opened the door and went inside.

It took her eyes a moment to adjust to the dim light. When they did, she saw that the only person in the shop was a girl with long purple hair washing her hands in a sink at the back of the room.

Ari stepped forward and cleared her throat. "Can you give me directions?"

The girl didn't turn around. "Where to?"

"I can't remember the exact address. I'm trying to get to my apartment. All I know is that I passed a theater on my way here."

"Two rights and a left." The girl dried her hands on a towel spotted with dye stains. "That's the closest place with apartments, and you have to pass the theater to get here from there."

"Thanks." Ari started to leave, but the girl cleared her throat aggressively.

"So you're new around here?" she asked.

"Yeah." Ari nodded to the girl's back.

"What made you want to come here?" She finally turned around to face Ari. Her expression was unfriendly, but Ari thought she could detect a sincere desire to be polite under her emotionless voice. So she reciprocated as best she could, glibly reciting the story she'd thought of on the flight.

"It's for character research," she said. "I—well, this sounds silly, but I wanted to be the next classic author. I've been told that my characters and storylines are too bland. So here I am, looking for some new scenery."

"That's nice."

"Have you been here long?"

"All my life. I was raised by the city." She rinsed a hairbrush in the sink, staining the water purple. "Name's Katya. It's nice to meet you."

"You, too." Ari hesitated. It felt unnatural to give away her real name, since she would never have done that in the military, but she had been instructed to be as authentic as possible. That was the only way she could keep up a lie for years, if necessary. "I'm Ari."

"What's it like being an artist?"

"An artist?" Ari hadn't heard writing described that way before. "It's tough to get a break. I haven't been able to get a single book published so far." Which was true—not that she had ever tried.

"Keep at it." Katya vigorously scrubbed the brush with a bristle sponge. "Seattle's a great place for people with talent."

"Thanks for the directions. I'll probably see you around."

"Right. Come back if you need a haircut or a tattoo."

Ari let herself out the front door, relieved. She'd managed to stick to her story and make it sound natural, and she'd made a new friend. Katya was exactly the kind of person who might be useful—she was scrappy, familiar with the neighborhood, and talkative. Though, Ari reflected, she had asked more questions than she had answered. And done it cleverly, too, in a way that Ari had barely noticed until afterwards.

Her phone vibrated.

Unknown: *Meet me in twenty minutes at the Bridge Theater.*

Ari: *Who are you?"*

That theater sounded familiar, and she wondered if it was the one she was looking for.

Unknown: *Yuri.*

And then, a moment later:

Unknown: *Never mind.*

Something moved in Ari's peripheral vision. Somebody was walking toward her. Somebody dressed a little too nicely for the neighborhood.

"Didn't expect to see you here," Yuri said.

"Me neither," she said cautiously. The NDEB hadn't forbidden them from socializing with each other, but it wasn't encouraged in public. And Yuri wasn't exactly in her good books after he'd left her stranded in her apartment.

"I told you it's not safe to walk around by yourself."

"I was just exploring," she answered.

"So, you want dinner?"

Ari could feel her stomach rumbling. "Dinner?"

"My treat. It's the first night."

"Umm . . . okay. Sure." She tried not to sound too enthusiastic. If he hadn't offered, she had no idea where or what or if she would've eaten that night. She'd have to think of a nice way to thank him later.

"Glad you're excited." He rolled his eyes and pulled out his phone. "There's some spaghetti place near here. Sound good?"

"Anything sounds good. Is Nika meeting us there?"

"What makes you think I invited her?" Yuri started walking down the sidewalk in front of Ari.

She trotted after him. "Well, you said it was a celebration of the first night, so I thought—"

"That's not a reasonable deduction," he interrupted. "Does your apartment have everything you need?"

"Yeah."

They continued in silence for three blocks. Ari liked silence, but things were starting to get awkward. She couldn't tell if Yuri wanted to say something or if he was just naturally quiet. And rude. She drifted off into her own thoughts, until Yuri stopped so suddenly that she almost ran into him.

He held open a smoke-blackened door. "Inside."

She hesitated. The outside of the building was covered with trash and a thick layer of smog deposits, just like her apartment. If it was anything like that on the inside, she knew she'd rather pay for dinner herself, even if that meant buying a donut from a gas station.

Then the warm smell of pasta drifted out. She sniffed it hungrily and went inside.

The walls, tile floors, and booths were pasta sauce-red, reminding her of something she couldn't quite put her finger on—an Italian restaurant she'd been to as a child, maybe? Or was it something from the military? It was clean, cozy, and quiet, the perfect place for a dinner meeting. There weren't many customers, but everyone who was there was nicely dressed, so much so that Ari almost felt out of place.

"Table for three, please," Yuri said to a passing waiter.

"Three?" She struggled to keep up. The room wasn't well lit, and she kept bumping her arms on the backs of chairs to her right.

"Why do you ask so many questions?" Yuri sighed. The waitress seated them alone at a booth and left them. "Mikael's coming. I just got a phone call from him an hour ago. He said he wanted to talk to us."

"Mikael?"

"I know what you're thinking. No, he wasn't supposed to be here. I don't know why he flew all the way out. I think he's just bored."

"Bored?"

"Stop repeating what I say," he ordered. "You're supposed to be old friends from the army, right? You should know what he wants. I think he's just tired of having less action than he's used to. Doesn't that sound like him to you?"

"I can't read people's minds," Ari snapped, finally losing her temper.

But before she could apologize, Mikael slid into the booth beside her, so silently that she jumped.

"All right so far, Ari?" he asked, ignoring her reaction.

"Everything's great. Thanks for asking." It wasn't the proper time to complain, even if Mikael could help change her living quarters.

"Quit shredding your napkin."

Ari started and guiltily placed what remained of her napkin on the table in front of her.

"Yuri, are you comfortable in your apartment?" Mikael continued.

"It's like asking if I'm comfortable in a trash heap," he said sourly. "It's not worse than where I came from before."

Ari hid her laughter in a cough. If she was going to be an author, these were the perfect people to write a book about—they were charismatic in the worst possible ways.

"I don't recall inviting you, Yuri. I specifically asked you to send Ari here by herself."

"It's too dangerous for her to walk alone."

"You could've left her here."

"That wouldn't be polite, would it?"

"Mikael," Ari interrupted, trying to keep the peace, "why'd you want to meet me ?"

"Business matters, which I'd rather not discuss now."

"Oh, so you wanted Ari all to yourself?" mocked Yuri.

Mikael stood up. "I think you should leave."

Yuri lurched from his seat and planted both hands firmly on the table. "Business matters?" His voice was starting to slur. "Business matters? That was your excuse?"

"You and I should step outside." Mikael tried to hold Yuri's arm and prevent him from faceplanting into the table, but he slapped Mikael's hand away.

"I'm going home." Without another word to either Ari or Mikael, he stumbled out the door and into the street. The front doorbell rang behind him, and the whole building shook when the door slammed.

"Mikael, we have to go after him!" Ari insisted. "He wasn't acting like that when we got here. Something's wrong."

But Mikael only seated himself and picked his menu back up. "He's drunk. That's how Russians are. I'll write a report, and that's the end of it."

Her conscience pricked her, but she had to look professional in front of Mikael. She'd find a way to make it up to Yuri later.

"Yes, sir," she mumbled, peeking out the window to see if she could spot Yuri. He had already disappeared.

And if you have any regrets, what are you going to do? She tried to brush the voice aside, but it was loud and insistent. *Is being nice to Mikael worth damaging your relationship with Yuri?*

"You can call me Mikael. Consider this an informal business dinner." Mikael smiled graciously at her from over his menu. "I've heard the lasagna is good here."

You should take better care of your teammates!

"Have you been here before?" Small talk would help quiet the anxious voices. Something must have been bothering her more than she realized, or they wouldn't feel so loud, but she couldn't quite tell what it was.

"No, but Yuri and Nika have. I heard about it from them." Mikael shut his menu with a snap. "First, let me say what I came here to say so we can enjoy the rest of the evening. I hope you know who you're going up against on this mission. You accepted without hesitation. Calvin told me. Why'd you do it?"

Ari was unprepared with her reply. "Well . . . I . . . " She fumbled for the right words—something that wouldn't make her sound crazy. "I've always been in this line of work," she said feebly. "It just . . . seemed like something I'd be good at." She knew that wasn't what Mikael was asking, but she couldn't figure out what he was really looking for. Why would he fly all the way across the country just to ask her why she'd accepted a job offer? There had to be something specific he wanted her to say.

Surely he knows you did it only because you had no other choice. The voices reflected her surprise. *Surely he knows you couldn't work anywhere else because it wasn't "exciting" enough,* they mocked.

"I want to make sure you're really up for the mission, since a lot depends on you." He made a note on his napkin and put it in his pocket. "Please don't forget that your apartment is in a very bad neighborhood, most of which is owned by Vita and his people. Actually, this restaurant is run by the head of the local street gang, Azure Cross." Mikael smiled at her obvious surprise. "Haven't you heard of the Italian mafia? They make pasta when they aren't selling drugs. I don't think you'll get bored around here."

"The Azure Crosses . . . ?"

"You'll probably end up joining them," he said. "Of course, it's up to you what strategy you use to get in touch with their leaders. But we shouldn't talk about that right now."

The waiter took their orders and gave Ari a new napkin, evidently thinking she hadn't gotten one in the first place.

"It's like chess," she said thoughtfully. "This whole game of trying to get into their good graces without taking the drugs."

"Quietly, Ari," said Mikael. "But you're right. I'm surprised to hear you call it a game when it's so dangerous, but the less worried you are, the better."

Maybe Mikael is actually worried for me? Ari puzzled disbelievingly. *But why would he be? If he was in the military, he should know I'm used to this.*

Maybe he's worried about *you. Maybe he knows you aren't really as good as you used to be. You're a liability.*

But no, there had already been plenty of opportunities for him to give her a different mission if he didn't trust her.

"I'll tell you why I'm here." Mikael leaned across the table and lowered his voice. "You won't be surprised to know that we get a lot of warning letters back at headquarters. They say things like 'so-and-so is running drugs—I just know it!' and a bunch of other groundless accusations and suspicions. But we received a strange one this morning. It was an encrypted email that we couldn't trace." He paused, staring straight into Ari's eyes as though he expected her to know something about it. When she didn't respond, he continued, "At first, it seemed like another spam email, but it was signed with your full name."

Ari sucked in a deep breath. "I certainly didn't send anything like that."

"We know. It didn't come from your email address." Mikael leaned back. "At first I thought you might've sent it without remembering. But now, having talked to you, I don't think you would've done something like that. I think there's more to this. That's why Yuno sent me out here."

"What exactly did the email say?"

"Nothing important. It was something like 'I have an anonymous tip for you. Please meet me in Vancouver.'"

"Vancouver? Why Vancouver?" Ari chuckled, relieved. "I guess whoever wrote it doesn't really know me that well."

"Vita lives there."

"I take it back," she said faintly. "You think it's connected?"

"Maybe." Mikael shrugged. "Or it could be nothing." He paused. "Do me a favor, Ari. Don't mention this to anyone else. I don't want to worry everyone."

"I think we should tell them," Ari said. "This seems important. I wouldn't like it if they were keeping a secret like this from me."

"Yuno's orders."

"What does Yuno have to do with this? Why is he in charge of everything? Aren't you supposed to be the team leader?"

The server approached their table, and Mikael's answer was vague. "Yes. But I answer to him, you know." A quick smile crossed his face. "Pun intended."

A few minutes after Ari had finally gotten home and gone to bed, she was startled awake.

She wasn't sure what had woken her from her impromptu nap. Nothing seemed out of place, and her room was silent except for a faint hum of distant machinery.

A light flashed in her window.

A car?

Then something banged on her front door.

Option one: she could answer and risk letting a serial killer into her apartment. Option two: she could refuse to answer and probably have her door broken down. She wavered for a split second, glancing around the room for something she could use as a weapon. Her gaze settled on her thermos, filled with cold water and sitting on her nightstand. That might be effective in a pinch.

She picked it up and opened the door a crack. A pair of anxious eyes met hers.

"Nika!" she cried. Her thermos clattered to the floor, and she stammered, "How did you—?"

Nika's face was pale, and it looked even whiter in the fluorescent streetlight. Ari glanced up and down the street, wondering if she'd been followed, but there was no sign of life. "Come inside."

Nika took a deep breath and shook her head. "There isn't time. Come with me."

"Where are we going?" Ari scrambled to tie her shoelaces in the dark.

"It's about Yuri." Her eyes glazed. "I think he was in an accident. I can't move him."

"An accident? Why didn't you call an ambulance?" cried Ari. She was already trying to assess the damage. Nika was out of breath, so even if she'd run all the way to Ari's apartment, she couldn't have come from anywhere nearby. "Why'd you waste time coming here?"

"Because if Yuri goes to the hospital, we'll have to release his medical records," said Nika. Her voice was flat and level, almost like she was sleepwalking. "They could trace him. The Azure Cross could find out. I thought maybe you'd be able to treat him yourself so we wouldn't have to get anyone else involved. You know first aid from the military, right?"

"Of course, but I don't even have any bandages," Ari snapped. "You took basic first aid classes—you should know it's dangerous to waste time." She pulled on a sweatshirt over her pajamas and bundled Nika out the door. "Shake it off, Nika. Take me to wherever you found him."

Nika ran off, and Ari followed, pulling her sleeves down over her hands and shivering. A few minutes later, when Ari had once again lost her sense of direction, Nika stopped in front of a dark alleyway and gestured Ari to pass her.

"Look in there."

Ari obeyed and at first saw nothing. Then she pulled her phone out of her pocket and turned on the flashlight. A man sat against the brick wall of the building to the right, his head slumped against his chest, hands resting loosely on the ground beside him. He wore the same suit Yuri had before dinner.

Ari's skin prickled.

Nika knelt beside him and raised his face to the light. Those pinched, blue lips and narrow, squinting eyes—there was no mistaking them. It was Yuri. And his face was so drained and colorless that Ari wondered if he was dead.

"He's been sitting here for at least an hour."

"T-that can't be right," Ari stammered. Yuri's eyes stared unblinkingly back at her. "He was at dinner with us tonight. When did you find him?"

"About a quarter of an hour ago. I tried calling you, but you didn't answer, so I had to find my way to your apartment alone." Nika laughed hysterically. "There's no way to know what happened." She collapsed to her knees, breathing heavily. Tears glittered in the beam of her flashlight.

Ari pressed two fingers against Yuri's neck. Surely he wasn't still alive, crumpled there with his eyes wide open and skin cold. But after a few breathless moments, a gentle flutter pulsed under her fingertips. She started backward and scraped her shoulder against the wall.

"That's it," Nika was mumbling, staring off into the dark end of the alley. "I'm not surprised that he was drinking, but there's no way he drank enough to kill himself."

"He didn't," said Ari firmly. "He's still alive, just like you said. Take my phone and call the ambulance." She pushed up her sleeves, laid Yuri flat on his back, and pressed her hands to his chest. "Now, Nika!"

Nika didn't move, and Ari's patience finally gave out. What was wrong with her, anyway—letting her friend die out in the cold because his medical records might give his identity away? What was wrong with everyone tonight? She paused and slapped Nika roughly across the cheek.

"Call the ambulance," she snapped. "Do it now."

Nika took the phone from her with shaking hands and dialed the number. Ari could hear Nika's voice clear as the operator asked her questions, and Ari sighed with relief. Then she tilted Yuri's neck back, opened his mouth, and blew gently down his throat. Two breaths, thirty compressions. She'd never attempted CPR before, not even in the military. Not once had she ever arrived before it was too late. This time, she swore, nobody else was going to die on her watch.

Especially not when you knew better than to let him leave alone.

A few minutes later, the alley lit up with bright red flashing lights. The paramedics bundled Yuri into an ambulance and drove off, sirens screaming. Ari plugged her ears and huddled in a corner, overwhelmed by the noise. All she could think about, strangely, was the first briefing she'd had with her teammates back in Virginia. "You're messing with me," she'd accused them playfully, half-expecting them all to burst out laughing as soon as she signed her name to the documents they handed her. Never had she dreamed they would end up like this.

A horrible sense of the reality of their work washed over her. This wasn't just a job that paid for her bread and butter. Lives were on the line, and she was once again expected to step in and do her best to keep everyone safe. She thought she'd completed that mission the day she left the military, but here she was again, just as needed, just as desperate, and just as indecisive as before. If only she'd followed Yuri home . . .

A policeman approached her with a notepad and pencil. She started to her feet, blinking tightly to clear her head.

"Can you tell us a little bit about the patient? Was he depressed? Often morose?" the policeman asked.

"Yes, he was all of that, but he didn't commit suicide." Nika pushed Ari out of the way. She was about to cry. "He didn't; I swear!"

The policeman nodded unconvincingly. "Yes, ma'am, we'll look into it."

Nika went white, and Ari thought she was going to pass out. She took the notebook from the policeman's hands and wrote her phone number at the top.

"Call us tomorrow, and we'll tell you everything we know," she said. "I need to get her to the hospital to make sure Yuri's okay."

"No," Nika said quietly, her eyes fixed on the ground. "I'm not going."

"Nika!" cried Ari, surprised.

"What are we going to do if we go?" she demanded, almost shrieking. "We'll just be in the way. We won't even get to see him!"

Ari opened her mouth to argue, but Nika turned away before she could speak.

"Goodnight," said Nika, her voice dropping to a whisper.

"You can't just leave!" Ari yelled after her. "What if Yuri wakes up tonight? Wouldn't you want to be there?"

But Nika didn't turn around.

Torn, Ari glanced back and forth between her friend and the police officer. "You have my number," she said at last. "Call me whenever you want to finish this questionnaire. I need to make sure she's okay."

"You both need to stay here and answer questions," he said, but Ari fished in her pocket and showed him her badge, and he sighed reluctantly. "All right, you can go."

Nika would kill me for that, Ari thought ruefully, hiding her badge and running after Nika. But she hadn't been left with much of a choice. *All I can do it hope he's not working with the Azure Crosses.*

Once they were out of the alley, out of sight of the police officers, Nika slowed to a stop and tapped Ari on the shoulder. "Who do you think did it?" she asked, trembling with nervousness.

"Nika . . . " Ari hesitated. "I don't think anyone did it. I think it was an accident. Maybe he drank too much. Or maybe it was some health condition he didn't know about. An aneurism, maybe. There's no reason for anyone to be targeting him." But she regretted the words the moment they left her mouth. Was that really true? Could she really believe that, even after everything Mikael had told her about the message the NDEB had received?

"But it makes sense," insisted Nika, seizing Ari's arm. "We're here on a secret mission, and this happens on the first night. I know Yuri never drank to excess—"

"He was drunk when we met him for dinner."

Nika turned away in frustration.

"I hope they investigate," was all Ari could say to comfort her. She was too shaken to think of anything better. "I really hope so. But I don't think they'll find much."

Nika nodded. "See you tomorrow," she said shortly.

"Yeah." Ari waved.

She crawled into bed that night—or early morning—with a vague feeling of dread. This wasn't right. There was a missing link somewhere that she couldn't grasp. Why was Nika so incapable of fending for herself and her teammates? Why hadn't she called an ambulance right away when she knew Yuri's life depended on it?

You're just as bad as she is. Why didn't you stop him from leaving by himself?

You could have prevented this.

If he dies, it's all your fault.

On the way back to her apartment, her phone rang. She answered.

"Is this Ari?"

"Who's this?"

"This is the police, calling from the hospital. You gave me your number."

"Right." Ari rubbed her forehead. "Can I call you back tomorrow?"

"Your friend didn't make it."

Long pause. A dull sense of dread washed over Ari, and she wondered if she'd heard him correctly.

"I'm not officially supposed to tell you, but I figured you'd want to know. The hospital ruled death by alcohol poisoning."

Ari gulped, suddenly sick to her stomach. "Are you . . . are you sure?"

"I'm sorry." The voice on the other end was gentle.

She hung up without another word.

The next day, Ari met with Mikael and a silent, subdued Nika at a nearby café. Calvin had been sent out to take Yuri's place, and he joined them later that morning. They all sat around the table, trying to avoid each other's eyes. Nobody knew what to say.

"The doctors ruled death by natural causes," said Nika eventually, her knuckles white around the handle of her mug. "So that's that."

"They're not investigating?" asked Ari.

Nika shook her head, and they went back to silence.

After a few painful minutes of hesitation, Mikael stood up. "I have to go," he said. "I was supposed to be back in Virginia this morning, but I didn't want to leave until Calvin arrived."

Ari didn't think it mattered whether he stayed or left. He, too, was responsible for Yuri's death. He was the one who had convinced her not to go after him—the serpent offering her the apple.

"It's like the life got sucked out of us." Calvin rubbed his eyes and sighed deeply.

"I need to leave." Nika stood up forcefully, shaking the table. A little of Calvin's coffee slipped over the edge of his mug. He raised a hand, either to wave goodbye or to stop her, but she disappeared before he could say anything.

"Ari," he said seriously, as soon as she was gone, "we need to talk. I've never seen anything shake Nika this much. She's taking Yuri's death pretty hard. I need you to keep an eye on her and make sure she doesn't do anything stupid."

"Okay." Ari nodded. She'd already been thinking about what she could do to bring Nika back to her normal self.

"Will you do it?"

"Who made you the leader?" Ari snapped bitterly. Then she regretted it. "I'm sorry, Calvin." She paused, searching for the right words. "I'll be honest with you. I don't know what to do with Nika. In the military, anyone who lost their presence of mind like she did last night would've been considered a liability to the team and sent straight to the psychologist or back to training. I've never had to salvage someone's sanity by myself. But I'll do my best. I hate seeing her like this."

"It's all right," said Calvin. He looked anxious. "I'll help you as much as I can."

Ari excused herself and left the café, wondering where to go from here. She finally settled on running errands—that would give her time to think about what she wanted to say to Nika.

To her surprise, before she'd walked two blocks back in the direction of her apartment, she met Mikael coming from the opposite direction. He smiled half-heartedly when he recognized her.

"I think I need to stay," he said. "Nika is on edge. Calvin is stressed. And you seem to be the only sane person here—if your kind of sanity counts for anything." He had dropped his usual formal speech, and

Ari thought he sounded tired. His eyes, she noticed, were surrounded by dark rings. "I'll just leave tomorrow or the day after. HQ can do without me for a few days."

"And the email?"

He sighed. "The cybercrime division is investigating it."

"Do you really think it's safe to stay here after what happened last night?" Ari's voice was tight. "We should have treated this email like a warning. We shouldn't have been so careless."

"So you think Yuri was murdered, despite the hospital's report?"

There was a long pause.

"No," said Ari reluctantly. "I don't. I just think we need to be careful."

"I agree. If everything that's happening is just a coincidence, we've still been incredibly unlucky. We have to change that." Mikael stood up. "Good luck, Ari. I'll see you later."

"Wait." She grabbed his shoulder. "We need to tell the others about the email."

"It's not our decision."

"But—"

"It's not your decision, either," he reminded her sharply. "I'll talk to Yuno about it. You should go home. It's not safe to be wandering around like this."

She watched him leave, debating whether to stop him again and beg him to change his mind. Dishonesty with her teammates—that was the one thing she abhorred most. Could Mikael really have been in the military if he was willing to keep a secret like that? But then again, he was just following orders, like they all were. Maybe there really wasn't anything he could do about it.

A few hours later, she finished her errands and carried everything back to her apartment, only turning once on the wrong street this time. It was while she was turning the key in the lock that she noticed it.

Taped to her door was a small white sign.

It was dark in the alley, so she had to blink a few times before she could make out the words written on it:

1/3

SUPPOSE THERE ARE FIVE CHARACTERS: A, B, C, D, AND UNKNOWN. ASSUME THAT A–D KNOW EACH OTHER AND UNKNOWN IS AN OUTSIDER. HERE ARE THE RULES OF THE SCENARIO:

1. A, B, AND C ARE AT DINNER.

2. D IS ELSEWHERE BUT NEARBY.

3. UNKNOWN IS ALSO NEARBY AND COULD BE ANY OF THE MILLIONS OF PEOPLE IN THIS CITY.

4. B LEAVES THE DINNER EARLY—BEFORE ANYONE HAS EATEN OR DRUNK.

5. D FINDS B DEAD.

WHO WROTE THIS RIDDLE?

IF YOU CAN SOLVE THAT, YOU'LL KNOW WHO KILLED B.

CHAPTER 8

First and most obvious conclusion—someone tried to kill Yuri because this riddle is clearly talking about him. And they don't know that they didn't succeed immediately because they say he was already dead when Nika found him. That means they couldn't have followed us, so how could they know who found him? Technically, only Nika should know that. But she would also know Yuri wasn't dead, so that doesn't make sense.

Second—one of these five people killed him. No, that's not right. Unknown could be anybody. We don't know who killed him.

Third—A must be Mikael; B must be Yuri; D must be Nika; and C must be me because the riddle says we all know each other, and I don't know anyone in this city but them. Unknown could be anybody in the city who might've had an interest in killing Yuri. Vita, maybe . . . ?

Fourth—the question at the end isn't "who killed B," but rather, "who wrote this riddle." If I can know the killer by answering that question, then the killer must be the one who wrote this riddle. And it doesn't necessarily have to be someone mentioned in the riddle.

Fifth—the killer is someone who knows all of us, where we were, and what we were doing last night.

Sixth—

She hesitated to even think about the last deduction.

If the killer wrote this riddle, that means they might kill again. And they probably know something about our connections with the NDEB.

Logically speaking, she wasn't in danger right away. The killer wouldn't come after her until she solved the riddle, or they might as well not have written it at all. But Calvin and Nika and Mikael—

Unless one of them was the killer?

She shook her head vigorously. None of them had any reason to play some stupid mind game with her. It was much more likely that the real killer was an unrecognized antagonist who wanted to create tension between Ari and her teammates.

Vita had a vested interest in destroying her team. But how could he have found out about their mission so quickly?

She picked up her phone and dialed Nika. "Be especially careful today," she said to the answering machine. "I can't explain everything right now, but you're in danger. Please don't forget that." Then she left Calvin and Mikael the same message.

She hadn't felt this much of an adrenaline rush since the army, and the old, familiar feeling she could describe only as "the fuzziness" was coming back. It was surreal, like she was looking into a world she didn't belong to. The risk she ran when she felt like this was forgetting, just like she forgot almost everything she'd experienced in the army. She hurriedly scribbled down a copy of the note in her journal along with a short explanation of the context surrounding it. This wasn't something to take chances with.

There came a knock on her door, and she leaped into the air, breathing heavily. *Surely it couldn't be—?* Opening her door to a tiny crack and looking out with suspicious eyes revealed a familiar face. Calvin.

He shoved open the door, almost knocking her over, and came inside before she invited him. She watched speechlessly as he threw himself down on the sofa and crossed his arms like he was planning to stay for a long time.

"I'm assuming you saw the riddle," he said after a long pause.

"You got the note?"

"You and Mikael had dinner last night . . . "

"That's right, but—"

"So that means you and Mikael are the prime suspects. I've known Mikael for a lot longer than I've known you, and he would never do something like this. So, who do we have left, Ari?"

She froze. His tone was short and sharp, and it didn't sound like him at all.

"I didn't do it, Calvin. I swear," she stammered. She looked down at her hands—they were shaking. Was she afraid? Guilty? But she couldn't be guilty, not if she hadn't done anything wrong. "You can send me back to Virginia for a polygraph if you must," she insisted.

He stood up, breathing heavily. "Then who did it?" he shouted.

She opened her mouth to reply, but he cut her off. In a split second, he was across the room, his hands on her shoulders, forcing her back into the wall. Ari was so caught off-guard that she couldn't fight back. His fingers squeezed tightly, and she tensed, trying to shrug off his grip His breath burned on her face as he shouted over and over, "Who did?"

Her voice choked in her throat. She tried to wriggle out of his grip, but he only held her tighter until she gasped with pain.

"I'll find you," Calvin panted. One of his hands slipped from her shoulder, and he reached behind his back. "I'll find you and kill you. I'll—"

A knife. Ari spotted the familiar shimmer instantly.

She dropped to her knees as the blade drove a hole in the wall right where her head had been moments before. She rolled under Calvin's upraised arm and backed defensively toward the other side of the room.

Her options were quickly running out. He was going to kill her if she didn't fight back. What could she use as a weapon? There was one knife in the kitchen. With one swift dive, she was under the counter and seizing it from the drawer.

"Don't come any closer," she warned, bracing herself with her back against the fridge. "I didn't kill Yuri. I don't know what you're thinking, but we can't fight like this."

Calvin didn't say a word in response. Instead, he lunged at her with the blade pointed right at her throat.

She never remembered anything about what went through her head, right at that moment when she felt her knife sink deeply into his chest. He gasped, and his knife clattered to the floor. Then, before she could think, she sliced her knife across Calvin's throat. He struggled briefly for breath; then his body went limp.

Ari glanced numbly down at the red splattered over her shirt. Her hands were covered in blood.

Two of your teammates in two days.

And guess what?

The voices laughed in unison.

They were both your fault!

"Shut up!" she screamed, covering her ears with her bloody hands. They smeared and tangled in her hair. "Shut up, shut up, shut up!"

Remember Kira?

That was where it all started.

The voices began to laugh so loudly that her ears rang. She couldn't join in, couldn't interrupt them, couldn't say a word in self-defense. After all, what was there to say? She had nothing, no excuse.

Shameless killer, one of them said mockingly.

She ran. She had no idea where or why or what she was trying to hide from. All she knew was that the faster she ran, the further behind she left the voices that were tormenting her. They sounded like distant echoes now. She was still running, flying, escaping as fast as she could. She ran into something that forced her to stop. Forced her to her knees. The voices approached.

The first thing she heard when she woke up was the echo of her own hoarse screams.

She sat up and looked around the room. She was alone in her apartment. Her hands were clean, and her shirt was a uniform, spotless gray.

Throwing the blanket off, she leaped off the sofa and ran to the kitchen. There was nothing there.

It was all a dream. A nightmare. Her imagination and nothing more.

Her knees wobbled until she collapsed onto the floor, laughing hysterically and wiping tears from her cheeks. She wasn't a murderer after all. Her mind could play tricks on her, but it couldn't make her into something she wasn't.

She crawled back to the sofa, still shivering, and picked up her phone. Should she call one of her teammates for help? Was it even safe to reveal her mental state had gotten this bad? She ran the risk of being sent to a psychiatric ward, and she'd certainly be kicked out of the NDEB.

No. No, she couldn't tell anyone. It was all downhill from here, no matter how she looked at it, and even a psychiatrist couldn't stifle her vicious imagination anyway.

She took a few deep breaths. *Relax.* That was what they taught her in the army. Her heart rate slowed until she could breathe normally again.

The voices snickered condescendingly.

You're just doing this because you're a selfish brat. Just like you were when you joined the army.

"I don't remember anything about it," she answered aloud.

That's because you don't want to.

"You *aren't* real," she insisted. She knew it was dangerous to talk to the voices, but she had to shut them up somehow. "You're my imagination."

Does that make it any easier?

Or any less your fault?

There was no point in arguing with herself, so she went quiet and tried to think about something else. Plans. She had to figure out how to continue their mission so she could solve the riddle. She slammed her hands down on the coffee table, startling the voices into silence, and started talking to herself—her real self, not the voices—to keep them quiet.

"If I can find who's selling drugs, I can find the gang. And if I can find the gang, I can find Vita, and maybe that will explain the riddles. But where do I start?"

The answer came to her after a few minutes of pacing. "People who buy the drugs will know. People who buy drugs go to recreational drugstores, too, so whoever works there must know something about it."

There was time left in the day to find out.

She slipped on a sweatshirt, trying to look edgy, then ruffled her hair. It wasn't difficult to make it look like she hadn't showered in days, and she chuckled at her reflection in the mirror. Shabby, but comical, and very disorganized—not at all what an NDEB agent should look like. She added some dark eyeshadow to make herself look sleepier, then too much eyeliner. The look complete, she tucked her hair under her hood and headed out the door.

It was hard to believe there were neighborhoods worse than hers, but the dark, shadowy alleys she was passing now were worse in every way. Lined with rusty, old dumpsters, from which trash spilled like a disgusting, putrid fountain, they offered plenty of corners to lurk behind. A few shadows flitted here and there between them—people ducking back and forth, whether to collect something from the dumpsters or put trash inside, it was too dark to tell. Occasionally a scream or yell or curse would echo off the walls with startling clarity. Every time, Ari's hand instinctively went to her waist where she was used to carrying a gun, but, of course, there was nothing there.

Ten minutes later, she found the dispensary. The whole area reeked of a disgustingly sweet smell, most of which emanated from one slouched figure on the steps leading up to the door. There was a deep, cross-shaped scar on his upper arm, which somehow seemed familiar to Ari. He was holding something cylindrical in one hand and a brown paper bag in the other. Marijuana, the easiest recreational drug to obtain.

She walked gingerly past him, but he didn't seem to know she was there. Inside the store, the smell was even worse, and there was so much smoke in the air that she had trouble locating the cash register. Although "cash register" seemed too technical of a word for the foldable table and locked money safe that did duty for a counter. There was somebody sitting behind it in a white plastic chair, somebody with long, tangled hair and a relaxed grin hiding behind an unkempt beard. His eyes were faded blue and glimmering in the dim light of the shop, and they were watching Ari closely.

She approached him with a friendly smile.

"H'lo," he said briefly, looking up at her. "Stuff's in the back."

Time for an artful lie. "I was reading what Huxley said about inducing hallucinations with drugs and how that helps people be creative, and—"

"Who's Huxley?"

These people of all people ought to know who he was and what he wrote about, thought Ari with a flash of superiority. Then she guiltily continued aloud: "I'm an author and I'm looking for some inspiration. What can you recommend? I want to see something new."

He stared at her closely, and to her horror, she saw that his eyeballs were tattooed black. They looked like holes in the misty half-light.

"We don't sell anything like that here."

There was no mistaking that shifty twitch of his eyes or his unintentional refusal to meet her steady gaze. "I know you do," she said, then added: "A friend told me about this place. They said it was the best for getting the—you know—the strong stuff."

His eyes were back on her. "Like what stuff?"

Ari had no idea what kinds of drugs Huxley had prescribed for hallucinations. "What do you recommend? I don't know what I should be looking for."

"So you're totally new to this?" He laughed maliciously. "Fine. You can try this sample free." His head disappeared beneath the table, and she could hear him rummaging among something made of paper. Then he handed her a brown paper bag. "Of course, that's on the condition that you come back as a regular."

"What's this?" She took it from him like he was handing her a bomb.

He answered with a wink. "Make sure you don't overdo it on the first try."

"Thanks." She couldn't stand any more of the stale air, so she escaped into the street, still clutching her paper bag. When she was far enough away from the shop that she was sure nobody could see her, she opened it and looked inside. White powder, nothing more. It had no smell, and she couldn't tell what it was.

"Now that I've got the drugs," she puzzled, putting the bag in her back pocket, "where do I find the people selling them?"

The tap of footsteps behind her caught her attention. They were purposeful footsteps, almost loud enough to sound like running. Somebody was following her. She quickened her pace. They did the same.

She realized she should be afraid, but instead, all she felt was a surge of pleasurable adrenaline. This was fun—something she hadn't done in a long time. She ducked around two corners in quick succession and waited for them to pass her so she could get a look at their face.

A few seconds later, whoever it was rounded the same corner and caught sight of her in the shadows. "Ari!" She recognized the voice at once and flinched. Calvin. "I was surprised to see you there. That place is disgusting."

She looked him up and down. "Are you the guy that was sitting on the front steps?"

He nodded and smiled widely. "I wasn't smoking, though. I just lit up and tried not to breathe too much. I've got the worst headache already."

"Then maybe you'll know what this is." She pulled the crinkled bag from her pocket and gave it to him.

He sniffed it and put a tiny pinch into his mouth. With an expression of disgust, he spat it out into the gutter. "Pure corn starch," he said, laughing at Ari's confusion. "It has the same texture as cocaine. Whoever gave this to you probably just wanted you out of the store as quickly as possible."

Ari couldn't help smiling, amused at her own naïveté. Apparently, she didn't quite look the part of the addict yet.

"So . . . were you looking for me?" she asked.

"No. I was looking for Katya."

"Who's that?" *Why did that name sound familiar?*

"You don't know?" He grinned. "I forgot you haven't been here before. She's . . . well, she's hard to explain. Let's keep walking so nobody listens in."

They walked in silence for a few minutes, until they'd left the dark alley behind. Ari noticed that Calvin seemed much less tense once they were out on a main street.

"Katya and Nika met last year," he began. "It's a really long story, and I'll let Nika tell you the details; but basically, Katya figured out that Nika was with the NDEB and threatened to report her. In turn, Nika said she'd betray Katya's whole group to local law enforcement. It was a stalemate either way. Nothing ever came of it. They mutually hate each other, but Katya agreed to work with us if we promised never to get her in trouble. And if we . . . well, you know. She doesn't exactly work for us for free. We call it payment, though, not bribery."

"So this girl is an addict?"

He nodded. "I think she's been to rehab several times, but nothing seems to help. It gives her a sense of purpose to work with us."

Ari paused. "Is there anyone else who's working for you?"

Calvin shook his head.

"Can this girl—Katya—can she get me into the gang?"

"Probably," he said. "But before she does, I should probably explain that the Azure Cross isn't a gang in the traditional sense. It's better described as . . . " He paused. "As a mafia. Vita isn't Italian and doesn't have any ties with the real mafia. But they're classy. There's a lower division which does the dirty work, and a higher division where criminal masterminds lurk in the shadows of high-rise apartments. Unfortunately, you and I are condemned to the lower division. Nika stays in the heights."

"If we are in the lower division . . . then what can we really do to help this mission? Just doing dirty work won't be enough to get Vita's attention."

"It's possible to switch divisions if you do anything especially noteworthy—and by that, I mean something so twistedly brilliant that you catch the higher-ups' attention. Other than that, I'm not sure. That's why Mikael predicted this would be a long mission. We're supposed to figure it out for ourselves."

Ari nodded slowly. "So what did Nika do?"

"What?"

"How did she get up into the higher division?"

Calvin looked uncomfortable. "That's—that's not for me to say."

"But you know?"

He sighed. "She'll kill me if I tell you."

What could possibly be that bad?

"It wasn't her choice," he added quickly. "It started by accident, and—and—she couldn't get out of it. She's ashamed of what she does. Maybe it's not anything someone else would be ashamed of, but for Nika . . . " His voice trailed off.

"If you say so." Ari could tell she wasn't going to get anything else out of him, no matter how hard she pressed.

His pace sped up slightly. "I'll catch you later then."

"Wait." She darted after him before he could make his escape. "Aren't you going to introduce me to Katya?"

He hesitated.

"The sooner we can get involved, the better," she prodded.

"Fine," he said reluctantly. "I guess you can come with me right now if you have time."

"Sure." Ari paused. He didn't know about the riddle and wouldn't understand why she was in such a hurry. "Hey, Calvin," she added casually, "did you get a letter or a note today?"

He looked startled. "What kind of note?"

"'One-third,'" recited Ari, quoting her letter. "'Suppose there are five characters . . .'"

"Stop," he insisted, covering his ears. "I really can't listen to that right now. I wasn't prepared for that today. Not after what happened with Yuri. I just need time to process it all."

"It's okay," Ari said soothingly. "We don't have to talk about it. I just wanted to make sure you knew."

He nodded, and they walked along in silence.

"Right here."

Ari looked up at the building next to them. Sagging, dilapidated, it looked just like all the other buildings she'd passed before. But the way it was positioned on the street corner felt familiar, and as they went inside, she realized why. It was the same tattoo parlor where she had asked for directions the first time she'd gotten lost.

Wait, wasn't that girl's name Katya, too?

"Back for a tattoo?" The purple-haired girl came to the front to greet them. Her eyes were a different color today, deep emerald green, and they matched her heavily artistic makeup perfectly. Ari couldn't help feeling the slightest bit jealous of how pretty she was, in an artificial way, like a beautiful human canvas.

"N-no," she stammered, caught off-guard. "I'm—" She made a vague gesture at Calvin.

"We've met before, Katya." He extended his hand, and Katya shook it, smearing dye on his fingers.

"I remember you." She nodded. "You're the one who nearly burned this place down last year trying to pretend that you were drunk."

Ari raised her eyebrows at Calvin. He clicked his tongue and pretended to be studying something on the wall behind Katya.

"No use asking him about it; he'll shut you up tighter than a clam." Katya turned away from them to sort some papers behind the counter. "So, what's the blackmail today?"

"Is that an unfriendly way of asking how you can help us?" Calvin smiled and stuffed his hands in his pockets. "It's simple. I want you to get us both into the Azure Cross."

She glared at him. "I'm not a member."

"Don't start with that. We both know you are and have been for at least the past four years." Calvin enumerated points on an imaginary list. "Five prior convictions that were directly tied to the Azure Cross, nine misdemeanors in company of alleged gang members—not to mention the fact that I saw you there last year, in person. Please don't tell me you're not a member of this gang."

"Quit calling it a gang," she interrupted. "They call themselves a syndicate. Anyone who says otherwise is gonna look suspicious."

"Syndicate, then. Can you get us in?"

"It's not like you've left me much choice." She laughed sharply. "You've heard about the initiation ritual, so you're prepared, right?"

Calvin nodded, and Ari shook her head.

Katya seemed happy to explain. "It's a real fun ceremony," she said. "It's where they take a—"

"Stop," interrupted Calvin hastily. "I'll tell her about it later, okay? When is the next initiation?"

"Wait, I want to hear about this," Ari said. "Initiation . . . ritual?"

Calvin's elbow dug into her side, and she paused reluctantly. Was he trying to keep a secret from Katya? If so, she couldn't force him to talk.

"I'll tell you later," repeated Calvin doggedly.

"Your timing is coincidentally perfect," Katya answered, as if she hadn't heard Ari's question. "It's tonight. Though you wouldn't have had to wait long anyway—they've started having them more often because of how many people want to get in on the fun. Stupid freaks. They just like seeing people in pain."

"Will Vita be there?"

Katya slammed the papers defiantly on the desk and looked up at Calvin. "You've asked me that before. I don't know him. The leader of this division is Ace. That's who you'll see tonight."

Calvin sighed, an exaggerated sigh. The corners of Katya's mouth pinched like she was trying not to laugh.

"Fine then. I guess I'll just have to keep looking for him."

"You go on, pretty boy," Katya said with a smirk. "And best of luck to you. There's nobody named Vita in this syndicate. You can search it from top to bottom."

"And what about Vika?"

She shook her head.

"Should we meet you here tonight? And what time?"

"Nine p.m.," she answered. "That's after most of the cops have had their donuts and last coffee for the night. Safest time. Not that anybody would mess with us, unless . . . " She eyed him suspiciously.

"Of course not," he assured her. "You have our word."

"All right then. I will see you both later tonight." She flashed them a peace sign and a wide smile, and then returned to her papers behind the desk.

Once they were out in the street, Calvin put his hands on his knees and laughed. Ari raised an eyebrow at him.

"She's the only person I'm really scared of," he explained. "If she hadn't gotten trapped in the underworld, she'd have gone to Harvard and found the cure for cancer. She's smarter than our whole team put together." His smile faded, and he shook his head. "Honestly, the only person I know smart enough to come up with this riddle game is Katya. Of course, that isn't proof of anything. I just think she's interesting."

"And what was all that about the initiation?" Ari asked. "You didn't want me to ask questions, but Katya had something to tell us. Shouldn't we have listened to her? Were you afraid someone would overhear?"

Calvin's gaze dropped. "When I went through the initiation, I would have preferred not to know what it was like until afterwards. Besides, Katya isn't supposed to tell anyone about it. If you show up acting nervous, the syndicate will assume that someone warned you what to expect, and they may make things worse for you."

"Is it some kind of test . . . ?" she began. But Calvin's expression pinched into a frown, and she paused. She wasn't sure which was worse—forcing the information out of Calvin and possibly losing his trust or walking blindly into a situation that seemed to terrify him.

"All right, whatever you think is best," she decided. "I don't know what you think could make me more nervous than not knowing anything at all, but I'll leave that to your judgment."

"Thanks." He chuckled nervously. "I promise you'll know all about it soon enough."

CHAPTER 9

"What are you doing?" Ari peeked over his shoulder at the computer screen covered in meaningless words and symbols. They flashed by almost too fast for her to read them as his fingers danced across the keyboard.

He paused to look up at her. His mouth twitched like he was trying to smile, though he looked like he was about to cry or fall asleep. "This is the project they gave me today."

The dark rings around his eyes had gotten worse since the last time she'd seen him, and his face was so pale she wondered if he was sick. Impulsively, she put a hand to his forehead, brushing his hair—what color was it again?—out of the way. It was damp with sweat.

"Kira, you're sick."

"So what?" He swiveled back to the computer. "Deadlines. And when not working, training. And when not training, watching—you know, the training videos."

She wanted to force him to rest, but she knew she looked the same as him.

"Can you leave?"

"We can't leave." He reached for the headphones on his desk but paused before putting them on. "You have it a lot worse than me, so I'm not complaining."

They both were trapped, slaves to something they couldn't even see.

Ari woke up smiling, surprised that she'd finally had a dream that didn't terrify her. A dream about *Kira*, no less—one she could wake up from without feeling empty and hurt inside. She was annoyed that she couldn't remember exactly what he looked like, but at least the dream had felt real.

She turned off her alarm and put on the sweatshirt she was wearing earlier that day. Her hair was appropriately messy after her nap, and her makeup had smudged. It looked awful, but she left it alone because it made her eyes look darker. She needed all the macho points she could get if she was about to be initiated into a "syndicate"—whatever that meant.

She ate half a can of refried beans and emptied her pockets of everything except her house key. Then she locked the door behind her and headed back to the tattoo parlor.

There were two people on the doorstep this time: Calvin and somebody else who was easy to recognize from the almost palpable aura of irritation surrounding him. Mikael.

"Why are you still here?" Ari asked before she could stop herself. "Weren't you supposed to—"

Calvin shushed her. He hadn't realized as quickly as she did that there was nobody to overhear them, and she couldn't blame him for being cautious.

"There's been a change of plans," he said in a low voice. "He's not here to call off the mission. He's coming with us." He popped his knuckles nervously, and Ari could see the lecture forming on Mikael's lips, just like the one he'd given her when she shredded her napkin.

But before he could say anything, Katya appeared in the shop doorway. She had changed clothes and was dressed in a cutoff tank, ripped black jeans, and several necklaces too many. The moment she noticed Mikael, her eyes narrowed.

"Who's he?" she demanded, glaring at Calvin. "You didn't tell me there was going to be anyone else."

Calvin cleared his throat and whispered, "We can't talk about that here. But he's with us."

"There's nobody else here," said Katya in her usual voice, loudly enough to produce a faint echo off the nearby buildings. "Well, it's your funeral if you get caught. I can always plead ignorance. They give me credit for recruiting the lovely little Nika, so I know they'll cut me some slack, even if they do get suspicious."

Calvin pressed his lips tightly together and fixed his gaze on the ground.

Katya led them through the maze of back roads through the city. It was dark outside and starting to get chilly. It felt strange to be in the city when it was quiet—strange and a little creepy.

"So you all three know about the initiation, right? I don't like to let people go without warning them." Katya stopped and looked back at them.

Calvin and Mikael nodded. Ari shook her head.

"You didn't tell her?" Mikael glanced sharply at Calvin. "She deserved to know. She won't back down just because of that."

"I thought . . . " Calvin mumbled. "I thought it would be better if she didn't have to worry about it."

"There's not much time left. You should tell me before we get there," said Ari.

Calvin stayed reluctantly silent, and Katya smacked him playfully on the shoulder. "You've got the personality of a flea," she remarked. Then she rolled up her sleeve and showed Ari her upper arm. It was knotted and pulled together with a burn scar that took the vague shape of a cross. "That's what you'll be doing," she said. "It's a test of loyalty. Nobody who wasn't serious about joining would want to get permanently burned like that, or so the logic goes."

So that's where Calvin got that scar.

The scar brought back a blur of memories—memories that took the vague form of distant screams, cries for help, something else she couldn't quite remember. She nodded at Katya, bit her lip, and looked away. It was too late for her to back out now—that was probably why Calvin hadn't told her in the first place. How badly could it hurt, anyway?

They turned the corner onto a one-way side street that was brightly lit with streetlights. The brick walls were lined with people, mostly boys who looked just out of high school. They all held beer cans or bottles, and a few were smoking. She could smell the dirty, sweet scent of marijuana and something else she didn't quite recognize, muffled by clean smoke from a wood fire. In total, there must have been thirty or forty of them, plus a few seedy-looking girls dressed in flamboyant colors.

Everyone was staring at them.

Katya stepped forward to break the tension. "They want to join," she explained, addressing the person closest to them. Ari looked him up and down and realized he must be the leader, whom Katya had referred to as Ace.

"Another Nika?" he asked, smiling at Ari. No, not smiling—smirking was a better word to describe it. "Or is she good for something else?"

Does everyone know Nika's secret except me?

"She's a runner," Katya explained. Ari puzzled over the term. Was that some kind of errand boy?

The man stood up and put his beer bottle down, extending his hand. "I'm Ace," he said. "If Katya says you're in, you're in. Welcome."

"Ari," she answered, shaking his hand. His grip pinched her fingers, and she bit her lip to avoid pulling away.

"How about the rest?" He glanced at Calvin and Mikael.

"I'm here strictly for business," Mikael said.

"Explain."

"Think of me as your supplier."

"Don't wear yourself out with talking." Ace was laughing, but Ari could see a faint spark of interest in his eyes. "Prices?"

"Low."

"Specifics?"

Mikael smiled. "You'll get those once you've agreed to the deal."

"Right. That's just good business," Ace agreed. "What's your name?"

"Mikael."

They shook hands, and Ace moved on to Calvin. "And what're you here for?"

"I'm Mikael's partner," he answered. "I just do deliveries."

Ace paused. "Wait, I remember you. Didn't you come here last year working for someone else?"

"I don't talk about past employers."

Ace laughed. "All right, so all three of you are interesting in your own ways," said Ace. "Want something to drink?"

Calvin and Mikael accepted. Ari hesitated, but Mikael motioned her to take the bottle Ace was offering. Curiosity got the better of her discretion, and she tried it. Though she couldn't quite identify it, she enjoyed the cold, sweet taste. But she wasn't willing to risk getting drunk, so she abandoned it discreetly on a trash can behind her.

"Tonight's initiation is going to be short," said Ace. He had returned to leaning against the brick wall, sipping his second drink. "There's just the two of you since Calvin already had his."

Ari shot a careful glance at Calvin. If he, of all people, had survived the initiation, surely she would be fine. She'd promised to trust him. But her skin prickled, and she felt sick to her stomach, no matter how hard she tried not to think about it.

Ace stood up again and smashed his bottle on the ground. The noise made Ari jump, and he laughed. "Who wants to go first?"

Better to get it over with, Ari thought. She raised her hand.

Three of the men—or more correctly, boys—standing near the opposite end of the alley silently stood up and disappeared into the darkness. They returned with a stack of firewood, which they dumped into an empty metal barrel. Ace produced a bottle of lighter fluid from somewhere in the shadow and emptied it over the wood. Somebody pulled a cigarette lighter from his pocket and set it on fire. The heat scorched Ari's face and she backed away.

"You've probably guessed what this is already, even if Katya didn't warn you," Ace began, lighting a cigarette. "We want to know if you're fully committed. And I won't even try to lie to you—we also want to keep track of you if you decide to pull anything funny." He grinned eerily in the orange light. "Keep that in mind and don't be sissies. It won't hurt for long."

Slowly, Ari pulled her sweatshirt over her head, feeling horribly exposed in her tank top and sweatpants. Everyone was watching her, the firelight reflected in their curious eyes. They could all see the scars on her back, scars from much worse pain—she hoped—than a metal brand could ever cause.

"Geez," Ace said. He bent down for a closer look and let out an admiring whistle. "What happened to you?"

Ari didn't remember and couldn't have told him if she'd wanted to. But he didn't wait for the answer. He moved so quickly that Ari didn't have time to feel afraid, seizing the metal poker from the fire and pressing it to her arm. First vertically, then horizontally, forming a cross-shaped burn.

At first it felt cold. Then it felt like a thousand needles were poking her all at once, not just in her arm, but all down her spine and all the way to her feet. She kept her teeth clenched, despite the temptation to bite her tongue, and squeezed her eyes shut.

When she opened her eyes again, the faces around her had turned into indistinct blurs. She stumbled back against the wall, covering the burn lightly with her other hand, dizzy and shaking. Her own touch felt hot like the fire all over again, but she couldn't pull her hand away. A tiny drip of blood seeped through her fingers, and she closed her eyes, nauseous.

Though she was still nauseous from the pain of her burn, Ari managed to drag herself back to the syndicate alley the next night. All she could think about when she saw it was how awful her memories from that place were. At least, she reflected ruefully, things could only go uphill from then on.

"Welcome back," said a very young-looking boy she'd never seen before. He offered her a beer. "Feeling any better today?"

"Yeah, thanks," she lied, accepting the drink and taking a deep swig.

"Great." He held out a hand, and she shook it. "I'm Lucas, Katya's brother. What's your name?"

"Ari." Then she stopped. "Wait, Katya's brother? As in, the Katya who brought us here last night?"

He nodded with a wide smile. Ari thought he looked nice, despite the company he was keeping and the fact that he was chugging alcohol at a rate which would've knocked her out in a few minutes.

"Nice to meet you. Where is everybody tonight? Am I supposed to be out doing something?"

"Ace will give you something to do eventually," Lucas answered. "They're just giving you time to get used to the people and the way we work."

"What do you do?"

"I'm mostly here because Katya is. She won't let me try anything, though." Ari assumed that he was talking about drugs. "But if Ace needs something done, I'll do it."

"What kinds of *somethings*?"

"Breaking into places?" He laughed at the surprised look on Ari's face. "It's fun once you get used to it."

"So . . . where do you keep the stuff you take? And what do you steal?"

"We have all kinds of things. Weapons, if we can get them. Anything we can sell."

"Interesting," said Ari absently. Her attention had been caught by the mention of weapons. "Where do you keep all this stuff?"

"In the storehouse. I'll ask Ace if it's okay to show you." He ran off to talk to Ace, who was leaning up against a wall, both fists clenching what looked like money. Lucas waved Ari over.

"These guys are arguing about who gets the mission," he explained, pointing to two men doing battle without any obvious rules in the middle of the street. Ari watched with interest. They were awful fighters—not at all what she'd expected. "Ace wants you to go, too."

Ari snorted. "Does that mean I have to get in the fight?"

Lucas was shaking his head no, but Ace interrupted with a laugh. "The psycho thinks she can get in on the fun? I'd like to see that."

She bottled her irritation at the nickname, pleased at a chance to take out her frustration on someone other than the voices in her head.

It was easier even than she expected. She caught the two men off guard, and they didn't know what to do once they realized who she was. She could read the doubt in their faces: *do we attack this girl? Block her? Tell her to stop?* But she didn't give them time to decide. The fight would've been over even quicker if she could've aimed for their knees, but—remembering how badly she'd injured Mikael—she took the more cautious approach of targeting their ankles. One quick kick, and the first assailant was down on the ground. She jumped on him before his companion had time to pull her off. Knocking him out with a pressure point felt like cheating, but she couldn't waste time winding up energy for a hard punch. Her fingers felt for the point on his neck, and she pinched. He went limp.

Sensing someone behind her, she rolled to the side, barely missing a wild swing. A quick glance back at the first man assured her he was out for the count, so she focused her attention on the opponent in front of her. This time, there was no hurry. If she'd been fighting to defend herself, she would've taken her time to make sure every hit counted and didn't sap too much energy. But she could hear everyone cheering her on, so she decided to give them the show they wanted. Her mixed martial arts were rusty, but there was one move she'd loved so much she'd practiced it until it was ingrained in her muscle memory—a roundhouse kick. One quick step forward, a twist to gather torque, and a leap. Her shoe hit the man's cheek, and he whimpered, then collapsed into a groggy sleep on the pavement. The cheers doubled into a roar of congratulations.

Ace laughed and slapped Ari on the back. Every slap felt like a battering ram. He wouldn't be as easy to fight as his subordinates were, Ari thought ruefully, and she hoped she never had to try.

"That was the greatest thing I've ever seen!" he cackled, spilling some of his drink on her shirt. "Want to fight someone else?"

"No, no, no, no," Ari refused, backing away to avoid getting slapped again. "I'm good. Wouldn't want to ruin my reputation now."

"You are definitely 'good' if you mean that you're a good influence," said Ace. Her opponents looked disgusted. "Hey, maybe that'll be your job from now on—beating up everybody who needs it. Sounds like a good job for someone named Psycho, doesn't it?"

"That's not my name," said Ari with a flash of annoyance. "It's Ari."

"Psycho suits you better." Ace's eyes flicked back to Lucas. "You can take her to the storehouse once she's been here a while longer. For now, why don't you show her around?"

Ari was disappointed that she wouldn't have the chance to acquire a weapon. Though she didn't want to admit it to herself, she had wanted to see how much she could get away with unnoticed. But there was nothing she could do about it, so she went back to questioning Lucas.

"Are you the only syndicate in the area?" she asked. "Or should we keep an eye out for . . . I don't know, rivals?"

"Of course we aren't the only syndicate." Lucas tipped his head back and nearly staggered back into the wall. He was getting tipsy. "But we've all got your back if anything happens. We're basically your family now."

"You trust me that quickly?" Ari steadied him. "I'm family already?"

"Anyone Katya says is safe is fine," said Lucas.

His confidence made Ari's heart sink.

CHAPTER 10

Joining the syndicate was like joining a club, Ari soon discovered. They met every night at the same time—nine o'clock—and stayed together until early morning, fighting, drinking, gambling. Occasionally, they were assigned "missions," some of which came from Ace or one of the other members and some of which seemed to come from a higher-up who was never named. Ari soon came to know everyone, if not by name, at least by personality. Lucas was right: the group really was like family. They accepted her without hesitation and treated her like one of them.

In her first week, she was assigned two missions: to rob a bakery cash register and to steal liquor from a grocery store. Ace called them "test missions." And she was good at everything sneaky—lockpicking, disabling security cameras, evading night guards—so she quickly earned Ace's trust.

Nika was around only during the weekly morning meetings. Sometimes Katya would tag along, and they would exchange vicious banter, which made everyone else uncomfortable.

Calvin was the only one who seemed discouraged. He wasn't acting like himself—at least, not the version of him that Ari was used to seeing. She was trying to be especially nice to him since her nightmare, so about a week after the initiation she pulled him aside and asked him about it.

"I'm fine," he answered with a smile. "It's just that I'm not getting much sleep."

"Why not?"

"Because we stay up late, and I'm used to waking up early."

No matter how hard she pressed, Ari couldn't get anything else out of him.

Mikael already had a reputation built around his air of mystery. The theories Ari heard about him never failed to make her laugh: some said he was a Russian spy or that he was from the Italian mafia. But nobody guessed that he worked with the NDEB, and he never set the record straight.

Sometimes Ari worked with him to re-package the drugs he'd bought to resell to the gang so their origin couldn't be traced. It gave her something better to do than sleep all day. Occasionally, he dropped his formality, usually by accident, and then Ari could have a real conversation with him.

"This should be the last of it," said Ari, stuffing the plastic bags filled with tiny crystals down into the cardboard box. "Your apartment looks like a warehouse."

Mikael finished writing down the box number on his clipboard before looking up. "If the police came now, they'd never believe I'm with the NDEB. Let's hope they don't."

"Did you clear this plan with the agency?"

He shook his head and smiled mischievously. "They were going to disapprove it anyway."

"My work here is done." Ari bowed gracefully. "Your apartment won't hold any more of this stuff." She dusted the powder off her hands and started putting on her jacket.

"Before you go," said Mikael, "I heard from the cybercrime division about that email I mentioned."

"Oh?" Ari had nearly forgotten about it, distracted by her new work with the syndicate. Now she realized she'd been slacking, and she tensed. "What did they say?"

"They traced it back to a bot that auto-generates emails with random names."

"You're kidding. My name's not that common. There's no way it was randomly generated."

Mikael rested his elbow on one of the boxes. "I know," he said after a short pause. "I told Yuno that."

"It must have something to do with the riddles," Ari said. "You already know what I'm going to say."

"And I don't disagree. We need to tell the others. It's just—" He stopped, clearly frustrated. "We'd be going against orders." Seeing that Ari was about to interrupt, he raised his hands. "I know, I know. I'll take responsibility for this. I'll send out an email to everyone tonight, okay?"

Ari studied his face closely, wondering if she should believe him.

"Send me a copy," she said at last.

"You don't trust me, do you?"

She shot him a rueful grin. "That's the whole point of the riddles, isn't it?" The annoyance on Mikael's face almost made her laugh. "It's not that I don't trust you. But I feel responsible for how things turned out. If I'd kept a closer eye on Yuri . . . " Voicing her feelings aloud made the guilt even worse.

"I should have done better," she mumbled. "I don't want anything like this to happen again."

True to his word, Mikael sent out the email a few hours later, courtesy copying Ari. She read it through several times, trying to make sense of its implications. The writer of the riddles—and, it seemed likely, the email—had no reason to make his presence known before they even left Virginia. Had they known that sending a message like that would force Mikael to travel to Seattle? Was he going to be their next target? That, Ari thought, would require either an incredible amount of foresight or an intimate knowledge of how the hierarchy at the NDEB worked. And even the latter might not be enough, since Yuno, head of the whole department, was directly in charge of the mission. How could the email-writer have known that he wouldn't have come to Seattle instead of Mikael?

Whoever sent it must know not only my name and that I started working at the NDEB, but also the whereabouts of every person on this team, the best way to get the agency's attention, and exactly what we're doing here in Seattle. So why haven't they killed again, if they have all the information they need to do so?

It was still bothering her in the morning when she gave up trying to sleep and went out into her kitchen. Her first project was to make coffee. While she waited for the water to boil, she went to the sofa to get her blanket—the only sweatshirt she'd brought had traces of the drugs she'd been packaging, and she was paranoid about breathing in the powder. Wrapping the blanket around her shoulders, she put her feet up on the coffee table. Something wet chilled her heels.

She looked up at the roof. No leak. Then she looked down at the coffee table.

Scrawled across in yellow spray paint was a blurry message:

2/3

WHAT BREATHES FIRE IN BLUE?
IF YOU CAN SOLVE THAT, YOU'LL KNOW HOW B DIED.

"Who are you to say I want to know? Or that I care?" she shouted at the ceiling. Then she stopped herself. Her mission was to solve the riddles, not curse until someone else did it for her.

She washed the paint off her feet and called Nika to ask if she'd seen anything like it, but she said no without hesitation. Then she asked Calvin. He'd gotten the same message on his door the night before, but he seemed to be in a hurry to get off the phone, and she couldn't get any details from him. Finally, she called Mikael.

"I saw the message," he said before she had a chance to explain why she was calling. "I already spoke to Calvin about it."

"What are we going to do?" she asked. At least she wasn't alone this time. "Somebody was in my apartment during the night, and I didn't even know they were there. I should've woken up, but I didn't. I don't want to play this stupid game."

"If you don't want him to keep playing the game, I'd suggest you do what Calvin and I are already doing—try to find an answer to the riddles," Mikael answered quietly. "There's no other way. The first riddle says it clearly—if you can find out who wrote it, you'll know who killed Yuri. Once we know that, we can have him arrested, and the game will be over."

"Calvin thinks this game is about revenge," Ari said. "Do you agree? Why else would someone play a game with us?"

There was a long pause. "I think Calvin's selling the killer short," he said at last. "Revenge is petty. I think there's a much deeper reason."

"Which is?"

"Who knows?" His voice had gotten staticky. "Sorry, the service is bad here."

"If this is a game . . ."

"What did you say?"

"If this is a game," Ari shouted into the phone, "what happens if we lose?"

There was a long pause. "Whoever did this is a murderer," he said at last. "I don't think they would hesitate to kill us all."

The familiar adrenaline rush that she felt whenever she was supposed to be afraid washed over her. "Great," she said sarcastically. "But where do we start?"

The phone clicked loudly. Apparently, his service had finally given out. But almost as soon as he hung up, Ari's phone vibrated again.

Lia: *Remember how you told me you didn't want me to forget anything else?*

Lia: *Well, I remembered, just like you said. I remember what happened at my wedding.*

Ari froze. She had been so stupid to think things could just go back to the way they were.

Ari: *I'm so sorry. I'll call you right now.*

Lia: *No need. I'm busy.*

She knew she didn't deserve another chance, but she had a nagging feeling that she had to try. Even if Lia hated her now, at least she would get the chance to apologize properly.

The phone rang until Ari started pacing frantically up and down, and then, at long last, it stopped.

"Hello?" asked an uncharacteristically dry voice.

"L-Lia?" Ari was relieved enough to cry. "I had to call you. I feel awful."

"I really don't have time to talk to you right now."

"Please listen for just thirty seconds," said Ari desperately. "I wanted to say I'm sorry. I'm sorry for disappearing after the—the thing with the army. I'm sorry for being a jerk to you every time we talk. I'm sorry for crashing on your wedding night. I'm sorry for never being grateful to you for anything. I'm sorry for—for everything. I mean it, Lia. You don't ever have to talk to me again after this, but I had to say it. I'm so, so sorry."

The silence that followed was so long that Ari pulled her phone away from her ear to make sure Lia hadn't hung up.

"So?" Lia said at last. "What good does that do either of us now?"

"None, I guess." Things were going just as Ari expected, and she felt miserable.

"So, let's just forget it."

"Forget it?"

"Yeah." Long pause. "I want my friend back, so let's just forget it."

Relief flooded Ari. Relief, and regret. "Thank you, Lia. I'm—"

"No need to say it again." Lia laughed, and she sounded like her old, cheerful self this time. "We all mess up. And I know you were going through some hard times after Kira died. We can leave all that in the past where it belongs. You don't have to apologize."

"Well, about that . . . " Ari hesitated. "Do you remember what happened? Back in the army? I had this strange dream about Kira recently, and it seems like something happened between us before he died, but I forget what it was."

"What *do* you remember?" Lia sounded surprised.

"I don't remember anything except that we were friends and that he was killed right before we disbanded."

This time the pause was even longer.

"Lia?"

"I'm here. I just don't know what to say."

"What's the matter?"

"How could you forget something like that?" Lia laughed again, but it was a short, bitter laugh. "Even I remember the gist of the story. You really don't remember?"

"I can't remember anything that happened while we were in the army. I remember who my friends were, and of course I remember you and Grey because I saw you afterwards, but the events . . . I can't. Every time I try to think about them, I hit a block. It's literally like crashing into a wall."

"I guess that's to be expected after everything that happened." Lia still sounded doubtful. "If you've forgotten what happened with Kira, then I don't think you want to remember."

"Why not?"

"Because it's not a pleasant story."

"I'm asking you to tell me."

"And I'm answering. No."

"Why won't you tell me?"

"The first reason is because I don't know all the details," Lia said. "And the second is, I don't think knowing would help you. There's a reason your mind won't let you think about it."

Ari thought carefully before she replied. Lia was a psychologist, known for her ability to make and alter memories, just like she did for herself. Ari dimly remembered how accurate her perception had always been. If she refused to say anything about Ari's past, it would be hard to force her to talk.

Then again, she might have insight about something else.

"Can I ask you something else then?"

"Sure."

Ari explained the context of the two riddles and read them aloud to Lia from her journal. "Why would someone play a game like this?" she asked. "It's awful."

"Oo!" Lia chirped excitedly. "Hold on, let me think. I've heard of something like this before."

She really is like Sherlock Holmes. Ari waited respectfully, scrabbling on her coffee table for a pen and paper to take notes.

"I remember now," Lia said at last. "There was a guy who—well, the story is long, but his fiancée was unfaithful the night of their wedding, and he resented her so much he wanted to send a specific, hurtful message. And he made it as creepy as possible—he left messages written in fake blood on his fiancée's house. He never killed anyone, but he made threats, and the police had a terrible time unraveling the case."

"But who is the killer trying to reach?" Ari asked. "Calvin and Mikael have also gotten the riddles. And they seem to hint that one of us four was responsible for the killing. Do you think—" Ari hesitated. She hated to blame someone specific, but what else was she supposed to think? "Do you think it could be Nika? She's the only one who hasn't gotten the riddles."

"No way." Lia didn't even hesitate. "If I'm understanding the first riddle, it says that whoever wrote the riddle is also the killer. Nika would *never* throw suspicion on herself by admitting she didn't have the riddles."

"But what if she knew we'd think that?"

"This whole plan is really just someone trying to scare you into doing what they want. There's no room for complex details, so I doubt the culprit went to great lengths to cover up their identity. We can rule Nika out. That leaves Unknown, you, Calvin, and Mikael. I'll take it on trust that we can rule you out, too."

"Why do you think I didn't do it?"

"Because you told me you spent the whole evening with Mikael, which is the same story I heard from Grey. That also rules out Mikael. All you have left is Calvin, if you think the suspect is someone in your group."

"How does Grey know anything about this?"

"The NDEB is doing an undercover investigation," Lia answered. "Grey is doing chemical analysis on a sample of Yuri's blood to find what killed him."

"So nobody really thinks Yuri died of natural causes." Finally, she would have good news for Nika.

"Not after the riddles."

"They think the riddles are real?"

"Whoever wrote them must have known when Yuri died and how many teammates he had," Lia explained. "They must be real, at least to that extent."

"Is there a primary suspect?"

"It's Nika. They won't listen to me when I tell them there's no way it could've been her. The head of the investigation, Yuno—that's the head of your division—said I was crazy and hung up on me." She laughed. "He's not wrong, either."

Ari couldn't help chuckling, despite her misgivings. "Thanks, Lia. I'm glad to hear we're not alone on this."

"We can't leave you out there by yourselves." Ari heard a masculine voice in the background. "Oops, that's Grey. I'd better go." Lia hung up in a chorus of giggles.

What now?

She had the whole day free, and she had to fight the urge to spend it doing nothing. She couldn't let herself fall into the same trap of apathy she had when she left the military.

First, she made breakfast—a bowl of cereal and some coffee. Then she cleaned off her table as best she could, curled up on the sofa under a blanket, and turned off her phone.

She spread her journal on her lap and re-read the first riddle:

1/3

SUPPOSE THERE ARE FIVE CHARACTERS: A, B, C, D, AND UNKNOWN. ASSUME THAT A–D KNOW EACH OTHER AND UNKNOWN IS AN OUTSIDER. HERE ARE THE RULES OF THE SCENARIO:

1. A, B, AND C ARE AT DINNER.

2. D IS ELSEWHERE BUT NEARBY.

3. UNKNOWN IS ALSO NEARBY AND COULD BE ANY OF THE MILLIONS OF PEOPLE IN THIS CITY.

4. B LEAVES THE DINNER EARLY—BEFORE ANYONE HAS EATEN OR DRUNK.

5. D FINDS B DEAD.

WHO WROTE THIS RIDDLE?

IF YOU CAN SOLVE THAT, YOU'LL KNOW WHO KILLED B.

"One-third," she mumbled. "No, that's not it. One out of three." The riddle from today was 2/3. That meant there was only one more left.

She wrote in her journal:

> TO SOLVE THE FIRST RIDDLE, I HAVE TO FIGURE OUT WHO WROTE IT. PRIZE FOR SOLVING = THE IDENTITY OF THE KILLER. SINCE THAT WOULD GIVE THE WHOLE GAME AWAY, I PROBABLY WILL SOLVE THIS RIDDLE LAST.

> TO SOLVE THE SECOND RIDDLE, I HAVE TO FIGURE OUT 'WHAT BREATHES FIRE IN BLUE.'

Odd word order . . . why wouldn't he say "what breathes blue fire?"

> PRIZE FOR SOLVING = HOW YURI DIED.

Why would the identity of the killer be the first prize? It would make more sense if he saved that riddle for last.

Maybe his identity is the most important?

Or . . . maybe his identity is the point.

What if Katya had informed Vita that they were NDEB agents? Ari wrote his name down on the suspect list.

Lia had said that Nika shouldn't be one of the suspects, but Ari didn't agree with her reasoning. If Nika found Yuri, then she should be the first suspect. "Too complex" was the only reason Lia had given for this idea to be wrong, so Ari wrote her name along with Vita's.

Calvin? It couldn't have been him, since he was in Virginia when Yuri died and the NDEB could corroborate that. Though, she reflected, he had shown up right after Yuri died. But he had told everyone that he was coming to replace Yuri on Yuno's orders, and if that was true, then he wouldn't have gotten on a plane until after Yuri was already dead. She could verify that easily enough. She picked up her phone and sent a quick email to the scheduler back at the NDEB. A few minutes later, she received a response confirming that Calvin's plane tickets had been booked after Yuri's death, and he had come to the office to pick up his tickets. So there was no way he was guilty.

Mikael? He had been at the restaurant all night with Ari, and Yuri hadn't eaten or drunk while he was there. There was the hour-long period during which she'd been at home and hadn't seen either of them. But from the way Yuri had acted at the restaurant—seemingly drunk, slurring his speech, bizarrely angry—she suspected his death was already set in stone well before they had arrived at the restaurant. A slow-acting poison could do that. So if Mikael was a suspect, he would've had to meet Yuri in person before they arrived at the restaurant. Ari didn't believe he had because Yuri had mentioned getting a phone call from Mikael asking him to bring Ari to the restaurant. If they had met in person, why would Mikael have called him afterwards? The timing simply didn't add up for Mikael to be a suspect.

That left her with only two names: Nika and Vita. That is, if she assumed the killer was someone they knew.

What about Katya?

There was no evidence that she'd been involved, and everybody seemed to trust her. Ari didn't have any particular reason to suspect her either, but she hadn't known her for very long. Unknown could technically be anyone, but the riddles strongly suggested the list was confined to people she knew personally. She wrote Katya's name down.

Nika or Vita?

If she made Vita her primary suspect, a whole new avenue of possibilities opened up. That would mean that Vita knew about the

NDEB's involvement in the Azure Cross, and he was probably watching them from afar—which didn't seem unlikely, given that he had already been brazen enough to confess to an NDEB agent that he was involved in illegal activities. Also, now that she thought about it, she remembered Yuri was the only one of the team who had met him personally.

Her fingers tingled with excitement. She was onto something at last.

She picked up the second riddle. *What breathes fire in blue?* Why, she wondered, would the author say "fire in blue" rather than "blue fire?" Either the fire burned in something blue—such as the sky—or word order was important. Fire that burned in the sky could be the aurora. But that didn't tell her anything about how Yuri died.

Breathes.

Fire.

In blue.

How else could you write that riddle so it means the same thing?

There wasn't another obvious way, except changing the ending. Ari tried substituting various words for the three keywords—breathes, fire, and blue—but nothing made any sense.

She closed her journal and put it on the table in front of her. Her time hadn't been totally wasted—at least, she hoped not—but she still hadn't found an answer to either of the riddles.

When she turned her phone back on, there was a message from Grey. She was surprised and wondered if something had happened to Lia.

Grey: *I got the formula.*

Grey: *The main components are arsenic and cyanide. Oxy—that's related to the chemical formula and then -ar-cyan. The process to make it is rough, couldn't figure it out in the lab. Don't try at home.*

Ari had forgotten all about the oxyarcyan experiment.

Ari: *Send it to me by email.*

Grey: *What are you doing with it?*

She didn't reply. There was no point in asking someone's permission to be stupid, and she didn't want to hear the warnings that she already knew about. Arsenic and cyanide were a vicious combination. But she had to know.

She texted Katya.

Ari: *Do you know someone who can make me a certain drug?*

The reply was almost instant.

Katya: *Prolly.*

Ari: *I've got the formula.*

Katya: *Formula?*

Ari checked her email. Grey had sent the formula, but she couldn't just text it to Katya on the off-chance that someone was spying on her phone. Yes, the information was technically declassified, but still. . .

She cropped the picture and sent the first part of the formula.

Katya: *This is lab stuff. Like . . . complicated lab stuff.*

Ari: *Do you know anyone?*

Long pause.

Katya: *I'll see what I can do. Gonna cost you a pretty penny.*

Ari: *That's fine.*

She put her phone down, relieved that Katya hadn't asked too many questions.

Somebody knocked on her door, and she peeked through the front window blinds to see who it was. Mikael.

"I need to talk to you," he said through the glass. "It's urgent."

Ari wondered why he hadn't just called her on the phone, but she opened the door.

Mikael's eyes were dark with stress. "Nika failed her drug test," he said abruptly. "And I was hoping you would talk to her."

"W-what?" Ari found herself stammering. "Drug test? *What* drug test?"

"Let's talk about it inside."

She stood aside to let him in, then shut and locked the door behind them. Mikael went to the window, glanced outside, and then pulled the blinds shut.

"NDEB employees are expected to pass the drug test once every two months," he said, leaning back against the wall and staring absently at Ari's coffee table, still smeared with paint. "You and Calvin aren't due because you had preliminary tests before we left Virginia, but Nika had hers done yesterday. I got the results via a private email. She tested positive for an unknown substance the lab is working to identify. All we know for now is she took something with oxycodone in it."

"Oxycodone . . . ?" An addictive opioid, easy to get because it was freely prescribed by doctors. Ari had taken it once for a pinched nerve. "She wouldn't do that."

"It doesn't matter whether she would or wouldn't. The fact is that she did. Although she's denying it." He laughed in bitter frustration. "As if we don't know without a shadow of a doubt."

"But couldn't it have been a mistake? A mix-up?"

"Why don't you talk to her yourself?" Mikael looked at his phone. "She said she was on her way here. And you'll want all the information you can get. Apparently, this is so important that the NDEB is flying us all the way back to Virginia as soon as possible to testify for her."

"They'd call us all home in the middle of a mission over this?" Ari pinched her lips together. "That doesn't make sense. How are we going to explain where we went? Or why we all left together?"

"Tell that to Yuno. This was his decision."

Maybe I should add Yuno to the suspect list. Everything that's gone wrong on this mission ties back to him somehow.

There was another knock on the door, and Ari unlocked it. Nika stopped in the doorway, halfway between the street and the living room. For once, she didn't look neat and prim—she looked chaotically stressed. Her eyes were a crazy mixture of blank and desperate, and her fingers were bleeding.

"I didn't do it," she burst out.

Neither Mikael nor Ari said anything.

"I didn't," she insisted. "I don't know what they're talking about. I haven't done anything wrong. I haven't taken anything."

Nika's gaze flitted back and forth between them. Ari tried her best to look sympathetic, but there wasn't much she could do in front of Mikael.

"Nika," Mikael said at last, "do you realize you're the primary suspect in the investigation of Yuri's death?"

She nodded.

"And that this isn't helping your case?"

She nodded again.

"And that we have concrete evidence that you've been using oxycodone?"

"No!" Her voice sounded scared. "No, no, no! You can't have evidence if I didn't do anything!"

Silence.

"Assuming you're not lying." Ari's voice was colder than she meant for it to be, and she gulped, trying to soften her tone. "How can you explain the test results?"

Nika glanced at her. "I can't. But I swear, I didn't do it."

Ari's gaze met Mikael's. She had seen hundreds of people lie to her with varying levels of believability, but she had never seen anyone lie as well as Nika. Which meant she was probably telling the truth. Mikael gave her a small nod. He knew it, too.

"I believe you," he said with a sigh.

Nika slid down the wall to the floor. "I didn't, I didn't, I didn't."

"We know," Mikael said irritably. "But a whole lot of difference it makes what we think."

"The only way to prove her innocent," Ari said slowly, "is to prove that she wasn't the killer and that the killer is trying to frame her. If they know she's NDEB, it would make sense for them to trick her into failing the drug test so she gets sent home."

"We don't know if that's true," said Mikael. "Even if she isn't the killer, why would they try to frame Nika?"

"Lia said Nika shouldn't be one of the suspects," Ari insisted. "And we can't even identify what drug she took, other than it has something to do with oxycodone. The first step is to find out what it was. Then we can make the case from there."

"Oxycodone by itself is a restricted drug. And they know for sure she's been taking it," Mikael answered hopelessly. "We can't get her out of that one. It's signed, sealed, and delivered."

Nika hugged her knees tightly to her chest. "I don't think you get it."

They waited for her to continue.

"I'm going back tomorrow," she said bitterly. "Back to headquarters. By myself. And you people are coming back with me, one at a time. They expect you to testify to what I've been doing."

"But we don't know—" began Ari.

"That's what I'm trying to tell you!" Nika was almost crying. "You don't know what I've been doing, so you can't say anything to help me."

"Maybe it's time for you to tell her," Mikael said quietly. "She may not be able to help you, but at least she can have a better idea of where you're coming from if she's called on to testify."

"No."

Nika sat silent, so obviously distressed that Ari suddenly wanted to hug her. But before she could do anything, Nika stood up and let herself out the front door without another word.

"You're late."

"Well, so are you."

Those were the first words they ever said to each other.

She had noticed him before, mostly because it was hard not *to notice him. He wore the stereotypically nerdy, plastic glasses, black ripped jeans, and t-shirt with a plaid flannel shirt on top. He even wore headphones around his neck. Ari had first seen him from behind, and the combination of orange headset and messy brown hair caught her attention. When he turned around, she saw his eyes. They looked exhausted, but nice. Friendly.*

After that, she wanted to talk to him out of sheer curiosity, but there was never a chance—at least, not until now.

She couldn't believe he'd actually come up to her.

"Mind if I sit here?" he continued.

She nodded, and he sat down on the bench beside her. They were on the roof, looking out over the city. It was quiet and should've been peaceful, but Ari could feel her anxiety kicking in like it always did when people got near her.

"It looked like you need a friend."

She nodded again.

"Training got you down?" He was persistent.

This time she felt obligated to explain—he was really trying to be nice, and she wasn't helping. "They were trying a new medication, and it makes me anxious." That was the best she could do.

"Oh." He took a sip from the soda in his hand. "They tried one on me last week that was supposed to increase productivity. It didn't work. I fell asleep at my desk. And woke up hallucinating about eating pickles."

Ari was finally brave enough to look at him. But she couldn't read anything other than good-humored cheerfulness in his face.

So she said, "What do you do?"

He put a finger to his lips. "Don't tell anyone, it's top secret!"

Was he trying to make a joke?

"I'm a hacker," he explained. "Thus these—" He poked his headset. "—and this." He pulled out his phone and flashed the screen, which was covered with green and orange text. "Can't get away from work even for lunch."

"I know how that goes."

They sat in silence until her companion finally stood up with a yawn. He stretched like a cat and cracked his wrists.

"Back to the grind," he said. "Keyboards and more keyboards. What's your name?"

"My real name?" she stammered.

"I guess I could find out by hacking your file, but I'd rather hear it from you." He smiled disarmingly.

"Ari." It had been too long since she'd told anyone—since anyone had asked. Usually, they wanted only her ID number.

He held out a hand, and she shook it. "I'm Kira," he said. "Nice to meet you. If you're up here again, let me know." He waved at her with his soda can. "See you soon!"

CHAPTER 11

Ari's cheeks were wet. As she quickly rubbed her tears away, pieces of her dream came back to her, and it played like a movie in her head. It made her want to cry again.

But before she had a chance to sort out her emotions, she realized what had woken her up: her phone was ringing. She rolled over with a sigh and answered.

"Ari?" asked a tense masculine voice.

"Calvin?" she said uncertainly. "Is that you?"

"No, this is Grey. Don't you have my number in your phone?"

"Oh." She felt a bit more awake. "I didn't look to see who it was. What's up? Isn't it . . . " She glanced at the clock on her phone. "Early? Even for you?"

"I've been up early every day because of you!" he shouted. Ari pulled the phone away from her ear, startled. "It's time to explain this game you're playing with me!"

"W-what . . . ?" she stammered. "What game?"

"Don't pretend like you don't know! Where did you send the oxyarcyan?"

"Oxy . . . ? Grey, what are you talking about?"

"You know exactly what I'm talking about, you—" He added a few descriptive curses. "Just tell me already so I can figure out what I'm going to do about Lia. This is killing me!"

145

"Take a deep breath," ordered Ari, "and explain from the beginning. I swear I have no idea what you're talking about."

"You can't be serious!"

"Grey. Calm down."

She could hear a few heavy breaths on the other side of the phone and some more muttered curses.

"So it wasn't you?" he asked eventually.

"No. The only thing I asked you for that relates to oxyarcyan was the formula. I have no idea what you're talking about. I don't have any oxy."

"So you didn't . . . you don't have the . . . ?"

"Have what?" Ari waited patiently.

"You haven't been getting the shipments?"

"Of?"

"Oxyarcyan."

A cold chill ran through her. "You've been making oxyarcyan? You told me you couldn't make it!"

"That's because I was told to say that." His voice sounded desperate. "And I thought you already had the formula. I'm sorry. I don't know what's going on. I'm as confused as you are."

"Explain."

"No, they said—they said if I try to tell anyone, Lia will . . . "

"Will what?" she demanded sharply.

This time she could hear him sigh. "They threatened her."

"Who's they?"

"I don't know. Look, it's too complicated to explain, and if they overhear—"

"According to Mikael, I'm going to be back in Virginia sometime this week to testify for Nika. Can we meet and talk about this?" Ari's chills changed to a rush of pure adrenaline, and the words tumbled out of her mouth. "I need all the information you can give me." She paced up and down, trying not to let on how nervous she was. Grey didn't need anything else to worry about. But she'd suddenly had an idea. "Everything ties back to the oxyarcyan somehow. I was right when I told you it was important. Now all I need is proof. You can help me with that." *Because it can't possibly be a coincidence that Nika failed her drug test because of a drug that starts with "oxy." And it can't be a coincidence that Yuri was poisoned with something the hospital couldn't detect in his system. And it can't be a coincidence that all this happened after I suspected I was poisoned with oxyarcyan.*

Grey laughed reluctantly. "I don't get what you're talking about, but fine. We'll discuss it when you get here."

"Great." Ari paused. "Hey, Grey?"

"What?"

"Don't worry about Lia. I won't let anything happen to either of you. That's a promise."

"Ari, I want you and Calvin to go with Lucas and Katya tonight," Ace ordered, stumbling into the wall. It was too early for him to be drunk, and Ari wondered what had him so excited.

"Where are we going?" she asked, trying to draw Ace's attention away from his drink.

"The four of you are going to try something new." Ace smiled mischievously, propping himself up against the wall. "There's a crack house near here. Calvin found out that the owners are on vacation, and there won't be anyone there. What do you think?"

Ari stifled a grin. Of all the jobs she'd expected when she started working in law enforcement, raiding a crack house on the side of the criminals was not one of them.

She looked around for her teammates, and the first she found was Calvin, sitting in front of the fire barrel. His eyes were invisible from her angle; but his shoulders were slumped, and his gaze was fixed in the distance. She yelled to him, but he didn't respond.

"Ace says we're going on a mission," she shouted hoarsely into his ear.

"Okay." He didn't seem startled by her voice.

She crouched beside him. "Something's going on with you," she said. "You're not acting like yourself. Not that I've known you for very long, but . . . you know what I mean."

Silence, broken only by the background of drunken laughter. Calvin didn't move.

"Ari?"

She whipped around, and there was Mikael.

"Ace wants you to leave as soon as possible."

Ari glanced back at Calvin. "You coming?" He still didn't move.

So she left him sitting there and went to find her other teammates.

"It's the ace of spades," she said to Katya, interrupting her magic trick. "I saw you flip them over."

Katya rolled her eyes. "Hey! They haven't seen this before, so could you keep it down?"

"No," said Ari with a sly smile. "Ace wants us to leave now for a mission."

"Oh, the crack house?" Katya perked up. "Just us two?"

"Lucas and Calvin are coming, too. Can you get Lucas . . . ?" Ari's voice trailed off when she recognized the expression on Katya's face.

It was fierce anger, all directed at her little brother, who was dancing dangerously close to the fire.

"Lucas," she roared, "I told you not to touch the booze!" She snatched the bottle out of his hand and smashed it on the ground. It shattered like a gunshot. Even in his half-drunk state, Lucas looked appropriately scared. All conversation in the alley instantly stopped, and everybody stared at Katya. She had Lucas by the shoulders and shook him until Ari could see sober sense flood into his eyes.

"I said that over and over, and this is what you're doing?" she shouted. "You're going to try the drugs next, aren't you?" Her voice was high-pitched with rage and a little shame. Her screams at her brother were the condemnations she wished somebody had screamed at her. Ari wondered why she hadn't caught onto that before.

Lucas was shaking now, backing away from his sister until his back hit the brick wall behind him. "N-n-no," he stammered. His speech slurred. "I didn't—I won't—I mean, I—"

"Get home right now," commanded Katya, "while you still have a home to go back to. I don't want to see you here again until you swear on everything you've ever believed in that you'll never do something like this again."

Everybody watched in dead silence as Lucas trailed away, staggering slightly. Several seconds after he'd turned the corner and disappeared, nobody moved at all except to turn their heads and look at Katya.

She dusted her hands off. "That's done," she said matter-of-factly. But her face was white, even in the orange firelight.

"Girl, you really sorted that kid," Ace said. He looked sober, too. "You sure you're up for this mission?"

"It's not like I've got anything left to lose." She smiled so widely that her eyes squeezed shut.

Ari put an arm around her shoulder, trying to be comforting, but the embrace was roughly shaken off.

"If we're going, let's go," Katya snarled, shoving her hands into her pockets. "Where are we going?"

"Just a few streets down," Calvin answered from in front of them. "It's not far away. The alarm is already taken care of—Ace sent somebody to do it a few hours ago. We just have to break in."

They were heading back in the direction of Ari's apartment, back to the sketchiest dump in town. She knew exactly where they were going—she passed the place every night on her way to the Azure Cross alley, though she had never thought twice about it before. It was a traditional brick warehouse sandwiched between apartments and a deli, and it looked like it was leaning off to one side. A constant stream of water dripped off the roof.

Sometimes when she passed by, she saw people outside—all ages, but mostly men not much older than her. They weren't the types of people she expected. Instead of being rough and street-smart, they just looked horribly exhausted. She was never afraid of them after the first time she saw them.

Tonight, though, there was nobody nearby. Even the typical city noise seemed quieter than usual. It echoed far away and acted like a backdrop. Ari thought the combination of silence and darkness made the place look like a haunted house. The closer they got, the more threatened she felt. She wondered how hard it would be to convince her teammates that something felt off, and they shouldn't get near the building.

Ari couldn't shake her uneasiness, and she crouched tensely behind a dumpster. The darkness and changing shadows made it feel like someone could jump out at them any second. It was an unreasonable feeling, but it wouldn't go away, and Ari had learned never to ignore it.

"Break the window," Katya said. "That's probably the easiest way. If the alarm is disabled, we should be fine."

"Do you want to just—" began Calvin, but Katya was ahead of him. With one quick movement, she produced a gun from her pocket and slammed the barrel into the glass. It shattered immediately.

"Where did you get that?" Calvin cried. "They're not legal here! If you get caught—"

He was interrupted by a flash from inside and a loud crash—a gun being fired in the dark, and a window shattering. Ari ducked her head behind the dumpster. Her first instinct was to fire back where she'd seen the flash, but she was unarmed and forced to wait helplessly. Two more crashes, both from her left—Katya was firing. Her shot hit somebody. From inside the building came a wild shriek of pain, and in the momentary silence between shots, it sounded like an echoing siren.

There were people behind her. Ari could sense them. But she couldn't stand up, not while somebody she couldn't see was shooting from inside the warehouse. Her head, silhouetted against the wall, would be the perfect target.

Something hit her at the base of her neck, and her legs crumpled under her.

"I'd prefer if all the doorknobs around here were brass."

Ari blinked and opened her eyes. Even then, all she saw was black.

"That way, every time you open the doors, you get that cold shiver down your spine, and it feels even more like a haunted house."

She blinked. She still couldn't see anything. Not sitting—lying on her back. Listening closely revealed nothing but the gentle hum of a few voices, which seemed to be coming through a wall.

"Why would you want your hands frozen off all the time?" another voice grumbled. "Why can't the doorknobs just be the normal kind?"

"Don't you like the es—esth—aesthetic?" He choked out the big word with a struggle that almost made Ari laugh. "Don't you think—"

She shut out the voices and tried moving her hands. They were securely tied in front of her with duct tape, and the sticky feeling against her skin reminded her of something she'd felt before. A test. *That's it.* Something from the military. She twisted her wrists against the tape. It stretched almost imperceptibly at first, then a little more, and finally she was able to worm her hands out. She rubbed her hands together to restore circulation, then wiped the sticky residue from her wrists.

The next step was to free her ankles, also taped. It was difficult without a knife, but Ari managed it after a few minutes of quiet effort. Now she could explore.

She reached out her arms in front of her and crawled until she hit a wall—about two feet from where she was sitting. In total, the room must have been about six feet long by four wide. Something metal and cylindrical was in the other corner, something bristly on a pole leaning against it. And she found some plastic spray bottles scattered around the room. Conclusion—she was in a utility closet, right next to a water tank.

Trying to stand up revealed that the ceiling was low, so low that she could feel herself touch it as she tiptoed around to search for the door. Her fingers brushed along the rough wall until they hit something rectangular. Not a doorknob—a light switch.

She flipped the switch and closed her eyes in the sudden light. A smile crept across her face.

As expected, the door was locked, but it was one of those cheap doorknobs designed for bedrooms that had a safety lock on both sides. All she needed was something long and thin to put in it, and the door would open. She glanced around the closet and noticed a mop submerged in a murky bucket of water in the corner. Even the idea of touching it made her gag, but she couldn't think of any alternatives, so she gingerly pulled the mop out of the water and wrung it out. Buried in the spongy mop head were two plastic pins holding the head to the wringer. She wormed them out, and the whole thing fell apart. Something metallic clicked on the floor, and she picked it up. A tiny metal spring. *Perfect.*

She stretched it out, then bent the tip into a hook. It fit the safety lock perfectly. The door swung open, and she stepped into the room outside.

It was lined with people—men and women, teenagers to adults. They were all laughing and chatting and drinking, until they noticed Ari. Then they dropped into abrupt silence. Every eye was on her, but nobody moved—they seemed too shocked that she'd even dared to try escaping to do anything about it.

She seized the opportunity and fled to the closest door. An interior door. She knew it as soon as she opened it. There was no draft like there should've been if the room led to an exit.

"Maybe get a map next time," a voice behind her suggested. Her wrists were squeezed painfully, and she was dragged backwards, stumbling over people's shoes.

She expected to be tied up in the utility closet again—this time with something more effective than duct tape—but instead, she was taken back to the open room and forced to sit in a chair in the middle. Everybody else went back to their positions against the wall, smoked, looked at her, and talked in low voices.

"—way to get back at the Azure Cross?" she heard one of them say.

"—others escaped—"

Ari sighed with relief. It sounded like her friends were safe. She wondered how they'd escaped and if anybody would come looking for her.

I don't need them. I can get out of this myself.

She couldn't tell what exactly she was feeling, but she wasn't scared yet. There were still so many tricks she could try, but she had to wait for the right moment.

The door at the opposite end of the room opened to reveal a little blond boy, his hands cupped around some change. His head was ducked into his chest.

"How much can I get for this . . . ?" he asked in a trembling voice.

They looked at him for a second; then one of them said, "Come in."

The boy shuffled inside, head still bowed.

"You little!" came a cry from outside. "Get back here, kid!"

And then came a surprise: Mikael jumped through the door.

He looked around the room for a second, and his eyes met Ari's. A quick grin flitted across his face; then he turned to the boy, his face pinched in a menacing scowl.

"I told you not to come here by yourself!" he said sternly, pulling the boy's hair. "What made you think I'd changed the rules?"

"Hey, don't be so rough with him." One of the men stood from his position against the wall. "Just take your kid and go."

"I'd rather see what I can get from you first, now that we're here." Mikael shrugged.

Ari wondered what the plan was. Nobody was looking at her, so she stood up very carefully. Mikael saw her from the corner of his eye and nodded.

"You want some crack, too?" the man asked. "You're gonna spoil that boy if you give him everything he wants."

"He won't get any of it. That's all for us."

"Us?"

Before anyone could answer, the door burst open again, and half the Azure Cross flooded into the room, Katya in front waving a crowbar and yelling until Ari's ears ached. The boy straightened and laughed—it was Lucas. Mikael kicked the man closest to him across the room like a football. His eyes met Ari's, and he grinned, a real ear-to-ear grin of pride and satisfaction.

Mikael was suddenly eclipsed by a man Ari didn't recognize, and she tensed defensively. His face registered utter confusion, and he made a wild swing at Ari, which she easily dodged. In a split second, with her favorite kick to the knee, she knocked him down. A punch to the temples finished him off. Someone else was attacking from behind. She tripped him and slammed his face into the wall. The room erupted in screams and yells and bumps and bangs, and Ari could barely keep track of what was happening around her. She'd never seen a full-scale fistfight with fifty participants in an enclosed space, and she got a few harsh knocks from elbows and feet that weren't even aimed at her. But she held her own, guarding her face with one arm and swinging at everything she could see with the other.

And then, suddenly, everything quieted down. Her captors were spread across the floor. The Azure Cross members were laughing, congratulating each other, and helping up the few unfortunate allies who'd gotten knocked down.

"Should we take one with us?" Katya poked a limp body with her foot. "Always good to have a hostage. They're gonna be mad about this."

"No." Ari recognized Ace's voice from somewhere on the opposite end of the room. "Too much work. After all, we're here to have fun, right?"

"Right!" Everybody cheered.

"Thanks, guys," Ari said, still confused by the bright lights and noise. "Who are these people, anyway?"

"They own that crack house you tried to get into. They're called the Barbers, or some funny name like that," Ace answered. Then he added slyly, "But you can ask Calvin. I'm sure he'd know."

"Why Calvin?"

"She's slow tonight!" interrupted Katya. "Hey, don't worry about it for now. You must have a splitting headache." She pulled Ari aside and hissed: "Stop asking questions. You'll get the story later, I promise. Now's not the time to bring it up. Ace knows you two were friends."

"Were?"

"Come with me." It was Mikael, tapping her shoulder from behind.

They squeezed their way through the crowd and ducked outside. Katya followed them and leaned back against the door, blocking it shut.

"What's going on?" Ari asked. She could feel blood trickling from her nose, and she wiped it impatiently with her sleeve.

"Ace thinks Calvin is responsible for the attack tonight," Mikael said softly.

Ari was startled. "Wait, back up. What happened after I went out?"

Katya grunted irritably. "There were guys waiting in the dark for us to show up here, and even though Calvin and I got away, it was a pretty close call." She tapped her arm, and Ari could see it was wrapped in gauze bandages. "Ace's reasoning is that since Calvin said the owners would be away, and they clearly knew we were coming, that Calvin might've betrayed us."

"Wouldn't he know we'd suspect him first?" Ari protested.

"Assuming Calvin really did have a deal with those guys, he would've just joined them after getting us out of the way. There wouldn't be anybody to get him in trouble."

"We can't even argue that he had nothing to gain from it," Mikael added gloomily. "Money. Drugs. Anything else they could've given him."

"He wouldn't do that, not after all the trouble we went through to get here." Ari glanced pleadingly at Katya, but she only shrugged.

Mikael ran his hands through his hair and sighed. "He hasn't connected with the syndicate like we have, and they've got every reason not to trust him. Even if he didn't do anything—don't look at me like that, I know he didn't—they might decide he did."

"What then?"

Mikael looked at Katya, and she shook her head. "They might kill him."

"There has to be some way to prove he didn't know they'd be there!" Ari cried. Her conscience pricked her crushingly. She should never have let him evade her questions. She should've pushed him to tell her what was wrong. If she could've helped him, if she'd been a better teammate, maybe . . . but she'd told herself all this before, after Yuri's death. She'd promised she'd do better, and here she was, repeating history.

"Can't we get him out before then?" she stammered. "There has to be something we can do. We can't just leave him."

"Get him out?" Katya laughed. "Sure, about as easily as you could get him to the moon. They'll have him locked up in the warehouse and guarded all day and night. And if he did get out, you two would be the first people they'd suspect."

"So we . . ." Ari stared at Mikael, but he refused to meet her eyes. "We have to choose between continuing the mission and saving Calvin?"

"Not 'we.' Me. I'll do the choosing," Mikael said firmly, finally turning to look at her with exhausted eyes. "I'm going home now. Ari, you should, too. You won't be able to pretend you're not upset if you go back tonight."

"But won't they think we went missing?"

"They'll think I took you home, and they'll be right," he answered shortly. "Come on."

CHAPTER 12

A soft sniffle broke the tense silence. "I have only five minutes."

"I'm sorry." Nika's pathetic voice made Ari want to cry, too. "I wish I could be there to help."

"You will be," Nika assured her. "I wanted to tell you that Calvin needs to come back here tomorrow. They're sending him his plane tickets, and they'll call to let him know. But I thought I'd tell you in advance so you could warn him."

Ari's throat tightened. "I'll tell him," she said quickly. It was the least she could do after having failed Calvin so badly.

Her eyes, as she looked in the mirror, were flat— totally lifeless, her eyelids half-closed. Forcing herself to brush her hair and shower and make decent food helped a little, but her whole body ached and insisted that she climb back in bed. She resisted because she knew that if she did, she'd only go back to her dreams.

The NDEB was supposed to be her chance to escape her dark apartment and have a fresh start, but it had been everything except that.

She pocketed her house keys and went out into the street. The rain beat on her head as she walked, soaking through her hoodie until her hair was dripping and her whole face was wet. Water poured down her cheeks, smearing her eyeliner into a dark shadow under her eyes.

The scene she saw illuminated by the fire barrel was different. Instead of the syndicate members being spread out through the alley with beer bottles and cigarettes in their hands, they were all standing in a tight group around the barrel. Nobody was drinking or smoking. Ari had never seen all of them sober at once.

She found Katya in the crowd and stood beside her, drying herself in the warmth of the fire and trying to clean up her smeared makeup.

"I told Lucas to get home," Katya said blandly.

Ari understood. Katya was protecting him from something she wished she didn't have to see.

"Apparently, this was interesting to him," she continued after a few minutes of silence, "so he's coming."

"Who? Lucas?"

"Nah. The Boss."

"Ace?"

"Well, I thought the boss *was* Ace, but he's already here, so it can't be him. And he's scrambling to get ready for whomever this VIP is."

"You've been a member of the Azure Cross for years, and you didn't know that Ace reported to a higher-up?"

"I sort of knew, but I thought this guy was just someone Ace paid off to keep the fuzz off our backs. I didn't realize he was actually involved in the syndicate. And I've never seen him before. I'm betting that nobody here has ever seen him before. I'm not sure what he's doing here now, but Ace said he was bored and wanted to play judge. Like it's all for fun." Katya squeezed the water from her long hair, and it puddled on the ground. "He must be the head guy that Ace gets orders from. That's all I can figure."

Ari nodded silently. The whole situation felt unreal, like she was acting in a movie. There should be cameras somewhere. Surely someone was going to say they had enough footage, and the game could end now.

Then everything went dead silent.

Ari strained to see over the people in front of her. Between their shoulders, squeezed tightly together, she could see Ace and someone else. This must be "the Boss," as Katya had described him. But he wasn't anything like the instant picture she'd crafted in her mind. He wasn't tall and burly; he was small and slender. He didn't look fierce at all; he looked a little bored. He wasn't dressed roughly like the others; he was wearing black gym clothes, with tight black leggings under shorts that looked like swim trunks and a zip-up hoodie on top. He wasn't holding a beer bottle; he was holding a sports drink. He looked like . . .

Ari's throat tightened. *He looks like Vita.*

She'd studied his Instagram until she'd memorized every identifiable feature, every little mark, every trace of individuality. There was no way she could be wrong.

The man's eyes somehow met Ari's, despite everyone standing between them, and she shivered. His eyes were coolly condescending, and she could've sworn that for a split second, the man recognized her.

"So, when do we start?" He finished the last of his drink and tossed the plastic bottle into the fire.

Ari stared, mesmerized, as it melted away.

"Whenever you want, sir," Ace said. He unfolded a camp chair and set it against the brick wall in front of the fire barrel.

The Boss sat down. From his position, he could see everyone and everything—including Ari. She shrank behind the people in front of her, wanting to see and not be seen. Would he notice, she wondered, that she knew who he was?

"Are you going to bring him out?" he asked. Ace nodded and looked at his men. They left, and when they came back, they were holding Calvin by both arms.

Ari had to do them justice: they didn't handle him roughly, and they didn't try to intimidate him. They just made him stand in front of the fire so that his face was illuminated, then retired back into the group to form a circle around him. They were scared. She hated that she couldn't even accuse them of making the situation worse.

Calvin stood still for a second, swaying back and forth, then dropped to his knees. His shoulders drooped as if he could barely hold them up, and his hands were limp at his sides.

Mikael, Ari realized suddenly, was standing on the opposite side of the fire from her. He was looking straight into the light, not at Calvin, but she could see the worry in his face.

"I'm the judge here, right?" The Boss crossed his legs and looked up at Calvin, a playful smile on his face. "What did you do?"

Calvin didn't reply, so Ace spoke for him. "We think he warned the Barbers that we were planning an attack last night." He recited the circumstantial evidence.

The Boss' smile hadn't changed at all while Ace was talking. It looked pasted on, like he was wearing a mask. Yet, despite its fixedness, it was sincere. The wrinkles at the corners of his eyes looked like he was laughing. Ari could picture pasting a white cotton ball beard on his face and turning him into something as harmless as a children's mall Santa. Perpetual amusement with the world was etched onto his face, and Ari found it difficult to dislike him. What if he just let Calvin go? What if he was simply amused at the unnecessary drama and had come to set things straight?

"What's the accused going to say?" He leaned back in his chair. "Speak up so we can all hear you."

"I joined the syndicate because I wanted to be useful to everyone here," Calvin said firmly. "I never had any reason to break your trust. I feel more at home here than I have anywhere else. I just want things to stay that way, and I swear . . . I never even thought of betraying you." He looked across the fire at Mikael, who nodded slightly. Maybe he'd told Calvin what to say.

"Great . . . touching . . . amusing," the Boss said sarcastically. He leaned forward in excitement, his fists clenching and unclenching as though he was trying to crack his knuckles. "Is there anything else? That doesn't seem to override the circumstantial evidence, does it?"

"I don't have any proof," Calvin said. "But you don't have any proof either. And if I was planning to betray you, why would I do it when there's so much evidence pointing to me?"

"That's an excellent point. I'm glad you brought that up." The Boss nodded sagely. "I think you're innocent. But I didn't come here to acquit anyone. And I also can't have people I'm not entirely sure about mixed in with my loyal subjects." He gestured to the audience. "He's guilty, and that's the end of it."

Ari waited expectantly for someone to protest. If they didn't, surely, she could kill this tiny man alone, even if the crowd rushed her and tried to pull her away. But nobody moved, either to help or hurt. They all seemed frozen in shock.

"Who wants to do it?" The Boss produced a gun from his pocket and held it out, barrel first.

Still nothing.

"No volunteers?" He jumped to his feet. His gaze wandered over the crowd. No matter how much she tried to hide from him, nothing seemed to work. His eyes always came back to her, fixing a mocking stare at her face and daring her to look away.

"You," he ordered and waved the gun at her. "Get over here."

She didn't say a word. This must be her voices talking to her again. Surely, of all the people in the crowd, he wouldn't have chosen her.

"Girl!" he shouted. "I said get over here!"

She felt numb as she stepped out of the group and took the gun, her gaze fixed on Calvin's huddled figure. She wanted to cry, but she felt like all her tears were frozen in her eyes. She could kill Calvin, kill the Boss, or kill herself. And the last two options were more or less the same.

"Ari, do it."

That couldn't have been Calvin's voice speaking—could it? She looked at him in confusion, her fingers clenched around the gun.

He nodded.

Her right hand shook as she raised the gun and pointed it at him, and she had to use her left hand to steady it.

Reality was fading away, and she knew it. She shook herself back to the alley, back to the Calvin she knew was real. He had never tried to hurt her. The dream—that was her mind playing tricks on her. Or maybe it had been a premonition. Or a conviction of guilt. But it had never been the truth.

What am I doing?

"There's something I can tell you only if you do this," he said quietly, so quietly that she could barely hear him, though they were only an arm's length apart. "Shoot."

She couldn't pull the trigger.

"Shoot!"

The Boss started chanting it over and over. "Shoot, shoot, shoot!" His voice rose in pitch until he was screaming in Ari's ear. "Shoot!"

"Ari, listen," Calvin said. His voice was loud enough to catch everyone's attention, but it sank immediately to a whisper. "I know who wrote—"

Something crashed in the crowd, and Ari's head snapped toward the sound. Mikael had stumbled over the fire barrel, sending it rolling across the cobbles. He straightened it up with an embarrassed grin at Vita.

"I don't think she should have to do this," he announced, having attracted everyone's attention. "I don't think we should do this at all. Calvin should be innocent until proven guilty, don't you think?"

Calvin was pulling on Ari's sleeve, but she couldn't hear his words over the rumbling crowd. She tried to look toward him, but with one quick bound, Vita appeared next to her and seized her chin, tilting it up toward him. He twisted her wrist backward so roughly that she yelped, until her gun was pointed at Calvin's head. His hand slid over hers and cocked the gun.

She shot him a defiant look, but Vita was stronger than he looked, and it was clear that nobody was going to help her. She didn't dare struggle while the gun was cocked.

"You don't get to tell me what happens around here," said Vita with a tight smile. "I've had enough of being yanked on your chain."

Calvin was yelling now. "I know who wrote the riddles!"

Horrified, she tried to twist around. But she was so firmly locked in Vita's grip that she could barely move.

And the moment she flinched, Vita's finger pressed hers down on the trigger.

There was an explosion, so loud and so close that Ari's ears ached. Filled with blind anger, she fought her way out of Vita's grip.

But it was too late. Calvin was on his knees, arms wrapped around his chest. He was still looking at her, still trying to say something. Vita pulled her away. She struggled to get close enough to Calvin to hear his words.

"—you know."

She wormed out of Vita's grip and caught him as he fell.

"Please." She shook him roughly. "Please tell me what you were going to say."

But he didn't move, no matter how loudly she shrieked.

And eventually, she had no choice but to give up.

Her first move was toward Vita. It was as if the crowd around her had faded completely away. She couldn't hear them, couldn't see them, wouldn't have cared if she could. All she wanted was to feel her hands around Vita's throat. She still had his gun in her hand. She'd shoot him. She'd shoot to kill, for the first time in years. And for the first time in forever, she'd have no regrets. His smirk was maddening. She raised the gun and pointed it directly at his smiling lips.

She pulled the trigger. Nothing happened. Distracted by Calvin's death, she had failed to notice that the slide had locked back, and the magazine was empty.

Her knees went limp, and she collapsed, sobbing and covering her face with her hands.

"So it was you all along," she snarled. "You killed him because he was about to tell us who wrote those nasty riddles. It was *you*."

"What?" Vita's voice was perfectly pitched with surprise. "What are you talking about?"

She raised her head disbelievingly and stared at him. His expression matched his voice.

He really doesn't know.

But maybe her instincts were playing tricks on her again. There was no way he didn't know. He had to know. There was no other reason for him to insist on Calvin's death. And to make her kill him—he knew, then, that they had been working together. He knew they were friends. The only person who could know that was the one who had written the riddles.

"You don't have to assign a reason for everything." He grinned. "You killed him because I decided you would. That's how it always works."

"Not always," said a quiet voice from behind Ari. It was Mikael. "Ari, get out your phone and call an ambulance."

"Hey!" Vita frowned. "It's too late for that now. I'm—"

"It doesn't look good to protest when someone's pointing a gun at your head." Mikael's voice was still soft. "Ari, do as I say. Now."

With shaking hands, she pulled out her phone, crouching under Mikael's extended arm. The gun he was holding glimmered in her peripheral vision, and it was all she could do not to stare at it, mesmerized. There was nothing she hated more than that particular shine. It was irreversibly burned into her memory.

Her voice shaking, she gave the emergency operator their address.

"Stand up, Ari," Mikael ordered. "Hold the gun. Don't be afraid to shoot if he moves."

She took the gun, warm from Mikael's hands, and aligned Vita's smiling face through the sights. Mikael bent down and leaned toward

Calvin. She didn't want to know what he was doing. Any moment, she expected him to stand up and say it was too late, that she might as well call off the ambulance. But he remained silent.

"I can't wait around for the cops to show up," said Vita suddenly. "I would've liked to see the outcome of this, but I'm afraid I have to go now."

Her grip on the gun tightened. "Don't move."

He held his hands up over his head with a disarming smile. "I don't think you realize the situation yet, Ari. It's been years since you've seen anyone like me. You've spent your time idling. Whereas I—"

Stunned by the implication of his words, Ari's reaction was too slow. He launched toward her and jerked her arm up to the sky. She pulled the trigger, but too late. The shot went over his head. Amid the confused yells of the crowd, he planted his knee firmly in Ari's chest and knocked the breath out of her. Moments later, he escaped into a side alley.

"What are you waiting for?" shouted Ace, who seemed to have finally come to his senses. "Go after him!"

The crowd dispersed uneasily. It was clear what they were thinking: was Vita still armed? And if he'd been able to defeat the near-invincible Ari without weapons, what would he do to them?

But they were loyal to their leader, and moments later, the alley was empty except for Mikael, Ari, and Calvin's motionless body.

"If you were armed, why didn't you kill Vita when you had the chance?" Ari hissed at Mikael. "You knew what he was planning to do, and you could've stopped him. What were you thinking?"

He was busy knotting his sweatshirt around Calvin's chest. "If I had shot him, I would've gone to prison. Guns are illegal here, even for self-defense."

"Well, you didn't seem to have much of a problem threatening Vita with your gun after it was already too late!" she shouted, furious. "Besides, you're law enforcement! We're allowed to carry guns!"

For a split second, his hands stopped moving. When he looked up at Ari, his face was gray and drained.

"You were between me and Vita the whole time," he murmured. "I wasn't going to risk shooting you."

"You're kidding me!" Ari wanted to scream at him, but she was afraid she would make him flinch and hurt Calvin. "So it was my fault you didn't shoot? My fault, again?"

"None of this was your fault," he began, but she couldn't even hear him.

"It was my fault that Yuri died. I should've followed him. It'll be my fault if Calvin dies. I should've seen that you couldn't get a clear shot and moved. I should've done anything but what I did. I should've—"

"Stop." Mikael disentangled himself from the makeshift bandage and stood up. "It's not your fault; it's mine."

"I should've—"

"If we're talking 'should'ves,' I'm the worst one here," he snapped, startling Ari into silence. "I should've called off the mission the moment I saw that email. I should've told everyone about it from the very beginning, just like you said. I could've stopped all of this if I had just taken that initiative." His face was tense with anger. "Don't you dare be blaming yourself. I let this all go too far."

The alley was illuminated with flashing red and blue lights, just like Ari had seen when the ambulance came for Yuri. Everything was repeating itself, and just like last time, she was the one to blame.

She covered her face with her hands and sank down against the wall.

"I'm so sorry," was all she could say, as she watched the paramedics bundle Calvin onto a stretcher. She didn't even know who she was apologizing to. "I'm so sorry. I won't let this happen again. I swear."

But you swore the same thing last time.

The past really does repeat itself.

That was all Ari could think when she received the phone call. Even the officer's words were almost exactly the same, and the inevitable, meaningless "I'm sorry" was tacked onto the end of every sentence, just like it had been when Yuri died.

"No, I'm sorry." She looked up at her ceiling, misty gray with dust, and held up her hand to filter out the light. "I'm sorry that nothing will ever be right."

Her arm collapsed limply onto the bed beside her. Burying her face in her pillow, she cried until her head ached and her body refused to stay awake.

CHAPTER 13

"He's not here anymore," said Ace gloomily. "I don't have any idea who he was or where he's from. You heard him mention Vancouver."

"Is he coming back?" Ari prodded.

"Dunno." He paused uncomfortably. "Look, I . . . I'm sorry about last night. There's no way I would've let things go that far if I had any say. Even if he was guilty—and I'm still not sure—I wouldn't have killed him."

"Katya said you would," said Ari before she could stop herself.

"It's not true. We're not awful people, Ari."

"I know."

"I didn't know that was who these mission orders were from. I just reported Calvin's discovery to HQ like I was supposed to. I didn't realize things would go this far."

"I know."

He handed her a beer bottle. "Drink?"

"Sure." She needed it. She tilted the bottom to the sky and poured it down her throat until the bottle was empty, and when she looked back for Ace, he was gone.

She checked the time on her phone. Mikael was staying in Seattle while she went to testify about Nika, and her flight left just after midnight. It was already time to head to the airport. Without saying goodbye to anyone, she snuck away from the group and walked back to her apartment, feeling painfully alone.

The next morning, she was back in her old Virginia apartment, staring at the familiar blackout blinds and messy floor. It felt like nothing had changed since she was there before.

She sent a quick text to Grey, reminding him of their plans to meet.

Ari: *Can you meet today over lunch?*

His response came a moment later:

Grey: *Afternoon coffee? Meet you at the café near HQ.*

Ari dressed herself neatly in front of the mirror, curling up the corners of her mouth in an unconvincing smile. This was the best she could do for Nika—show up looking like a respectable witness rather than an exhausted drifter.

On her way to the office, she thought about what she was going to say. She couldn't answer any specific questions, especially if they pertained to what Nika had been doing in Seattle. The only thing she knew for sure was Nika hadn't been at dinner when Yuri was killed, which was probably a point against her if it even came up in the interview today. She couldn't go into a long explanation of why she believed Yuri had been poisoned well before he ever came to the dinner because she didn't have a shred of concrete evidence to back it up.

Her phone vibrated, and she checked it as soon as she was parked.

[Restricted]: *She sat up with a start when her phone rang. She'd forgotten where she was. She looked around the room, terrified, and then answered the phone. It was her friend's wedding day.*

A chill shot down Ari's spine.

Is it talking about . . . that day in my apartment . . . when Lia called?

She remembered the loud noise, her dark room, her confusion. Somebody had seen her . . . or maybe it was just a coincidence. Anyone who knew she'd been shut up in her apartment—probably half the NDEB—could've written it as a prank.

Her palms were sweaty as she deleted the message and blocked the number, but a few seconds later, another message popped up:

[Restricted]: *The shrill of her phone was the last thing she wanted to wake up to, and it took all her self-control not to curse when she realized what it was. Instead, closing her eyes, she dropped back against her pillows and reached out a lazy arm. Her phone wasn't on the nightstand where she expected it to be, and all her fingers touched was empty candy bar wrappers. She was forced to open her eyes and look around. There was a glow somewhere across the room on the floor—that must be her phone. Was it worth getting up?*

[Restricted]: *I know authors don't usually add commentary, but don't you like where this story is going?*

Ari: *Who are you? Stop messaging me.*

[Restricted]: *You don't want to miss the rest of the story.*

[Restricted]: *Talk to you later, Ari Nomura.*

She blocked the number again and slammed her fist against the steering wheel. Too much, too fast. Yuri. Riddles. Nika. Calvin. And now these messages. Ari couldn't take much more.

But it wasn't the time to think about things she couldn't change. She needed to be there for Nika. Even if she couldn't get her out of trouble, at least she could be a welcoming shoulder to cry on.

She asked the secretary for directions and was pointed down the hallway to the opposite end of the building. It was the same room she'd been interviewed in for her current position.

Behind the desk on the right side of the room were three people. One was Yuno, the department head. The other two, she guessed, must be interrogators. Nika was nowhere to be seen. Apparently, she wasn't allowed to listen in.

"Sorry to bring you all the way back here," said Yuno, stacking some papers neatly on the desk in front him. "We won't take too much of your time. This investigation, as you know, is centered on whether Nika intentionally took illegal drugs during her time in Seattle. We're not concerned with her role in Yuri's death—that's a separate matter. All we want to know is what you can tell us about what she was doing."

"To the best of my knowledge, she was working the whole time." Ari tried to sound official with the meager information she had. "She was always on time or early to the weekly meetings, and she never seemed off at all—I mean, nothing ever seemed wrong with her. She—"

"This isn't evidence, Ari. Please stick to what you know for sure."

I don't know anything for sure.

"That was all true." She tried again. "Nika was on time. She was her normal self. And as I said, she was working the whole time."

"That's all you know?"

"Yes." She couldn't lie—she had no information to work with, and Mikael's testimony might contradict hers if she tried to be specific.

"Then you can leave now," said Yuno, glancing between the other two interrogators. They nodded. "I'm sorry we flew you all the way out here. We could've had this discussion on the phone."

"Can I . . . " Ari wondered what the most tactful way would be to ask, then gave way to honesty. "Can I see Nika?"

Yuno nodded grudgingly. "Go down to the basement and turn left. They'll tell you where to go from there."

"Thanks." She stood up, nodded stiffly—the NDEB equivalent of a salute—and walked back into the hallway.

Once safely outside, she sighed deeply, trying to catch her breath and give herself time to think. She couldn't leave without seeing Nika, no matter how much she wanted to hide from all her prying questions. Maybe this was why nobody ever told her anything. Maybe she asked too many questions, and they were afraid of her like she was of Nika.

She went downstairs, talked with the guard, and was told to sit in the waiting room. She seated herself in a chair so tall that her feet couldn't touch the ground and swung her legs impatiently, eyes focused on the blank wall in front of her. A few minutes later Nika came in, her hands in cuffs.

"Thanks for coming," she said as she sat down, her eyes looking everywhere but at Ari. "I'm sorry for making this hard."

"It's all right," said Ari gently. "You said there was something you wanted to tell me."

"Yeah."

Ari waited.

"It's . . . just about . . . well, do you remember how when you first came to the NDEB, you were asking me why I have a different partner each mission?" Nika was talking so fast that Ari could barely understand her. "And I just said that's normal here. I kind of lied. Not really. But kind of. It's normal for me. Because—"

"Slow down," interrupted Ari.

Nika did not slow down. "Because they always . . . something always happens to them."

Ari understood immediately. "So you change partners because they're killed?" she said softly. She'd seen all this play out before and couldn't understand why Nika was afraid of explaining. If anyone had asked her why she changed partners in the military, she wouldn't have known better than to answer honestly.

"Why did you have to put it that way?" Nika sighed, hiding her face in her hands. They were too heavy for her to hold up for long. "That's right."

"They die on missions?"

She nodded.

"And you're just now telling me this—why?"

Nika bit her lip. "Because I feel responsible. Maybe if I'd told you earlier, this wouldn't have happened."

"Nika." Ari fought the impulse to laugh. "You're not cursed, if that's what you're thinking. We all knew before we left for Seattle that the mission was going to be dangerous. Besides . . . " How could she explain it? She knew the reaction she'd get if she used the word "normal" in the same sentence with "death."

"We knew it was dangerous," she repeated vaguely.

"It's not just that."

"What is it, then?"

"They died because of me."

"Who did? Yuri and—" Ari stopped.

Nika looked up at her. "So Calvin is dead."

There was no point in denying it now. Ari nodded slowly.

"I thought so."

Silence, and then Ari said, "Please tell me what you were going to say."

"I don't think it was my fault they died," said Nika. Her hands were tightly clasped together. "I just feel guilty for not saying anything. Because my previous mission partners . . . they . . . "

"Died because of you," finished Ari. "I know."

Nika started, and Ari wondered if she'd gone too far. "How did you know?" Her voice shook.

"I guessed. You're telling me this about your partners, and you're saying it like it's your fault. There's no reason for you to tell me this if that's not true, and besides, I've seen all this before. It's not news to me."

"Then I don't need to tell you the rest."

"Please, Nika," begged Ari. "I'm listening now."

Nika obviously wanted to say something, but no matter how hard she tried, nothing came out.

"I—I'm such a filthy person," she choked out after several minutes of silence. "My teammates are out there doing actual jobs, and I . . . all I do is sit around and wear makeup and go to dinner and . . . "

Ari patted her shoulder.

"The only reason the NDEB hired me is because I look pretty enough to make people think I'm easy." Nika squeezed her eyes shut. "I don't do any real work besides flirting with everyone in sight, trying to act like the worst kind of cheap, artificial woman who'll do anything for money or affirmation or . . . " Her voice trailed off. "And sometimes my mission partners would find out the details about what I was doing. They were all so disgusted because they were risking their lives, and they thought I was sitting in the lap of luxury. That I got everything I wanted without even trying. They never said anything to my face, but I knew what they were thinking because I heard them talking to each other about me. Sometimes I had to choose between—between what I was doing and risking their lives, and I chose—to risk their lives, and—" Her voice was broken by sobs. "And they died because of me. Because I didn't want to compromise my nice, easy position up there with the rich, old people who were selling drugs to the gangs my teammates were forced to join. That's why."

"How could they say something like that?" asked Ari bitterly. She stood up and wrapped her arms around Nika in a tight hug until her tense shoulders relaxed. "It's not your fault. And you're not a filthy person because of it. It's just your job."

"I lost so many friends over it," said Nika's muffled voice. "That's why I couldn't tell you. I thought it'd be just like the others, and I'd have to make the choice again."

"No." Ari sat back in her chair. "There's no way I'd leave you because of that."

"Why not?"

"You're making a sacrifice to keep people safe, Nika. You're not doing this for fun. It's your work, and you're good at it, or you wouldn't still be doing it."

The only reply was a sniffle.

"I'm not going to stop being your friend," said Ari. "Is that what you were doing this week?"

Nika nodded.

"That's why you want to be discharged? Because you feel guilty about it?"

Another nod.

Ari took a deep breath. "Did you set this up so you would be kicked out?"

This time she shook her head. "No, no, no. Even if I hate this place, I didn't mean to give up my position. Because then somebody else would have to do it."

Ari finally understood. "Then I'm not going to say anything else in your favor. You're probably going to get kicked out, and if that's what you want, I'm not going to try to prevent it. But I need to know for sure that's what you—"

"You don't get it!" cried Nika. "I want to leave, but I don't want to make anyone else take my place. Somebody else would just end up here, and what's the point in that?"

"Nika." Ari shook her by the shoulders. "You've done enough. Someone else won't be hurt by this the same way you are."

"Then why did they pick *me*?" she choked.

"Because they're a bunch of callous bureaucrats," answered Ari viciously. "No matter what happens, you're not doing this anymore, so stop worrying and let Mikael and me take care of it. We won't leave you here."

Nika hung her head, her shoulders shaking. Ari watched in pitying silence until she looked up, a smile on her face and her eyes filled with tears.

"Thank you."

Ari met with Grey that afternoon at their local coffee shop, the same one where she'd met with Nika during her first week at the NDEB. She seated herself at a booth near a butterfly bush, which filled the air with incongruous sweetness, and tried not to think about Nika. She could fight only one battle at a time, and she already had too much to worry about.

Grey's arrival gave her something else to focus on. He looked exhausted, like he hadn't slept in days. When he plopped down in the chair across from her, his eyes fixed on the space over her shoulder, and his head drooped to the side. Just when she thought she was going to have to shake him awake, he blinked and started talking.

"I got a letter," he began, looking around suspiciously, "and it said that if I don't make the oxyarcyan and put it in a certain place at a certain time, once per week, Lia's going to be killed."

Ari nervously pinched the hem of her shirt between her fingers. *Exactly what I thought.*

"I thought it was just some kind of scam at first, so I ignored it. Then I got another letter saying they'd prove it to me. That same day, Lia got sick. Really sick—I thought I'd have to take her to the emergency room. But she recovered, and I knew the letter was real. Since then—"

"Since when?" interrupted Ari.

"Since a month ago. I've been making the oxyarcyan like the letter said." A flicker of terror crossed Grey's face. "I don't have a choice."

"And why exactly did you think I would do something like that?"

He rubbed his eyes and sighed deeply. "I didn't really. I just couldn't think of another option. After all, you had the formula, and you'd asked me to make it. I didn't think anyone else would know that I was capable of doing it." He paused. "I know you'd never do something like that, Ari, but I thought maybe if you were having . . . you know, episodes . . . " His voice trailed off, and he couldn't meet her eyes.

"That doesn't even make sense." Ari couldn't quite hide her irritation. "You've been making it since before I even asked you for the formula. I haven't worked at the NDEB for a whole month yet."

Grey sat quietly, twisting his hands in his lap. Finally, he said, "I know. It was just easier to think that it was you because I knew you'd never really hurt Lia."

She relented. There was no point in asking him to stop sending it—he'd never compromise on Lia's safety.

"Thanks for the information." She pushed her chair away from the table and stood up, draining the last of her coffee in one long gulp. "I need to get some sleep before my flight leaves."

"Okay." His head lolled onto his chest.

"Grey," she added quickly, "the letter's real. Take it seriously, for Lia's sake."

He nodded without looking up. "I know."

CHAPTER 14

"Maybe you've got a stalker." Mikael sipped his coffee.

"But whoever sent this text message spied on me," Ari insisted, annoyed by his complacency. That was what had gotten them all in trouble in the first place. "That's the only way they could've known all these details." She paused. "And come to think of it, whoever submitted my application to the NDEB also knew enough to fill out the paperwork. So maybe they're the same person."

Mikael looked mildly surprised. "They never told you who submitted your application?"

"No."

"That's strange. There's no reason for you not to know. I did it."

She blinked. "What?"

"I had a list of names from our unit in the military," he explained sheepishly. "I remembered yours, so I filled out the paperwork and sent it in. Yuno was supposed to tell you that when he called you for an interview. I guess somebody got it mixed up. You must have been awfully surprised."

"So how did *you* fill out the paperwork?" Ari asked, frowning. "Didn't they ask for personal information, like my address or something? And you had to give them my phone number because Yuno knew exactly how to find me. How'd you know all that?"

"It was in the records. You haven't changed your number since you left the army, have you? Or your address?"

She couldn't remember, so she shook her head vaguely. "During my interview, Yuno said he learned a lot about me from those. I should have read my own file, I guess." She paused. "But Nika asked me for my address even after having read my file. If it was in there, shouldn't she have known?"

"I meant your military file, not the one we have at the NDEB." Ari scrutinized his face, but there wasn't the slightest trace of hesitation or unease in his response. "Anyways, that should answer one of your questions. I don't think you need to worry about the text messages. You're a girl, and you're—don't call HR about this, please—but you're pretty enough that someone might want to follow you around. It wouldn't surprise me if you had a secret admirer." He winked. Ari couldn't quite hide a disapproving grimace. "We have other things to worry about. Are you ready to get to work?"

"Work? Aren't you supposed to be in Virginia the day after tomorrow?" Ari asked as she cleaned up the table and put her empty coffee cup into the trash. "You have to testify for Nika."

"Correct. You're going to Vancouver by yourself. But try not to do anything dangerous until I get there. A little scouting is fine, but don't try to corner Vita on your own."

"But we don't have much time. If Vita was the one writing the riddles—"

"What exactly makes you think that?" Mikael interrupted. "I know you think he killed Calvin because he was about to tell you who wrote the riddles." His voice lowered. "But doesn't it make just as much sense that he did it as a power play? He seems like the type."

Ari bit her lip. "Maybe. But it's our best lead, and we can't afford to waste it." She paused, trying to decide whether voicing her doubts was worth it. "Why have you been so reluctant to take action on this?"

"Excuse me?"

"We didn't tell the others about that email until it was too late." She enumerated her points on her fingers. "We've barely done any investigation into the riddles. You're telling me *not* to go after Vita without you, even though we have fifty eyewitnesses who saw him commit a murder. We could arrest him on the spot and have him in prison for the rest of his life. *Why* aren't you telling me to do it?"

"You and I are the only ones left. I don't want to put you at risk." His back was turned to her, so she couldn't see the expression on his face.

"That doesn't explain why you were fine with putting everyone else at risk."

He turned to face her, and she could tell that he was struggling not to get angry at her. Perhaps she'd been too direct after all.

"I answer to Yuno," he said briefly. "We served in the military together. You, of all people, should know that we were told not to question our superiors, no matter what. I didn't realize what a lie that was until it was too late. Neither did you. You could've gone against my orders if you disagreed, but you didn't. You're guilty of the exact same thing you're blaming me for."

They fell silent. Ari was so choked with things she wanted to say that she couldn't speak a single word.

"See you in a few days." Mikael gave her a curt nod and left the coffee shop.

"I could've helped you with that."

Ari recognized the voice and smiled automatically. When she looked up, Kira was standing in front of her, twisting his headphone cord around his fingers. His glasses were smudged with fingerprints, and his eyes were dark as if he'd been rubbing them. He looked exhausted.

"Don't worry, I'm almost done," she assured him, stacking the last box onto the shelf. "How have you been?"

"The usual." He laughed. "Being a hacker at home is much better than being a hacker here. Too bad I got found out."

"What do you mean?"

He sat down on the floor against the wall and rested his arms on his knees. "I was doing this hacking project just for fun. I tried getting into a big organization's database because I didn't think I could actually do it, but I did. I hadn't bothered to cover my tracks, so the police showed up at my door the next day. They said I could either go to prison or come here. This sounded more exciting. Boy, was I an idiot back then. I'd much rather be in prison. In fact, I would've probably been out by now."

"How long ago was that?" She sat down beside him and hugged her knees to her chest.

"I forgot. Maybe a couple of years."

"Didn't you have to leave your family? And friends?"

"Friends?" He raised his eyebrows. "Hackers don't have those—they sit in their basements all day. And I didn't have any family either. They—well, they kicked me out. Long story."

"Oh." Ari didn't know what to say. She had never seen him look serious before—it was hard when he always dressed like a character from a videogame.

"How'd you end up here?" he asked curiously. "I'm assuming you didn't get yanked out of prison like me."

"No. I was . . . "

She paused, and he waited expectantly.

"I forgot."

"We have a fun mission tonight," Katya announced. "We're going to get that oxy-whatever-it-was that I ordered for you. And on the way, Ace wants us to steal some crack from the Barber dudes."

"Sounds fun." Ari hadn't heard a word Katya said.

"Really?" Katya looked suspicious. "You've been acting weird ever since you got back from—where did you go again? To visit family in Virginia? You should be at least a little worried about this mission. Look at what happened last time. You almost got killed, and I almost got my arm taken off. Ace is getting greedy, or he wouldn't be sending us back in there."

"It's not that," Ari snapped.

Katya raised her eyebrows.

"Sorry," Ari added guiltily. "We can talk about it on the way. It's not important."

"Curiosity killed the cat, but not the human," shrugged Katya. "I'd like to hear about it."

"Where are we going?" Ari asked, stuffing her chilled hands into her pockets.

"Some sketchy back street. We're getting your stuff first." She sighed impatiently. "I'm not stupid. The NDEB is headquartered in Virginia, and that's why you went back."

"Yeah." Ari mumbled reluctantly. "It's about Nika."

"What about her?"

Ari shook her head. It wasn't her place to tell the story.

They sloshed on for a while, and then Katya said, "I don't really get what you guys do; and to be honest, I really hate that Nika girl. She used my addiction as a weapon against me to get me on your side. No way am I gonna forget that. And if your organization-bureau-thing could've saved me from this stupid life, I would've liked you better. But since *you*, specifically, are trying to do something about it, I'm on your side." She paused. "What I'm trying to say is, ask me if you need any help. You and I are friends now."

"Thanks," was all Ari said aloud. *Is she just saying that, or does she mean it?* But she suddenly, irrationally, felt that the icy water soaking her clothes was a little less cold.

"And I know your little, suspicious, psycho self is back there wondering if I'm telling the truth," added Katya with a chuckle. "I meant what I said."

Ari nodded silently, hiding her smile behind her coat collar.

A few minutes later, Katya stopped and motioned for her to be quiet. Ari concealed herself in the shadows. Katya glanced both ways up and down the street and knocked on what looked like the back door to a restaurant. It opened after a few seconds of tense silence, and a little, old man looked out at them.

"You here for the chemical?" he asked in a cracked, decrepit voice. "Forgot what it's called."

"We're here for the oxy-something-or-other," Katya said.

The man straightened up and smiled. "Great! Hold up just a sec; I'll get it for you."

When he reappeared, he handed Katya a bottle.

She examined it for a moment, then tugged on the lid. "This is empty."

"Whoa, don't open that!" He snatched it from her. "It's a gas. Didn't you know what I was making?"

"Holy . . . " mumbled Ari. *It makes sense now—why I didn't notice when my drink got spiked. Because it didn't, not if they used a gas instead. That could also be why the drink had no traces of any drug.*

Then she realized Katya and the man were both looking at her curiously. She forced a grin and held out her hand. "Thanks for making it."

The man shrugged and then gave it to her. "Be good customers and come back, 'kay?" The door shut with a click and the alley went dark.

"So what *are* you gonna do with that?" Katya asked curiously. "Hey, this way. We can't go back without the crack."

Ari followed mechanically, her thoughts elsewhere. "I'm going to inhale it," she said. "I was going to drink it, but I guess that won't be happening."

"You're going to *what?*" cried Katya. "Are you an idiot? Didn't you say that stuff is made of cyanide or something?"

Maybe I shouldn't have told her. But I need an ally. I can't find out the secret if I'm just going to die afterwards.

"Oxycodone, cyanide, and arsenic," she said aloud. "I won't do it until I'm home." She never got tired of the adrenaline rush shooting up her spine when the end of her mission was in sight. Once she had tried the drug, she'd know for sure whether that was what had been used to knock her out back in Virginia. And then she'd be well on her way to solving that mystery, at least.

"But why—?"

"Don't worry about it," said Ari quickly. "Let's go."

Katya eyed her silently. "You're not acting like yourself."

Ari shrugged.

"Just please tell me one thing, and then I won't ask any more questions." Katya hesitated. "You're not going to—you know, you're not going to kill yourself or anything, are you?"

"No, I'm not," chuckled Ari. "I'm sorry if I gave you that impression."

"But then why would you?"

Ari walked away from her, tucking her sweatshirt hem safely over the bottle and shrugging mysteriously.

"Weirdo," snorted Katya, rolling her eyes and flipping her hair over her shoulder. "If you die, I'm not taking any responsibility. Where are you going now? It's this place right here."

To their left was an apartment building whose roof sloped noticeably to one side. It was sandwiched between two other buildings, but it looked like it might topple at any second. Glare from the streetlights showed huge cracks in the brick and missing windows that looked like dark holes.

"Do we just sneak in?" asked Ari doubtfully.

"Pretty much."

They both stood in the street and looked up at it for a while.

"Do we have a plan?" asked Ari at last.

"Not unless you do."

They stared for a while, until Katya suddenly broke down laughing.

"They've definitely seen us by now," she gasped. "And we must look ridiculous staring at them like this."

"At least we don't look like threats." Ari smiled. "More like idiots, at worst. We could try getting in through the back if there's a window."

"The back? We'd have to go to the next street over." Apparently, that was unthinkable because Katya shook her head like the next step was obvious. "We have to get in here."

"A distraction?"

"There's nobody inside to distract."

"Huh? Then what are we waiting for?"

"Ace said there might be security cameras. But I don't see any, do you?"

Ari choked on her laughter and snorted. "If there are, it's a bit late to avoid being seen. We really are stupid."

"We just don't want them to recognize us." Katya gasped. "And they won't recognize our late-night selves with the ones they see during the day. Especially not you. You aren't depressed enough."

"Too late." Ari marched up to the front door and kicked it. The whole building shook. "I don't think it'll be hard to get in. What say we just go for it?"

"Sure!" cried Katya enthusiastically. "Take that!" She flung herself against the door, and it caved in with a crash, a sopping pile of wet wood.

They both instinctively looked up and down the street again before going inside.

"Is there a light switch?" Ari asked, patting her hand along the wall.

The air inside smelled like sweet, stale smoke. The only light in the room came from the streetlights through the windows, bathing the room in an eerie silver glow. A thin cloud of dust floated through the air.

Katya was rummaging through some cardboard boxes stacked in the corner. The floor squeaked under her feet as she stood on her tiptoes to look inside. "Look at all this!" she said, satisfied. "Here, catch."

Ari held out her arms, unable to see what Katya was throwing. Something soft and cold collided with her chest. It was a plastic bag filled with something squishy. She squeezed it and felt a fine powder coating on her hands.

"That's probably enough," said Katya, emerging with hands and pockets full. A little trail of white followed her across the floor. "Ace'll be happy with it, anyway. Ready to get out of here?"

There would be a party that ended with the ambulance if they took any more. Ari cautiously let a little of the bag she was carrying dribble out onto the ground where Katya couldn't see. "Sure, let's go."

There wasn't a sound from the empty building as they sneaked out into the street. Ari's intuition told her that nobody was watching and nobody was nearby, and she had learned to trust it, so her tension magically melted away. Katya whistled nonchalantly as they walked back to the syndicate alley.

Everybody stood up and cheered when they arrived. Katya tossed the bags up into the air, and whoever caught them was the lucky winner. One fell and burst and spread powder everywhere. Ari couldn't believe they were walking on such an expensive drug, but nobody seemed to mind. Their inhibitions were long gone, and the only ones who didn't participate were her and Mikael and Lucas. Mikael had left for the night, and Lucas was nowhere to be found.

Ari crept away from the group as soon as she knew she wouldn't be noticed. There was no point in staying any longer since she couldn't participate in the drug festival, which was getting louder and louder behind her. And Katya was obviously too busy to help with her experiment right now—so much for everything she'd said about caring, Ari thought. Then she felt guilty. It wasn't Katya's fault that she couldn't control herself. It had been once, but that time was long gone. The best thing Ari could do was go home and get one more good night of sleep, just in case something went wrong later.

She had a premonition the whole way home. At first, she assumed it was just a result of being sleepy, but she changed her mind when she saw the note on her door.

At least it wasn't a surprise this time.

3/3
WHAT'S YOUR PAST?
IF YOU CAN SOLVE THAT, YOU'LL KNOW WHY B DIED, HOW HE DIED,
WHO KILLED HIM, AND YOUR OWN FUTURE.

It was written with pen on a torn piece of notebook paper and taped to her door with one weak strip of Scotch tape. The tape was a message by itself. There was a brisk breeze blowing through the alley, and one strip of tape barely held the note to the door. It hadn't been there for very long, and the sender clearly wanted her to know that. She tore it down with contempt and stuffed it into her pocket.

Half of her wanted to puzzle over the riddles, and the other stronger half wanted to go immediately to bed. She compromised by checking her phone to see if the anonymous number had sent her any more messages. They hadn't, but there was a short text from Lia.

Lia: *Is Mikael coming to town tomorrow?*

Ari: *Yes.*

Lia: *Then you can tell him to check his email. He doesn't need to come. They've already decided to discharge Nika, and they're not going to punish her.*

Ari: *What???*

Lia: *More details tomorrow. I'll read the report tonight.*

What could've changed their minds?

Ari took the bottle of oxyarcyan gas from her pocket and put it on the kitchen counter. It was a surreal moment. She knew there was probably enough cyanide in the bottle to kill her instantly if she breathed all of it, but here it was, sitting in her room like nothing was wrong. The bottle was a normal, one-liter water bottle, the kind sold at the cheap grocery store down the road. It looked innocent. The excitement she got from that was worth the risk.

You aren't supposed to get your thrills from that, she chided herself. She knew better. Her constant longing for risks she wasn't allowed to take was what had left her depressed and directionless after she left the army.

And yet, she could never remember being genuinely scared before. She'd gone on missions that she never expected to come back from, but she always abandoned herself to fate, never doing more than was expected to keep herself and her teammates alive. Her philosophy had always been "whatever happens, happens." But now, as she stared at the bottle, trying to visualize what might be inside it, she could feel her heart racing. Her pulse beat in her palms, and she licked her lips nervously. Maybe, for once, she was scared to die. Since when had she ever valued her existence that highly?

"Bad timing," she chided herself. Her eyes were fixed on the bottle.

Impulsively, she picked up her phone. Was it really that bad to rely on someone else? There weren't many people she could ask for help. Mikael would never let her go through with the experiment— he'd recognize the danger immediately and stop her. Grey and Lia, too, even if they'd been nearby. She needed someone who wouldn't know what was happening until it was too late, yet who could get her to a hospital immediately. Someone who wouldn't take advantage of the opportunity to kill her . . . *probably*. Ari would never be able to stifle all her mistrust, but now was as good of a chance as ever.

"Wow, your apartment is in a worse part of town than mine," remarked Katya.

Ari was used to it by now, and she'd long stopped looking nervously into the alleys when she walked. Nothing had ever happened yet, and if it did now . . . well, what was she going to do about it anyway? She didn't even bother locking the door behind them when they went inside.

"So you know what you're doing, right?" she said, squeezing the bottle between her fingers until her knuckles were white. Now that the time had finally come, she couldn't fight a pang of nervousness. "Stay in the other room until I yell for you. The bottle will be sealed by then, so you'll be fine if you come inside. All you have to do is make sure I don't stop breathing."

"And if you do?"

She shrugged and grinned slightly. "Send my regards to Mikael, I guess."

"Well, this seems like a brilliant idea," grumbled Katya. She plopped down on the sofa and crossed her arms, tapping her shoes against the floor. "I don't know CPR, by the way.

Ari took the bottle from the counter and shut the door to her room.

I thought it was mixed in my drink, but could it have been a heavy gas like this? One that wouldn't dissipate around the room?

She knew that if she spent too much time thinking, she'd never have the courage to go through with it. So, with trembling fingers, she opened the bottle lid, put her nose to the opening, and took a tiny sniff.

Immediately the room started to spin. She staggered to the door and opened it for Katya, who came running as soon as she saw her face and helped her sit back on the bed.

"Can you hear me?" demanded Katya, shaking her roughly.

Ari nodded dizzily. "I hear you just fine."

"Are you sure this is the real stuff?" Katya looked at the bottle. "You seem to be okay."

"Not—'kay." That was all Ari could manage without throwing up.

She blinked slowly at the ceiling right before she passed out, wondering if she'd been wrong this whole time about how many ceiling fans there were. Three? Four? No, she was wrong. Was that construction that sounded like a hammer, or was it the blood pulsing behind her eyes?

When she woke up she was still on her back, and Katya was sitting beside her.

"Good grief," were Katya's first words. "That scared me, young lady!"

It worked.

Ari sat up and rubbed her throbbing forehead. She felt the bed shift as Katya stood up, and the movement almost made her sick. But it was worth it. Her guess had been confirmed, and she hadn't died. Not yet, anyway. She was probably going to wish she was dead until the hangover wore off.

"It feels exactly the same," she said out loud. The words didn't come out clearly. "It's the stuff from when I got roofied."

"I have no idea what you're talking about," said Katya gruffly. "All I know is, don't ever ask me to do that again. I was seriously worried you were gonna kick the bucket there."

"Sorry." Ari lay back down and hugged her pillow to her chest. "I don't feel very well."

"No wonder!" Katya answered sarcastically. "You're lucky to be feeling anything at all."

"I'm going to sleep," mumbled Ari, burying her face in the pillow.

"I guess that's my invitation to scram." Katya went out into the living room and paused before opening the door. "Sure you're okay?"

"Yup." Ari gave her a weak thumbs up.

"I'm leaving then." Katya slammed the door behind her, and Ari felt it inside her head like an explosion. If she could've gone to the window and called for Katya to come back, she would've, but it was a bit late now. Sleep was her only respite from the horrible, throbbing pain.

She tried to sleep, and her thoughts got mixed up with her dreams.

They really did use oxyarcyan. And they didn't put it in my drink like I thought—it was a gas. How come they didn't breathe it in?

The only other possible answer, since the chemical formula was known only to former army members, was Lia or Grey or someone else from the army she hadn't recognized. Nobody had any reason to poison her—at least, not that she knew of. Certainly Lia and Grey were innocent. They had both risked their lives for Ari back in the military days.

Her head ached with the light from her window, and she pulled the blankets over her head.

When she arrived at the syndicate meeting that night, everybody stared at her like they were seeing a ghost. She wasn't surprised. She'd seen herself in the mirror before she left the house. There were dark circles under her eyes, and her face was a dead, pasty gray. She had also just woken up, and her hair was a mess. Her head ached so badly she could barely hold it upright, and every little light burned her eyes like fire.

"For not being at the party last night, you look awful," Mikael observed.

Ari dropped her head on her chest. "Thanks," she mumbled. Her throat was so tight that she could barely choke out the words.

"Would you prefer that I lie?" He looked amused.

Ari wasn't in the mood for teasing. She walked past him without replying, but she could hear him laughing in the background, and the sound annoyed her. She found a dark corner and slid down against the wall. Cold comfort.

"Hey." Katya appeared and sank down next to her. She didn't sound like her usual confident self. "Since I helped you out with that experiment thing, could you do me a favor?"

Ari nodded, unable to say anything out loud. Her head would crack open like a walnut if she did.

"It's about Lucas." Katya hugged her knees to her chest and stared at the fire. "You've probably noticed that he hasn't been here for the past few nights. I try not to let him come when they bring the party stuff out." She sighed. "I feel like I'm ruining him. He comes here because of me."

"Really?"

"I'm afraid I'll have to go back to my family without him one day. He'll either refuse to leave, or he'll end up in the wrong place at the wrong time, and something'll happen to him. I hate myself so much." Katya twisted her fingers together. "It's my fault he even knows about this place."

Ari pulled herself together for a short speech. "Don't blame yourself," she said. Or mumbled. "You can still change, and if you do, he will, too. You're right about him looking up to you like that."

"If I changed, what would I change to? I'd have to go to therapy, which I can't pay for. Then find a job, which is gonna be hard with my . . . history. Then my family will just give me the 'I-told-you-so' look and keep on inviting me to the awkward dinners. There's nowhere for me to go." A tear glimmered brightly at the corner of her eyes.

"How do they feel about Lucas?" she asked.

"They don't know he comes here. They all go to bed early like grandmas, and he sneaks out. I'm the one who showed him how to do that." Katya dropped her head onto her knees, and her shoulders trembled.

"What makes you think I know any more about this than you do?" Ari lifted a heavy hand and patted Katya's head. "Do you really want my honest opinion?"

"Not really," she admitted with a poorly disguised sniffle, "but give it to me."

Ari tried to force her eyes to stay open. As long as she stared at the light, she could stay awake. "I think you should check yourself into a hospital, fail the drug test, and get forced into addiction recovery. You won't have to pay for it that way. Then when you get out, you can get a basic job that doesn't require a background check. With your prior experience, I wouldn't be surprised if the NDEB hired you, as long as you're clean."

"Seriously?" Katya looked up. "You think I might have a chance with that?"

"Yeah, of course." It was a lie. Ari didn't think they hired addicts, recovered or otherwise. But Katya needed something to hope for, at least for a little while.

Katya sat silent for a minute. Then she stood up and smiled. "Thanks, Ari."

"Where's Lucas now?"

"Probably at home," Katya shrugged. "Getting lectured by Pops."

"It's nice to see you two on friendly terms," interrupted Mikael. He had finished his story and had been watching them, Ari realized suddenly, since they'd started talking. "Did I hear you mention Lucas?"

"Oh, so you're an eavesdropper, too?" asked Katya sassily, putting her hands on her hips.

"No, I just wondered if you'd found him yet."

"Found him . . . ?" Katya's smile disappeared. "What are you talking about?"

Mikael looked confused. "He hasn't been here in two days."

"Yeah, so he's at home. Where he should be. He just texted me this morning and said he'd be coming back this afternoon."

"Ace sent some people around to check, and they couldn't find him. Also, there's . . . " He stopped.

"There's what?"

Mikael pulled out his phone, typed for a few seconds, and handed it to Katya. "This."

Ari read it over her shoulder.

LOCAL NEWS: PARENTS ARE FRANTICALLY SEARCHING FOR A YOUNG BOY BELIEVED TO HAVE BEEN KIDNAPPED BY A GANG KNOWN AS THE AZURE CROSSES.

She didn't have time to read any further before Katya locked the phone and handed it back to Mikael.

"Ace!" she roared, marching across to the opposite wall. "Get over here!"

Ace looked immediately guilty. "What's wrong, Katya?" he asked airily, sipping his drink and looking at everything but her face.

"You know what's wrong!" She seized his shirt at the neck and shook it. "Where's my brother?"

Ace looked over Katya's shoulder at Mikael. He shrugged. "I didn't know she hadn't seen it," he said apologetically.

"Oh, good grief." Ace shook Katya off. "I have no idea where your brother is. We've been looking for him for two days, and I didn't want to say anything to you until we found him. Thanks a lot, Mikael!" he added loudly.

"Forget about Mikael! Why does the article say you kidnapped him? Why? Explain, Ace!" Every punctuation mark was accompanied with a rough slap, which Ace didn't bother to dodge.

"You know everything like that gets blamed on us." Ace rubbed his eyes. "Katya, please listen to me. We didn't kidnap him, and we have no idea what happened to him. We're doing our best to find him, and I just didn't want you to worry until we were sure something was wrong—"

"Of course, something's wrong!" Her voice was getting hoarse. "My brother's gone, and you're not sure if something's wrong?"

"Ari," whispered Mikael, bending down to her ear. "Forget about Vancouver. We can't lose her as an ally. We have to stay and help."

She nodded, her gaze fixed on Katya.

"We think this might be in revenge for helping Ari escape from the Barbers," said Ace. "We aren't sure. We're looking, I swear."

Katya was silent for a second, eyes fixed on the ground. Finally she said, "I'm going home. To my parents. Lucas has to be there. I just heard from him this morning."

Without another word, she turned away from Ace and disappeared into the side street.

"Follow her," ordered Ace, turning to Ari.

"Are you sure that's the best idea?"

"Do it," he said roughly. "Her parents will kill her if she comes back without her brother. Go, before you lose her."

Ari stood up and slipped off into the darkness, trying to ignore her throbbing head.

She caught up with Katya a few minutes later and trailed behind her, wondering if she should say something or try to stay undetected. But Katya stopped suddenly and sighed.

"I know you're there," she said without turning around. "Go away."

"I can't. Ace told me to come." Ari sped up and walked beside her. "He said your family would be mad. I think he thought they'd hurt you."

"So what if they do?"

Ari didn't know how to reply to that.

They walked for about half an hour, twisting and turning until Ari had completely lost her sense of direction. Katya didn't say a word or even look up the whole time. Her attention was clearly elsewhere, and Ari couldn't blame her. She'd never had a brother—not that she remembered, anyway—but it was easy for her to guess what Katya must be feeling.

This was a much nicer part of town. Instead of being crammed together, the buildings were spread out, and the streets were well-lit. Ari and Katya weren't the only pedestrians, and there was a continuous stream of cars on the road to their left. On the right was a high-rise apartment building surrounded by a cozy garden. Katya turned in to the first entry, typed a code into the keypad on the front door, and let herself inside. Ari followed silently.

They took the elevator to the top floor. It was a glass elevator, and Ari fixedly watched the ground disappear beneath them as they went up. Somehow, the smooth rhythm made her headache feel better.

Katya didn't look out the window. As soon as the doors opened, she was out in the hallway and banging on one of the doors.

"Let me in!" she shouted. No response except an echo. Ari leaned against the wall and looked inconspicuous, just in case one of the neighbors decided to call the police.

Finally, several rounds of angry yelling later, the door opened, and Katya almost fell into the apartment. A woman with dyed red hair dressed in a silk bathrobe looked out disapprovingly. "Are you coming to apologize? If not, this could've waited until tomorrow."

Ari stiffened. *She doesn't even know what's wrong yet.*

"No, Mom, I'm coming to figure out where my brother is." Katya pushed past her into the apartment and blocked the door from closing behind her. "Let my friend in, too."

"Ahh . . . hi." Ari waved and tried to look supportive. "I'm the friend."

"Katya, your father's asleep!" cried the woman, but it was obvious that Katya wasn't going to take no for an answer. So she gave in, reluctantly holding the door open. "Who are you?" she demanded as Ari slipped nervously inside.

"I-I'm Ari," she said with a bright smile. "Katya . . . we . . . I mean, I met her at the shop."

"So you were probably buying drugs," said the woman disgustedly.

"I don't use drugs."

Katya's mother made them both sit down on a plush, white sofa next to the window. Ari pretended to look outside and admire the view, but she was listening carefully. She had never met someone quite like this woman, and she had a feeling there was going to be a battle before Katya got the information she wanted.

"Get Dad out of bed," ordered Katya.

"He has work tomorrow."

"Isn't Lucas more important than his stupid work?" cried Katya. "I need to talk to both of you!"

"Lower your voice," commanded her mother. "Ari, if she's this rude all the time, I don't see why you'd ever stay friends with her."

"I think she's just worried about her brother," said Ari soothingly. "I can see why. She didn't know he was missing until tonight."

"Because you never let me see him," snapped Katya. "How was I supposed to know?"

"Oh, please. If you kept in touch with your family, this wouldn't be a problem."

"Where's Dad?"

"I told you. He's asleep, and I'm not waking him up. Say what you want to say and then leave." Her mother sat down opposite them, her back straight as a pole, and stared at them.

"I want to know where my brother is."

"I don't know."

"How long has he been missing?"

"Three days."

Ari stole a pen from the table next to her and quietly took notes on her hand.

"Any ideas where he could've gone?"

"No."

"Was he acting strangely before he left?"

"No."

"Did you see him leave?"

"No."

"Do you ever pay any attention to anything he does?" Katya bounced up.

"Sit down."

Katya didn't stop. "Come on, Ari," she said, heading toward the door.

Ari looked back and forth between them, laughed nervously, and stood up. "I . . . uh . . . thanks for letting us in on such short notice," she stammered between polite nods. Then she escaped out into the hallway without waiting for a reply, dropping the pen on the table as she left.

Katya was fuming. "She doesn't know anything about Lucas."

"Hey, does he keep a journal?" asked Ari comfortingly. "Or have a computer or anything?" There was no point in braving Katya's mother if they didn't get a chance to investigate.

"Yeah."

"I'm going to go ask for them." Ari knocked on the door again, and Katya's mother reappeared, her eyes as flaming as her hair.

"What—?" she began, but Ari cut her off with a shower of politeness.

"I'm so sorry to bother you again," she said sweetly, "but Katya would like to see her brother's computer. He did leave that behind, right? If it's not too much trouble—"

"Go in and get it." Her mother stepped aside. Ari heard her yell out into the hallway, "Katya, don't dye your hair anymore! It doesn't look good on you!"

Ari had no idea where Lucas' room was—there were at least three doors that might lead to bedrooms. She picked one, and it was pink and purple inside. *This must be Katya's old room.* It felt like looking into a private diary, and she closed the door hastily. The next room was the right one. There was a closed laptop on a desk in the corner. She tucked it under her arm and put the charger in her pocket, then went back into the main room. Katya's mother was waiting for her with her arms crossed.

"Did you get it?" she asked.

"Yes, thank you, ma'am." She scuttled out the door and stopped in surprise. Katya was sitting against the wall next to the elevator, crying. This time, she wasn't even trying to hide it.

Ari looked back at her apartment door, ready to attack her mother if she was still there. But the door was already closed, so she turned back to Katya with a sigh.

"I'm sorry," she said gently, hugging her tightly. "Look, I've got the computer. This way, we'll have something to work with."

"It always ends this way," sobbed Katya. "Is it something I did? Why does she hate me so much?"

"I don't understand your situation," said Ari truthfully. "But your mother is a—" She stopped herself. "Your mother doesn't seem very nice. I don't think it's just you."

Katya wiped her eyes and tried to stop crying. "I'm sorry for being like this," she sniffled. "I shouldn't have let you come. I didn't mean for you to have to deal with this."

"It's okay. I'm glad I was here." Ari sat down beside her and waited patiently, tapping her fingers on the laptop lid.

After a while, it was obvious Katya wasn't planning to leave anytime soon. So Ari opened Lucas' computer and tried a few different passwords.

"Leave it alone," said Katya irritably. "Somebody at the syndicate can figure it out."

Ari obediently shut it.

Katya stood up, wiped her eyes with her sleeve, and pressed the elevator button. "It's fine. Let's go so they can get started on it."

Ari's head ached as they took the elevator down to the first floor. She could tell that Katya was crying again, but she had no idea what to say. Words alone wouldn't make the situation better.

"Can you take this back to the syndicate and ask them to figure out the password?" asked Katya, stopping so suddenly that Ari almost ran into her. "I'm going home. I can't deal with this anymore right now."

"Okay." Ari nodded. "How do I get back?"

"Just go straight."

"Then how come we made all those detours on the way here?" asked Ari innocently.

Katya groaned. "Don't be like that."

So you really didn't want me to come.

Ari sat down on the sidewalk, her back against a light pole, cradling her aching head. Her fingers reached for her phone, and she unlocked it and ordered it to call Mikael. She didn't usually like using the voice feature, just in case someone overheard, but tonight she had no choice. If she looked at the screen, she was convinced her eyes would pop out.

"Hello?"

"Please come get me," was all she could say before the world slid back into darkness.

"You can't be serious." His look of total disbelief tore at her heart, but she nodded. She had to. It was the truth, and there was no point in lying to him. He would know eventually anyway.

"You turned me in?"

She nodded again.

"Ari, why?" He looked like he was about to cry. "I didn't do it!"

"I saw the evidence. I know you did it. Please just confess so we can all go home." Her voice was flatter than a pancake. Somehow her real feelings weren't translating to her voice.

"I thought we were friends. I thought you knew me better than that." It was easy to tell what he was thinking. His voice was broken with hurt. And yet he still didn't want to give up on her. "I thought you knew I would never do something like that."

Ari turned away from him.

"I hacked the database because you asked me to," he said pleadingly. "I thought you were trying to find out about your own past. That's what you told me."

"I was."

"Then why did you do this?"

"Stop lying."

"Get away from me!" she gasped. Strong fingers were wrapped around her throat. She tore at them, trying to get them off. Then she realized the pressure was nothing but her sweatshirt collar.

"I don't know what you're high on, but I wouldn't recommend doing it again," said somebody dryly.

Ari opened her eyes and looked around. Above her was a soft cloth ceiling. She was vibrating slightly, so she was in the back seat of a car. And that voice belonged to Mikael.

She struggled to sit up. "Where's the laptop?" was her first question.

"I have it."

"I need somebody to find the password for me."

"It's Katya's name and Lucas' birthday."

"What?" Ari was surprised. "How do you know?"

"Because I figured it out while I was waiting for you to wake up."

How do people just know how to do these things? Isn't it almost impossible to hack a computer password that quickly?

"How long was I out?" she asked, rubbing her eyes. Her head felt a little better.

"About ten minutes after I found you."

"Where's Katya?"

Mikael chuckled. "I don't know the answers to all your questions. I'm not psychic, and I wasn't here when she left. I'm assuming she went back to her apartment."

"Okay." Ari leaned back against the car door and shut her eyes. She was out of action for the night, no matter how much better she felt.

Mikael dropped her off at her apartment and left the computer. "I changed the password to your full name," he said, setting it on the counter and watching Ari stumble wordlessly to her room. "Are you okay?"

She tried to nod, but the movement threw her balance off, and she stumbled against the doorframe.

Mikael caught her and set her upright. With his help, she made it to the bed, and he pulled the blankets over her.

"Sleep tight," he said, shutting the bedroom door behind him.

CHAPTER 15

Katya was sitting on her sofa when Ari came out to breakfast the next morning, rubbing sleepy eyes and trailing a blanket behind her. She snapped awake as soon as she saw the intruder, but Katya didn't seem to notice. Her eyes were fixed on her brother's computer.

There was no point in disturbing her, so Ari went to the kitchen and started to make coffee. Somebody—probably Katya—had already made it, so she filled her cup and sat down on the sofa, peeking at the screen over her shoulder.

Katya shut the lid with a snap. "His search history is amazing."

"Inappropriate?" asked Ari.

"No, that's why it's amazing. Apparently, he's a huge fanboy." She laughed. "I always knew there's something wrong with him."

"But did you find anything about—?"

"Well, thanks. I was trying not to think about that." Katya put the computer on the sofa beside her. "There was nothing. I even found the file where he keeps his journal, but he didn't say anything strange. The entries just suddenly stop three days ago—four, now."

"The day before we raided the cocaine stash?"

"Yeah."

Too much could have happened in that amount of time, and Ari didn't want to think about all the possibilities. There was no point in wasting time on wrong ones, anyway. The obvious question was— did Lucas run away, or was he kidnapped? After what she'd seen of his mother, it didn't seem unlikely that he might have left out of his own free will. But then, why wouldn't he ask Katya where to go, if he was close with her and knew she would sympathize?

"Did he ever say anything to you about leaving?" she said aloud.

"No. He didn't get along with Mom and Dad, but he didn't see running away as an option. At least, he never said he did." Katya stood up and paced back and forth between the front window and the kitchen. "Maybe I don't know him as well as I thought I did. Maybe he was keeping secrets from me."

Ari opened the computer and logged in. There wasn't much to see. Lucas' folders were well-organized and named by whatever was inside. Inside the music folder was only music, inside the photos folder only pictures of—*wow, he really is a fanboy.* Ari smiled.

Though she felt uncomfortably like she was invading Lucas' privacy, she clicked open his text messages. The last thing Katya had received from him was a message, sent the previous morning, saying that he was at home. But much to her astonishment, there was no such message in his records. According to them, the last message he'd sent Katya was from two days ago, and it read: "Do you have someone from the syndicate following me?"

Lucas wasn't the one who sent that message.

Could it be that the same person who's been texting and following me also spoofed that message? That would mean they know where Lucas is.

She pulled out her phone to check her texts, and sure enough, there was a new message from the restricted number.

[Restricted]: *You're tired of listening to Katya pace, aren't you?*

Ari looked up. "So, you're watching me right now," she said to the ceiling. "Tell me where Lucas is."

[Restricted]: *Do you want a hint?*

[Restricted]: *It's obvious when you think about it. You've probably already guessed that I wrote the riddles and that email Mikael told you about.*

[Restricted]: *Here's the hint: Yuri.*

Ari jumped up from the sofa without a word to Katya and ran out the door.

I'm going to be too late. Her mind was racing. Three days. There was no way she'd find him alive. Even if he'd been there for only a fraction of that time.

Five minutes later, she was back in that same alley. Everything looked familiar, down to the positions of the dumpsters and the little slumped figure against the wall. Except this time, the figure was smaller.

"Lucas!" she screamed.

No response.

She felt his pulse. At first there was nothing, then she felt a little movement.

Hastily, hands shaking, she pulled out her phone and dropped it on the ground beside her. "Call 911!" she shouted at it, pushing Lucas down to his back. His breath was slow and shallow.

The phone rang briefly, and somebody on the other end calmly asked her for location and details. She gave them as quickly as she could and started CPR.

Not this again. Not again. This can't be happening again.

The ambulance showed up a few minutes after, and the paramedics bundled Lucas onto a stretcher. Ari stood back, panting, and watched as though she was watching a movie. She barely heard the paramedics congratulate her on saving Lucas' life. They patted her on the back and asked if she was all right—at least, that's what she thought at first, until she realized they were actually asking her if she'd given CPR. She nodded. Her mind was elsewhere.

There was a score she had to settle now that she was free. Her fear and frustration was slowly being replaced with quiet rage.

As soon as the ambulance was gone, she picked up her phone from the ground and looked defiantly up at the sky.

"You're lured me into this same trap three times in a row, but I swear this is going to be the last time. Come out from wherever you're hiding and explain why you're doing this!"

[Restricted]: *That would ruin the fun.*

"How could you leave him like that? How could you think that's fun?"

[Restricted]: *I knew he wasn't going to die. I would have saved him if you hadn't. There's no reason for me to run around killing innocent people. You'd know that if you had any idea who I am.*

"Oh, that's lovely, really generous of you," said Ari, her voice bitter with sarcasm. "But I don't know *anything* because you won't tell me."

[Restricted]: *I did tell you, but you couldn't figure it out. At least, not yet. I'm hoping it doesn't take you a hundred years to solve those riddles. I thought they'd be too easy.*

"Are you saying I'll understand everything once I've solved them?"

[Restricted]: *Allowing for how slow you apparently are, I think you will.*

"Then I'll do it," she yelled. "For Lucas and Yuri. And Calvin. You killed Calvin, too, didn't you?"

[Restricted]: *Well, no. But you could say I was responsible for his death.*

[Restricted]: *You should really be doing this for yourself.*

"All of this was you." Ari lowered her voice to a venomous whisper. "You roofied me at the bar. You killed Yuri and Calvin. And you know what? I bet it's your fault that Nika failed her drug test. You must have been the one who asked Grey for the oxyarcyan."

[Restricted]: *Good!*

[Restricted]: *Oh, but not so good. Thanks for letting me know he snitched. I thought he might've, but I wasn't sure until you said so.*

"What are you going to do to him?" Ari screamed, her voice breaking. "Why are you doing this?"

[Restricted]: *I'm not.*

[Restricted]: *You are.*

[Restricted]: *If you'd solved those riddles, I wouldn't have needed anything else. But now I need to get your attention back.*

[Restricted]: *You really can't see how you brought this on yourself?*

"No, of course not." Ari dropped to her knees. "Please, please, I'm begging you to stop. Just tell me what you have against me, and I'll do anything to fix it. I can't solve the riddles. I've tried, and I've asked for help, and I can't do it. I can't let anything happen to Grey and Lia. They're all I've got left. I'll do anything you want, I swear."

[Redacted]: *Asking for help will get you nowhere. You're the only one who has all the pieces to the puzzle.*

A car pulled up beside her, and Mikael rolled down the window. "Katya wants us to go to the hospital with her," he said. "I think she's afraid someone might try to hurt Lucas again."

"All right." Ari jumped in the back seat. "Hold on. How did you know I was here?"

"The hospital said this was where the ambulance picked Lucas up," Mikael answered. "I didn't think you would've left yet."

That struck Ari as an odd deduction, but she was too distracted with trying to remember the riddles to think much about it. Though she'd left her journal with copies of the riddles at her apartment, she'd studied them so much that she could recall them word-for-word.

1/3

SUPPOSE THERE ARE FIVE CHARACTERS: A, B, C, D, AND UNKNOWN. ASSUME THAT A-D KNOW EACH OTHER AND UNKNOWN IS AN OUTSIDER. HERE ARE THE RULES OF THE SCENARIO:

1. A, B, AND C ARE AT DINNER.

2. D IS ELSEWHERE BUT NEARBY.

3. UNKNOWN IS ALSO NEARBY AND COULD BE ANY OF THE MILLIONS OF PEOPLE IN THIS CITY.

4. B LEAVES THE DINNER EARLY—BEFORE ANYONE HAS EATEN OR DRUNK.

5. D FINDS B DEAD.

WHO WROTE THIS RIDDLE?

IF YOU CAN SOLVE THAT, YOU'LL KNOW WHO KILLED B.

2/3

WHAT BREATHES FIRE IN BLUE?

IF YOU CAN SOLVE THAT, YOU'LL KNOW HOW B DIED.

3/3

WHAT'S YOUR PAST?

IF YOU CAN SOLVE THAT, YOU'LL KNOW WHY B DIED, HOW HE DIED, WHO KILLED HIM, AND YOUR OWN FUTURE.

"They're in the wrong order," she mumbled, accidentally out loud. Mikael glanced at her. "The first riddle is subjective and doesn't have a definite answer. That means the second riddle should be first, since it's objective, and the first riddle should be last. The third riddle—"

"You're really working on the riddles right now?"

"I was just thinking out loud." Ari clammed up, realizing that Mikael couldn't understand why she was suddenly in such a hurry.

The car screeched to a stop in front of the tattoo parlor. Mikael left it running and went inside. While Ari was waiting, she unlocked her phone and typed a message to the restricted number.

Ari: *I need to know one thing.*

No response.

Mikael returned with Katya, who slipped into the back seat.

"Mikael says you called the ambulance," she demanded as soon as she was inside. "Ari, how did you find him?"

There was no choice but to be honest, though Ari knew how ridiculous her story sounded. "I got a message from an unknown number," she said. "And he told me—"

"What did he say?"

He said that Lucas died the same way Yuri did. But how can I explain that?

"Do you remember Yuri?"

"What's he got to do with this?" Katya leaned into the front seat.

"The message said that Yuri was a clue to finding Lucas. I remembered where Yuri was found before he died and got there as quickly as I could, and that's where I found your brother." Ari squeezed her thumb nervously, hoping Katya wouldn't ask any more questions. If she did, there was nothing left Ari could tell her.

Nobody said anything else on the way to the hospital. When they arrived, Mikael asked the receptionist where Lucas' room was. She told them, but only Katya was allowed inside.

"I'll be outside," Ari told Mikael. "I can't explain everything right now, but I have to solve those riddles. Now. Today. Just keep an eye on Katya and Lucas and make sure they're safe."

There was a round, concrete planter beside the front entrance, and she sat down on the edge, trying to focus.

Solve the second riddle first, she reminded herself. She'd tried before without success, but she had so many clues in her hands now that she should be able to do it.

The killer said that they're responsible for Calvin's death. If that's true, Vita is the most likely culprit, since he is directly responsible. The circumstantial evidence points strongly to him. Though he did seem surprised when I told him about the riddles. Could he have been acting?

But I can't think like that now. I just need to know what the riddles say, not who wrote them.

Riddle #2.

Breathing. Flame. Blue.

Air. Burning. Sky?

No, that's too much of a stretch for blue.

Breath, fire, blue.

That seems reasonable.

Oxygen, fire, blue. That seems logical. Fire can be blue, and fire uses oxygen.

Oxygen, oxygen, oxy, oxy—

Her eyes snapped open.

Oxygen.

That could be the beginning of a very familiar name.

But then what would the next word be?

Ar—ar—ar . . . son?

Arson. Fire. Arsenic.

Once she'd gotten that far, the next part was obvious.

Cyan. You could say that's a shade of blue.

Breath, fire, blue. Oxygen, arsenic, cyanide.

Oxyarcyan.

And she knew that the promised reward for solving the second riddle was learning how Yuri had died, which meant . . .

If he was killed with oxyarcyan, then the same person who got the oxyarcyan from Grey must be the one who killed Yuri, just like the text messages said. And because the only people who could know about oxyarcyan are from the army, specifically the special agents division . . .

She couldn't rule out Grey, Lia, and Mikael as possibilities. Of course, it was also possible the culprit was somebody *else* from the army. But if the riddles—or the messages—were targeted at her, and she was the only one with all the information, then it was probably somebody she knew personally. She couldn't think of anyone else she was friends with from the army days. Of the three suspects, they all seemed equally unlikely.

Is Vita an ex-army member? Wouldn't there be a record of that somewhere?

There was no point in trying to solve the third riddle. She couldn't remember her own past, but she knew someone who could. She texted Lia.

Ari: *I need your help. Please call ASAP.*

Then she focused her attention on the first riddle.

Assuming the oxyarcyan points to the army special agents division, the only person mentioned in this riddle who fits the conditions has to be Mikael or Unknown, unless Nika was lying about her past. Her prior service history should've been mentioned in her records, though, so that seems unlikely. Lia and Grey aren't mentioned anywhere, so they're not likely suspects, unless one of them is Unknown.

Why, she wondered, would somebody illegally obtain oxyarcyan when they could use a more ordinary poison? There was only one possible answer: they wanted to draw her attention back to the army days. That hypothesis was confirmed by the third riddle, the one that said she would understand everything if she could just remember her past. That and the fact that somebody had used it on her—obviously without intent to kill because they wouldn't have thought up this elaborate scheme if they wanted to kill her at the beginning—all meant one thing. They must've wanted her to know about it. Those three things were enough to convince her. This had something to do with what she'd done in the army. There was something she couldn't remember, something important.

She checked her phone anxiously to see if Lia had texted or called. There were no new messages.

The door to the hospital squeaked open, and Mikael came out.

"I wanted to see how you're doing," he said, leaning against the planter.

"How's Lucas?"

"He's stable, and it looks like he's going to pull through." Mikael ran his hand through his hair. "I'm glad you found him in time. They said if he'd been there much longer without medical help, he probably would've gone into cardiac arrest."

"Do they know what he was drugged with?"

"Drugged?"

"Because I know," continued Ari feverishly. "I've solved the riddle. He was drugged with oxyarcyan."

Mikael twitched like she'd stung him. "How can you be sure?" he murmured. "Why do you think that? Only people from the army could know about that drug."

"From our special division in the army." Ari repeated her long chain of reasoning as simply and clearly as she could. "There's no other possible answer," she finished. "I'm sure I'm right."

"So you think I did it?"

"Yes," she answered. No hesitation. She didn't really believe it was Mikael, but there was only one way to find out for sure. She had to see his reaction.

And he just looked disappointed. Which was justified, she thought—she was deliberately wrecking a bond they'd struggled for months to form. They had never really liked each other, and ever since he had killed Calvin, she hated him. Though he had done nothing but what she would have done herself.

Didn't he? Would she really have done that?

It didn't matter. If Mikael wanted to make her suffer, there were plenty of ways he could have done it. Why would he choose a roundabout way like this?

"No, I'm sorry. I don't think it was you," she said. It felt like a weight off her shoulders.

"Thanks." He sat back on the planter and buried his face in his hands. "Our team can't fall apart now."

"And it hasn't, so cheer up," she said gruffly, looking away. "But I do know that the culprit must be someone from the army. Is there a list of people who were involved with our division?"

"We know there were exactly a hundred people involved. Beyond that, we're not sure. The list was destroyed after everything happened."

"Everything?"

"Oh, that's right. You don't remember. Ari, you've done enough worrying about this for today. Can you just relax a bit?"

His gentle voice somehow made her tired, but she was still too keyed up to stop hypothesizing. And she had no time left to waste. "Isn't there anyone who has a list?"

"The third riddle was for you," said Mikael. "It said, if I remember correctly, that you'll understand everything if you remember your past. I think that's where you have to start."

"How did you know? Did you get a copy?"

"Mine was probably a little different." He closed his eyes and recited it. "'Three of three. Ari has to remember.' Then the reward for solving it, just like yours."

"So this really is up to me."

"I wish I could've figured out that this was going to happen to Lucas before it actually did. I wish I could've predicted—" She froze.

There *was* something left that the riddles could help her predict. Distracted by Mikael's sudden appearance after she'd found Lucas, she'd forgotten the last part of what the restricted number told her.

"Thanks for letting me know he snitched. I thought he might've, but I wasn't sure until you told me." He's going after Grey and Lia next.

She pulled out her phone and dialed Grey's number. The ringer dragged on painfully, and then the call went to voicemail. She tried Lia's number. Still no response. Her throat tightened.

"Mikael, I have to get back to Virginia," she choked. "When I was solving the riddles, I forgot something important. Grey was the one manufacturing the oxyarcyan, and the killer found out that he'd told me. I have to go back and warn him if I can't get him on the phone. And neither he nor his wife are answering."

"If you say so," he said hesitantly. "But what about Katya?"

"I'll be back tomorrow. Can I borrow your car?"

"I've seen your traffic record," he said, but he handed her the keys. "Come back safe."

"I will." She sprinted off to the car, then paused. "Can you get my tickets?" she shouted across the parking lot.

Mikael gave her a thumbs up, silhouetted against the glass hospital door.

She waited in the airport for two hours before her flight took off—the longest two hours of her life. She spent every spare second trying to call and text Lia and Grey, and when she stopped after boarding the plane, exhausted, she realized she'd left them over a hundred messages. No response, and nothing new from the restricted number no matter how many texts she sent. She was on her own.

A few hours later, she had arrived in Virginia. She rented a car from the booth nearest the door and drove well over the speed limit all the way to Lia's apartment. They would both be asleep by now—it was after ten o'clock at night, and they weren't known for being night owls. She knocked as loudly as she could on their door and shouted their names. If the neighbors woke up, so much the better. They'd know to be on guard, too.

Eventually, after what felt like an eternity to Ari, the door opened a crack, and one shimmering brown eye peeked out. Then the door swung wide.

"Ari!" cried Lia, squeezing her tight. "Amazing! You're here!"

Ari wrapped her arms around her and picked her up off the floor. "You're safe." She couldn't let her voice tremble, couldn't let Lia know just how worried she'd been. She didn't want to trigger Lia's forgetfulness because that might put her in even more danger. But she couldn't stop herself from breathing a deep sigh of relief.

"Are you all right?" asked Lia curiously, her voice muffled by Ari's coat. "You seem worried."

"Yes." Ari disentangled herself and laughed apologetically. "I didn't mean to wake you up. But I need to come inside." It wasn't time to celebrate yet.

"Of course!" Lia was so excited that she jumped up and down. "Come in, come in, come in!"

Ari put her hands on her shoulders and forced her friend to stay still. "Lia, please listen to me. I have to talk to Grey." She was talking so quickly that her words slurred. "I need to talk to him now. And I need you to go into the bathroom and stay there."

"Bathroom?" Lia frowned. "Why?"

"Just get Grey and do it right away," Ari insisted.

Lia nodded and knocked on the bedroom door. "Grey!" she chirped. "Come out here!"

He came out wrapped in a bathrobe, rubbing his eyes and blinking. His eyes widened when he saw Ari. "What are you—"

"Lia, get in the bathroom." Ari pushed her inside and shut the door after her. "Don't eat or drink anything."

"What would I eat in the bathroom?" Lia asked through the door, but Ari ignored her.

"He found out," she told Grey.

His face went pale. "How do you know?" His voice shot up in pitch. "We need to tell Lia."

"You can't. She's the one in danger, and if we tell her everything, she's not going to remember any of it."

"Why wouldn't she . . . ?" His voice trailed off. It was Lia's job not to remember anything that could hurt her.

"He's going to try to kill Lia using the oxyarcyan," continued Ari "When you gave it to him, was it a gas?"

Grey shook his head. "It was a pill."

"Then he'll try to put it in something she eats or drinks. Or he might be able to get it as a gas and force her to breathe it. You can't let it happen, Grey. You need to get her out of the state. Out of the country if you can."

Her phone buzzed.

[Restricted]: *Good advice, but it won't work.*

So you can still hear me.

"Thanks for reminding me," she said aloud with a sarcastic smirk at her phone camera. Then she turned off her phone and put it outside on the front step. Her voice was quieter when she spoke again. "Grey, I'm serious about this. Lia is going to die."

"I'll do anything for Lia."

"Okay. Leave now. Not tomorrow—now. I've already had two friends die this way, and the third one is in the hospital now. I guarantee you she'll die if you stay. I don't know how he does it, but he—"

"I already know how serious this is," Grey interrupted. He slipped behind her and opened the bathroom door. "Lia, go get packed. We're leaving for a while."

Ari was impressed that Lia didn't ask questions. Obviously, she trusted Grey—or maybe she'd heard the whole conversation. Maybe she even knew something about it from her research at the NDEB. Ari hoped not, but it was hard to tell. Lia's face never expressed anything but childish happiness.

"Thanks for the warning, Ari." Grey pulled his bathrobe tighter and shivered. "Weren't you in Seattle?"

"I flew back because I couldn't get you on the phone."

"I checked my phone right before we went to sleep. I didn't have anything from you."

"Me neither," piped Lia from the bedroom.

"But I called you hundreds of times!" Ari cried.

Grey pulled his phone out of his pocket and showed her his call log. Lia, Lia, Lia, Work, Lia, Lia, Pizza, Lia. That was it for the last two days.

"Someone has control over my phone then."

"We've got an old one around here that Lia was going to sell online," Grey said. "Babe, where is it?"

Ari smirked at Lia, her mischievous humor getting the better of her. "Pet names?"

"We're married." Lia rummaged in her nightstand drawer and gave Ari the device. "Put your SIM card in here. It should work fine."

Ari retrieved her phone from the front porch and followed Lia's instructions. Nothing seemed out of the ordinary, but she couldn't take too many precautions.

"I'll get tickets for the next international flight, wherever it's going," Grey assured her. "I can't thank you enough for the warning." He lowered his voice. "If anything happened to Lia—"

"Nothing will happen, and you'll get a nice vacation." Ari couldn't imagine living without that high-pitched voice somewhere in the back of her mind. "I won't let anything happen."

CHAPTER 16

To say that Katya's reaction when she met Ari at the hospital was explosive would have been an understatement.

"Mikael told the doctor to test Lucas for signs of that oxy-whatever-the-heck-it-was," she shouted, so loudly that every patient in the waiting room looked up at them. "And guess what? He was right! So who do we know that just went out and bought a whole bottle full? Who was the first to find Lucas? You'd better have a flawless explanation for how my brother ended up here!"

"Katya, there's nothing but circumstantial evidence—" Mikael broke in.

"And I have the messages to prove—" Ari added.

Katya interrupted them. "I don't care what you do or don't have. All I know is that my brother's in the hospital on a ventilator and you have the poison that nearly killed him in your house. I want answers, and I want them now!"

Ari tried her best to explain. She had transferred the old messages to her new phone. She pulled it out of her pocket to show Katya. But when she clicked on the restricted number, there was only one message.

[Restricted]: *Nice work.*

Katya and Mikael watched silently as she scrolled desperately through all her messages. It was no use. They were gone.

226 WITH LOVE FROM THE PAST

"Oh, great." Katya rolled her eyes. "So there aren't any messages. That was going to be your evidence? Nice try, but I find it hard to believe they just up and vanished."

"I saw them," said Mikael. "I know she had them."

"But she doesn't have them *now*!" Katya was yelling again. "And guess what, Mikael? That's all I care about! I want to know what she did with that oxy-whatever-it-is!"

"I'll look into this," he assured her. "For now, Ari, I think you'd better leave."

"Is your brother okay?" she asked timidly, standing near the door so she could escape if Katya rushed her.

"Yeah," Katya answered shortly. "As 'okay' as anyone would be given the circumstances."

"Then I'll leave." Ari let herself out of the waiting room and exhaled deeply.

Mikael came out after her. "I'm sorry about that," he said. "But I didn't know you'd gone and bought oxyarcyan. I only told the hospital to test for it so they could administer the proper treatment. Why'd you do that?"

"Because I wanted to know if that was what this Unknown person used to drug me back in Virginia," she answered wearily. "I took it myself as an experiment."

"You did *what*?" He had the same incredulous look on his face that Katya had when she first found out. "Ari, it's an assassination drug, not a party trick!"

"But I had to be sure," she persisted. The idea sounded worse and worse the more she talked about it. "It ended fine. Obviously, I'm fine. And that's why I had it in my house. Katya can testify that I did actually take it because she was there."

Mikael was silent.

"I know the evidence is against me—" she began defensively, but he cut her off.

"The evidence is strongly against you."

"You trust me, don't you?"

He sighed. "I'm trying, Ari. But what am I supposed to think? I'm obligated to investigate. In all honesty, the best evidence you have going for you is the fact that you don't have an obvious motive to kill Lucas. If you did, I'd have to send you back to Virginia for trial."

Trial. The word evoked a vivid picture in her head. The hard bench. The officer uniforms that didn't look like hers. The eyes that looked through her and saw a dossier, not a person. She couldn't place where the vision came from, but it chilled her with fear. No matter what, no matter how, she would never let that happen again.

"They set me up for this," she said, "the person sending me those messages. They have to be framing me."

"I don't know about that," Mikael said. "We might be able to subpoena the phone records, but a really good hacker could erase or modify them. Ari, I think you should go home and rest. I'll try to think of something."

"I can't rest." She shook her head. "I have to solve these riddles, which means I either have to track down my military records, or I have to find someone who remembers."

"Be careful what you investigate, please."

"Why?" His voice caught Ari's attention.

"There's no reason to awaken old grudges. There are plenty of people who aren't happy about what happened, and a lot of information got swept under the rug to stop people—politicians, especially—from losing their jobs."

"I thought it was all declassified."

Mikael hesitated. "Who's going to take the time to read through all those official reports when there's already a publicized story that makes perfect sense? There's no need to stir up a national investigation."

But she had no choice—the riddles demanded an answer.

"I can see you're planning to ignore me." Mikael sighed. "That's fine. I wish you the best of luck."

"Where are you going?" asked Ari. "You could help me find those reports if you aren't busy."

He stiffened visibly, and she flinched.

"I'm going to help Katya," he said, his voice strained. "She's worried the killer might hurt Lucas again. I don't have time to look for the records."

Ari bit her lip. Fireworks of indecisiveness were screaming at her to stop and reconsider, but she couldn't afford to waste time interrogating Mikael.

"Didn't you say that someone you know back in Virginia was making oxyarcyan?" Mikael continued. "If so, then they must be ex-military. You could try asking them."

"Why would he remember if you don't?" asked Ari. "If the answer to the riddle is something that anyone other than me would know, you could've solved it yourself, and it wouldn't matter if I remembered."

"You have a point. But you don't remember me, and you *do* remember this Grey person. So maybe you spent more time with Grey than you did with me. You and I weren't on the same team, so it wouldn't be strange if there's something he knew about you that I don't."

"Grey wouldn't know," Ari said doubtfully. "But his wife was my team psychologist. Maybe I told her what was going on."

"A psychologist wouldn't remember much of anything, especially not if it was something traumatic. You know how they were."

"Well, it's not like I have much of a choice!" cried Ari. "I don't even know if I want to remember. I've had this conversation with Lia before, and she refused to tell me anything. But at this point, if there's even a chance, it seems like I have to try."

Mikael fell silent.

"The hacker has control of my phone," Ari said. "Where could I find a different one?"

"You could use mine," Mikael offered, but she shook her head.

"It can't be one of ours. Who knows—they might be spying on you, too."

"There's a hotel down the street. They might have a pay phone in the lobby."

"Okay." Ari took a deep breath. "Mikael, I promise I'm not crazy. I'm just running out of options here."

He smacked her shoulder playfully. "Then get going."

Slightly cheered by the realization that she hadn't yet hit a complete dead end, Ari sprinted down the street toward the hotel Mikael had suggested. Sure enough, there was a pay phone in the lobby. She dialed Lia's number, and much to her relief, the call connected immediately.

"Ari, Grey told me everything!" she said enthusiastically. "It's great—just like the army days! I love being in danger!"

"That's . . . " Ari didn't know how to respond. "I was calling to ask about the riddles. I've gotten a third riddle, and I think you're the only one who can answer it."

"Oh. What is it?"

Ari read it off from her journal, then waited.

"Are you still there?" she asked after a long thirty seconds.

"Yeah. But I don't know if I can help you. The question is so generic, there's no way to know if it's talking about a specific event, or even what that event might be."

"Then just tell me what you know."

"Ari," Lia interrupted. "We've had this discussion before. I don't want you to remember your past. I don't want—"

"People are going to die if you don't tell me!" Ari shouted, finally losing her temper. She smacked her fist against the wall of the phone booth, causing a flutter of feedback in the phone speaker. "I don't have time for this, Lia. Answer the question."

There was a long pause, and she could hear Lia discussing something in a low voice with Grey. At last, Lia came back to the microphone.

"All right."

"You're going to tell me?"

"Yes, on the condition that you don't let this information out."

The special agents division—which Lia referred to as the S.A.D.—was a secret part of the army that did "dirty work," or anything that couldn't be officially recognized and endorsed by the government, including everything from political assassination to human experimentation. Recruits who enrolled in the S.A.D. were forced to undergo desensitization training, which was a combination of hallucinogenic drugs and horrifically violent videos that permanently altered their personalities. The S.A.D. was a breeding ground for sociopaths.

There were a few exceptions, like Lia and Grey. Instead of desensitization training, they were given a course of drugs that made them abnormally happy and outgoing. Once, Lia said, she'd caught herself laughing hysterically during one of the most disgusting videos because it really did seem funny at the time. Recruits like them were meant to cheer the others up. But despite their best efforts, everyone was afraid of them.

Due to the total secrecy of the division, there were only a hundred members. They were divided up into twenty teams of five by specialty. Every team had a sniper, a psychologist, a chemist, a doctor, and a computer expert. Ari, according to Lia, had once been a sniper.

Lia's memory was hazy on what exactly their missions were because they were given drugs to erase some of their experiences so they couldn't leak information. But from her position as team psychologist, she knew what was happening to the other members, and she could recall a few details of their lives. She knew that Grey was testing his chemistry skills on real people, and she knew that Ari was being experimented on.

Lia watched as Ari, weakened by her constant training, became quieter and quieter until she had shut everyone out. For weeks, Lia never saw her say a word to anyone. But that changed when she met Kira.

Kira was the best hacker in the whole division, and probably, from what Lia knew, one of the best in the world. He was literally chained to his computers nearly all day every day, but whenever he wasn't working, he was with Ari. Slowly, Lia watched her open up to him, and Ari relaxed back to her normal self. Whenever she would leave work crying, Kira would be waiting for her with bandages and morphine from the infirmary. He never asked for anything in return except Ari's friendship, which he jokingly said was the only thing that helped him remember to speak English instead of code.

One day, they all woke up to find their names were in the newspapers. The secret division wasn't a secret anymore, and the media flew into a moral outrage against the atrocities they discovered. Nobody had any idea a place like this existed. The recruits were all turned out into the streets with no past and no future. They were forced to build their own lives from nothing, and they were shunned by everyone because of what had been done to them and what they were accused of doing.

"This is where it gets complicated," continued Lia hesitantly. "Ari, right after the leak happened, you told me you had proof Kira was the one who told the media. I don't know what the proof was because you never showed it to me. But the next day you took it to the general in charge of the S.A.D. program, and the day after that, Kira disappeared."

"What happened to him?"

"You were at his funeral that weekend. How can you possibly have forgotten?"

Ari shifted in her seat.

"I think I remember who the real traitor was," she murmured.

"You do?" Lia's voice was surprised. "Then who—"

"I need to go." Ari replaced the phone on its rest without another word.

She rubbed her eyes wearily. Slowly, the details of Lia's story began to fall into place. She remembered how the bandages Kira gave her felt against her skin. She remembered what he looked like. She remembered her room number, and the way she'd gotten the burn marks on her back, and where that odd, white scar on her wrist came from. And when Lia mentioned the traitor, it was like she'd never forgotten at all.

Of course, it was me. All along, this was my fault.

Maybe she really had deserved the voices' incessant mockery. Maybe they were right to tell her that Kira's death was all her fault.

There's no "maybe" about it.

Don't try to justify yourself. It's too late. They'd never been so loud, so insistent. She could hear them like they were in the room with her, filling her mind with their accusations.

All along, you tried to blame the person writing the riddles. When it was your fault all along.

"All right, fine." She slid back against the bench until her knees touched the wall of the phone booth and cradled her head in her hands. "It was me. I told the media. I blamed Kira. I got him killed when it should have been me instead. I brought this all on myself, didn't I?"

Keep going.

"There's no more to say!" she shouted. "If I were Kira, I'd want revenge, too. I don't blame him for *any* of this. It's all my fault. Happy now?"

Keep going.

"I just wanted to live a normal life!" Her voice raised to a scream, and through her tears, she could see the horrified faces of the restaurant guests outside the booth. Quickly, she cupped her hand over her mouth and choked herself quiet.

"I thought things would go back to normal. I thought one sacrifice would be okay," she mumbled after a few seconds of struggle. She wiped her tears with the back of her hand. "I was wrong. I get it. I'm sorry. I'm sorry to everyone."

She pulled out her cell phone and typed out a message to the restricted number. Maybe there was still a chance, if she was the only one who knew who the real traitor was. Maybe it was best if nobody else ever found out. She could determine her own punishment later.

Ari: *Kira.*

Ari: *How are you still alive?*

CHAPTER 17

Ari: *They lied to you about me.*

[Restricted]: *You turned me in for a crime you committed.*

Ari: *What else did they tell you? And who are they?*

[Restricted]: *I know exactly what you did. I can even appreciate why you did it. What I don't know is why you decided to make me take the blame.*

Ari: *I didn't betray the organization!!*

No reply. It was obvious that Kira knew the truth, and he wasn't interested in her excuses.

In sheer frustration, she picked up the phone again and texted the restricted number.

Ari: *You can't be alive. I went to your funeral. I saw you dead in a box.*

Still no reply.

While she was thinking, she emptied her closet into her suitcase and filled her backpack with snacks. She was finally heading to Vancouver, and it was a long drive. She didn't know what would happen once they got there. Hotel? Apartment? How long would they stay?

You did this to him.

The voices refused to leave her alone. They'd finally gotten her to respond, and they weren't going to let her get away with ignoring them anymore.

You can't use Kira as an excuse. After all, look what you did to him!

She jerked her head around in terror. These voices weren't like before. She could hear them somewhere in the room.

"You made his life miserable!"

"And you knew exactly what you were doing."

Ari covered her ears. "No, I didn't! I didn't mean to!"

"You turned into a cold-hearted killer."

"Betrayed your friend!"

She screamed in terror, but even that didn't drown them out. They grew louder and louder the more she begged them to stop.

"Does my voice still sound the same?"

"Did you forget to take your medicine?"

"Shut up!" Ari shouted. "Shut up, shut up, shut up!!"

"You're shirking. You have to leave now."

"Who are you shouting at?" asked a surprised but very normal voice.

Instantly, all the other voices stopped, and Ari looked up.

"K-Katya?" she stammered, blinking in the bright sunlight from her open front door.

"I thought I heard somebody talking in here, and then you just started to—"

"You heard them, too?" Ari cried excitedly, shaking Katya's shoulders. "You heard them?"

"I heard voices, but—"

"Oh, thank goodness." She sank down on the sofa in a puddle of relief. "I thought I was going crazy." Her phone vibrated, and she glanced at it.

Mikael: *Meet me at the syndicate alley ASAP.*

"I don't know what you think you're doing," Katya said, "but I came here with good news. Lucas woke up."

She sighed deeply, relieved. "Did he say who attacked him?"

"Yeah. It was . . ." She hesitated. "Well, I think it might've been Mikael."

Ari burst out laughing. "It could've been anyone in this city, and you think it was Mikael?"

Katya perked up. "I guess that doesn't make sense, does it?"

"There must be a lot of other blond Russians around here." Ari was still laughing hysterically. "You—why would you—*how* could you think that?"

"Are you okay?" Katya stared at her in disbelief. "'What's wrong with you? First voices and now this creepy laughing. Something's definitely wrong."

"Nothing's wrong; that's just too funny."

It is ironic, isn't it?

"I didn't think it was quite that amusing." Katya crossed her arms.

The way you thought somebody was on your side. All this time, if you hadn't lied to yourself, you would have known. If only you'd been able to see the situation clearly from the start, none of this would've happened.

"It really is," Ari said, finally controlling her laughter and switching to sporadic giggling. "I don't even know what to say. Everything fits together so nicely."

Still, you can't prove anything. Maybe someone's framing Mikael now, too.

Katya edged toward the door. "See you tomorrow?"

"No way. You won't be seeing me for a long time." That thought made Ari laugh even harder. She collapsed to her knees and snorted until Katya fled out the door and down the cross street.

Then she controlled herself by rapidly drinking a glass of ice-cold water. Katya wouldn't be back for a long time after what she'd just seen, and that gave Ari time to work out her plans.

"I've got to meet Mikael," she said aloud, forcing a deep breath. A quick pause in front of the mirror revealed an almost expressionless face—except a slight smile that she still couldn't get rid of—and a neat enough appearance to go outside.

Right before she turned into the alley, she caught sight of Mikael pacing back and forth across the road. He was paying no attention to traffic, and with every few steps, he took a long drink from a bottle of—was it red wine? It was too big to be a beer bottle. Ari raised an eyebrow disapprovingly. She needed him sober.

He saw her approaching and took one last swig from the bottle before tossing it across the street. It shattered on the pavement and barely left a stain. Empty. She could only hope that it hadn't been full when he started drinking it.

"Vita's back," he announced shortly. He didn't seem drunk—his speech was icily clear. "He's in the alley now."

"How did you figure that out?" She glanced in the hallway to look for Vita's familiar athletic figure. She didn't see it. "And why were you here in the middle of the day? Did you really drink that whole bottle?"

Mikael looked startled at first, but then he laughed. "Yes, I did. Don't worry about it. I wouldn't be drinking if I thought I'd get drunk. I just . . . well, I needed something to get me calmed down after finding out that Vita's here."

That doesn't sound like him at all. Well, on second thought, maybe it did. If her instinct was right, this was a moment he'd been waiting for. There could be a chance to finish their mission, one way or another, before Vita left. *If what Katya said is true, and Lucas isn't just seeing things, then he should be excited. Happy, even.* She frowned and looked away from him, hoping he couldn't read her expression.

"How long is he staying for?" she asked.

"I don't know. Ace asked him about that, but all he said was that he'd stay as long as he needs to." Mikael's eyes were wide and dilated. "Let's go talk to him."

"What are we going to talk about?" Ari demanded, but Mikael was already halfway into the alley, hands in his pockets, whistling nervously. Ari tiptoed after him, half-expecting to wake up any minute safe in her bed. This was a nightmare. It had to be.

She followed him into the alley, still looking for Vita. Eventually, she found him, leaned back against the wall beside an anxious-looking Ace, draining the last of a bottle of fruit juice. She smirked, thinking that fruit juice must be the closest he'd ever come to alcohol. At least she had an excuse to let out a little of her pent-up nervousness.

Mikael was ahead of her, and he started the conversation.

"It's nice to see you again," he said, a little awkwardly. "What are you here for this time?"

Vita laughed mid-swallow and spilled the juice. "Sorry," he said, choking. "Anyway, I'm here for the same reason I was last time—something entertaining! It's been too long. What have you got for me this time?"

Ari studied his face thoughtfully. *The killer poisoned Lucas. The killer had blond hair and blue eyes. Vita . . . has green eyes and blond hair. Could Lucas have possibly been that far off? Could I be on the wrong track entirely? Was it really Vita, after all?*

"Hey, it's the psycho chick," Vita said. "They told me that was your nickname."

"It's not," she said, biting back a sarcastic reply. "Pleasure to meet again."

"Indeed." He turned back to Mikael. "I've been paying you quite a bit of money for the drugs you've passed on to my boys. Where has it all been going?"

Part of it, Ari knew, went to pay Mikael's salary. The rest went back to the NDEB and was generally used to buy up more drugs to keep them off the market.

"I'm saving it for now," he said evasively. "I'll use it to invest once I don't have to worry about losing it. The drug trade is risky. I'm sure you know that."

"Oh, sure!" Vita said sympathetically. "You gain, and you lose; but you always gain more than you lose, and that's the point." He winked. "That's how I ended up a minor fitness celebrity." His expression was playful, but there was something in his eyes that caught Ari's attention. She knew that expression. It was the same look he'd had when he was teasing her about killing Calvin. He had a plan. The fact that he and Mikael were together was enough to confirm that. The only question left was whether Mikael knew about it.

"I've seen you on social media," was all she said aloud, dropping her eyes to the ground.

"Do you like the picture of me and the big kale leaf?" He fished his phone out of his pocket and stuck it in her face. The lock screen wallpaper was a rather racy photo of him wearing kale leaves as clothes.

Ari fought the impulse to laugh hysterically. "That's . . . " What was she supposed to say? "That's great," she continued hastily. *Do I really have anything to worry about? There's no way they could have come up with this all on their own. Not when they're wasting their own time like this.* She bit her lip. Whatever was about to happen, she consoled herself, she deserved it. She didn't get to fight back anymore.

"I've thought of a good use for some of the money," Mikael said. "Why don't you come to dinner tonight, Vita? Then we'll have a chance to discuss some future deals and potential clients. I'd like your help in connecting me with anyone you know."

"Absolutely," grinned Vita. "Especially if you pay."

"Of course. You're my guest." Mikael held out his hand, and Vita shook it. "I look forward to working with you tonight."

"Oh yeah!" cried Vita happily. "Looks like I'm going to get my share of the excitement after all. Wasn't sure when you walked in with that poker face of yours, but I guess this is going to be good."

Ari rolled her eyes. They weren't even trying to hide it anymore.

Mikael, when this is over, I'm going to choke you.

No, you can't think like that. You lost that privilege a long time ago.

"Ari, I'll need your help to get the paperwork ready," said Mikael.

"See you guys tonight then." Vita waved as they walked away. "Meet me at that Italian restaurant on Fifth at six o'clock sharp."

As soon as they had safely escaped the alley, Mikael turned to Ari. "Now's our chance to get on his good side." His voice was shaking. "We can end this right now. Nobody else has to die if we do it right."

"Okay, but—"

"Give me your phone," he ordered, holding out his hand.

"Why?"

"Because I don't want you distracted by that stalker who was texting you. We need to focus on Vita tonight. Please give me your phone."

She obeyed hesitantly. *You can't fight back. You can't. This is what's supposed to happen.* But giving up her phone meant giving up her last shred of self-defense, and it took every last ounce of her willpower to hand it over.

"I need you to be ready to answer questions—why you're here, how you know me, and anything Vita might think to ask. Can you work on that right now? We have an hour before we'd have to leave to get there on time. And we can't be late."

"Of course," said Ari. She couldn't stop herself from adding, "But what's the plan exactly? Are you going to ask him to find you clients? Will you be selling directly to him? Are you going to make a deal over dinner? What's your—"

"I don't know for sure," said Mikael. "I'll have to think about it for a bit. I'm a little—maybe it's the alcohol. I'm not feeling well. I need some time."

Ari nodded. "Okay. I'll see you tonight then."

She couldn't back out now. She needed proof. Firmer proof than a kid who'd almost died and offered a very vague description of a face that could fit almost anyone.

Almost. But he didn't die. Kira would never do that.

Would he?

"See you." Mikael started up the street, perpendicular to the direction he usually went. Ari watched him until he realized his mistake and ducked into a side street.

"So he's a heavyweight drinker, too," she mused. "I should have seen it before."

Maybe I'm like Lia. I know how to forget whatever I want to forget, whenever it suits me.

She wanted to live with the knowledge she had. She didn't want to die, didn't want to forget, didn't want to be punished. But forgiveness—the only other option—that was too little, too late. She and Kira both had already gone too far. She'd already betrayed him, and he'd already killed Yuri. And Calvin, too. Their names, all three of them, were on a list that could never be erased.

She couldn't quite stifle one single frustrated, thought.

How could you accuse me of betraying you, then treat me like this? How could you fall to my level?

The same restaurant where we had dinner with Yuri. How fitting. Ari glanced around uncomfortably. There were no allies for her here, and Mikael's tall figure loomed in front of her like a wall.

"There you are!" said a loud voice from behind them. Ari jumped. "I thought you'd never come."

Beside the door was a bench on which Vita was perched, his eyes shadowed behind a pair of black, plastic glasses. He was smiling—*of course, what else did you expect?* Ari wondered if it was possible to make him mad or sad or anything but psychotically happy.

He's just like Lia . . .

"Sorry," said Mikael briefly. Even his voice was starting to shake. Ari wondered if he was feeling even just a little bit guilty. He opened his mouth to continue, but nothing came out.

She pulled Vita aside. "He's drunk," she whispered firmly. They wouldn't go through with their plan, she thought, if they found out that she knew. She had to play innocent until the last moment if she didn't want her judgment to be postponed.

Vita laughed for a full ten seconds before he said anything. Ari watched awkwardly.

"Mikael's drunk?" he gasped. "Best thing I've heard all day. All week. Mikael, she says you're drunk!"

"No!" cried Ari, feigning embarrassment. "Why would you tell him I said that?"

Mikael just smiled, not very cheerfully.

"I wanted to take you two on a tour of my warehouse," said Vita, sitting down at a nearby table. Ari and Mikael slid into the seats across from him. "Should we go now or after dinner? Either is fine with me."

"Later," said Mikael hastily, hiding his face behind a menu.

"Oh, you spoil all the fun," complained Vita, leaning back in his chair. "You just hate talking, don't you? Let's have a completely silent dinner! I'm making the rules now—nobody gets to talk except to order. Sound fair?" He winked at Ari as if they had an inside joke.

She wondered how they were going to even pretend to arrange a deal if nobody could talk, but there was no point in worrying about it. Perhaps, if Vita was exceptionally perceptive, he'd already figured out that she had no intention of resisting. Or perhaps she'd fooled him into thinking she didn't know what they'd planned.

Obediently, she ducked her head into her menu.

Vita and Mikael didn't say a word, except very briefly to order their meals. Ari was too awkward to break the already awkward silence, which just got longer and longer. They drank in silence. They waited for their food in silence. They ate in silence. The only noise around them came from the other diners.

It gave Ari a good chance to study Vita. His smile never left his face, and reading his expression was like trying to read a dictionary straight through. There was nothing there except a randomly chosen expression—no story, no thoughts, nothing. Just like Lia's face had been right after she left the army, before she and Grey partnered to make their lives a little more normal.

How, Ari wondered, had she missed it for so long? How had she not recognized that look?

Mikael was completely different, too. Ari had never seen him so expressive. A plethora of minor emotions were easily visible on his face, but the dominant one was nervousness. Why hadn't he been nervous until now? Was there a chance . . . he hadn't been involved? Was he really just as confused as she was?

You expect me to believe you just ran into Vita on the side of the road and asked him to meet up for dinner? If you are who I think, you've lost your mind since the last time we met. Ari bit her cheek and winced from the pain. Never—she was never going to have any happy memories with him. She had to stop thinking about it.

"Are you finished?" Vita's voice startled Ari. "Then come on. We've got a deal to make, and I want you to see the warehouse."

Ari watched Vita steal a mint from the glass bowl on the hostess stand like it was the sneakiest thing he'd ever done. The more she saw of him, the harder it was to believe that he trafficked drugs. There were only a few people—twenty, in fact—who could hide their true natures so well. Lia was one of them, and apparently, so was Vita.

"Somebody's getting distracted," Vita mocked, breaking her train of thought. He was holding open the back door of a black BMW parked in front of the restaurant. "Get in, psycho missy."

A BMW? At least they're kidnapping me in style.

She hesitated for a moment. This was her last chance to turn away, to make them wait until she could call for backup. But there *was* no backup. She was cursed the moment she opened her mouth to accuse them. She couldn't protest her innocence without revealing how badly she had sinned.

So she got in the car. Mikael slid in beside her and immediately looked away. So much the better. She didn't want to see him, either.

Vita sat in the front, and the ride was as silent as dinner had been. Ari looked out the window the whole time to avoid looking at Mikael, but no matter how hard she tried to ignore him, she couldn't. She could feel his eyes on her back, and her spine tingled. For the first time since she could remember, she was afraid. What was she about to walk into?

The car slid to a glassy stop in front of an old studio apartment building. Was this what Vita called his warehouse? It must've cost him a small fortune if he owned the whole building.

His chauffeur walked ahead of them and unlocked the front door with a keycard, which he swiped across a hidden reader. Ari looked at the wall around it carefully, but no matter how hard she searched, she couldn't see it. So nobody would find her if they left her body inside.

Which they have every right to do. Don't you forget it.

The chauffeur retired back to the car, and Vita graciously held the door open for them.

The whole first floor was one wide, open space—at least, it would've been open if not for the multitude of crates scattered everywhere. They took up at least half the floor, and they were stacked to the ceiling. There was a familiar, sweet scent in the room.

"This is what I have left to check in," said Vita with a grand gesture around the room. "It's quite a bit all by itself, isn't it? And every floor above you is filled exactly like this."

No reply. Ari was too busy looking around, and nobody expected the tongue-tied Mikael to say anything.

"But I didn't come here to brag," said Vita briskly, producing a foldable chair from a closet and placing it in the center of the room. "Mikael, are you ready?"

He didn't respond, except to look at Ari with a distressed expression on his face.

"Mikael," she hissed, "what's he talking about?"

Still nothing.

"Mikael!"

"Stop being so dramatic!" cried Vita. "I don't have all night!"

Before Ari could react, he lunged toward her and forced her down into the chair. She didn't have time to cry for help before she was tied too tightly to move. Not that it would have mattered if she did—she knew there was nobody outside. Her hands were behind her, and her mouth was stuffed with some dirty canvas that tasted stale.

"Fwhetsh shoinsh om?" she demanded through the gag. Answers. That was all she'd come for.

Vita nearly choked on his own laughter. "I can't believe it!" he cried. "This whole elaborate plan you had, and she still has no idea. How about it, Kira?" He slapped Mikael on the back. The look of fury on Ari's face was enough to get him laughing again. "Kira put together this whole scheme," he giggled, "and even asked *me* for help! He was so sure it would work, I can't imagine how he feels now."

"Fwhash ii ey oo oo oo?" Ari struggled to speak. "Iirraaaa!"

Mikael—*Kira,* Ari mumbled to herself—bent down and untied her gag.

"What did I do to you?" she snapped as soon as she could be understood.

"How can you ask that?" he said flatly, backing away. "You know what you did."

"All right then, don't tell me what I did. Instead, tell me what you did." All she really wanted was an explanation of why he'd let her trust him. Why he'd become just like her, the one person she truly despised. "I thought we were teammates. Friends."

"So did I." He sighed and ran his hands through his hair. "A long time ago, anyway."

Ari could picture him with his headphones looped around his neck. The only thing different about him now was his eyes—they weren't nearly as blue. How had she missed it? How had she forgotten?

"You two lovebirds want to have a chat?" mocked Vita. Kira's hands twitched with anger, but Vita sauntered out the door into the street before he had a chance to say anything.

"You manipulative, little liar," snarled Kira as soon as the door shut. "How can you ask what you did to me? You know what you did. I know you remember. I heard your phone call with Lia. And you didn't even confess to her."

"Yes, but I—"

Stop trying to defend yourself.

"I never meant to—"

Yes, you did.

"If I had known—"

You're the only one who knew all about it.

Ari's chin dropped. "Please get this over with, whatever you want to do," she said, suddenly defeated. "I didn't come in here expecting to leave. I just wanted proof it was you." No, that wasn't right. "I wanted to see Kira again."

"You have to know the whole story first." Kira stood up and paced back and forth in front of her, arms crossed. "Before Vita comes back," he added tightly.

"You're going to tell me?"

He nodded.

"Kira," she said desperately. "I know I did wrong. I know all about it. I just want to know why you had to do this."

"Because I wanted you to know how I felt, Ari!" he shouted. "It wasn't just revenge—it was trying to get a piece of my sanity back. I wanted to believe you did it because you were crazy; but I did it, and I'm crazy, and it still hurts!" Ari flinched.

"K-Kira," she stammered, "I didn't do it because I was crazy, I just—I—I had to get out of there."

"So you used me as your excuse." He went quiet for a second. "And then betrayed me after everything I did to help you. If you had never said anything, I could have come with you, and none of this would have happened."

"I didn't do it because I wanted to!" protested Ari, shaking her head vigorously. "The generals said they had evidence that it was you. They already thought it was you, and there was no way I could get you out of it without implicating myself."

"Without implicating yourself," he repeated thoughtfully. Suddenly he turned around to face her, and his eyes glimmered wetly in his pale face. "It was always about you, wasn't it? It never occurred to you that I was even worse off than you. They chained me to my desk for eighteen hours at a time." He rolled up his sleeves and showed her his wrists. They were marked with thick, white scars that made her cringe—the visible remains of something wide and chafing attached to his wrists. "We could've escaped together, and they would've never known. But instead you got *them* involved." He smirked and kept on pacing. "Those generals who barely knew any of us and couldn't have called us by anything except our badge numbers if they'd practiced for a year. *They* gave you the evidence. *They* took me away and supposedly shot me. But they didn't. I wish they had."

"What did they do to you?"

Kira sat down against the crate again.

"Let me start from the beginning," he said quietly, his eyes fixed on the floor in front of his shoes. "If you really want to know."

She could make a guess at everything she wanted to know that she still didn't remember. But she had no choice except to listen, now that she'd come this far.

"Let's start by talking about *them*," he began bitterly. "*They* were, of course, the group of five generals with TS clearances who controlled the special agents division. What you and I didn't know at the time was that they were totally under the thumb of one man. He was a recruit, too—a psychologist—who had enough money outside the military to bribe them all into abject submission. We'll call him K. No reference to me. K gave the generals the 'evidence' that you saw against me, and he made it all up himself.

"You betrayed the division's existence to the media. Don't worry about how I know—we'll get to that later. Then you used this 'evidence' provided by K to blame me for the leak. I didn't know anything about that until the guards showed up at my dorm and said they were taking me away. I managed to get past them because I thought they were going to kill me, and I had to say goodbye to at least one person.

"But when they caught me, they didn't kill me. They took me to a building in the middle of nowhere, and that's where I met K. He wouldn't stop laughing, and that's how I knew that he must have been from our division. He told me all about how you betrayed us. I could've forgiven you for that—in fact, I could've blessed you for doing it because anything was better than staying there. But then he said that the only reason I was locked up now was because of you. He said you'd taken money from him to make me the culprit. He said you'd spilled the made-up evidence to everyone you could. He said—"

If it wasn't for the money he gave you, you wouldn't have survived when the division disbanded.

"I didn't know—" she began.

"He gave me proof that you did it—proof I could verify myself." Kira cut her off coldly. "And then he made me his slave for six months. It was worse than the division because there was no reason to let it happen—not patriotism, not honor, nothing. I couldn't get away until K let me go. He told me that he wanted me to find you. Yuno, the department head of the NDEB, is one of his agents. So he got me hired, and then I hired you."

That explains why he seemed so disorganized. It was all to further Kira's plan. No, Vita's plan.

"I put the oxyarcyan in your drink because I wanted to see how much you remembered about the army. I poisoned Yuri because I wanted to see how you'd react—if you'd have any remorse at all. I did the same to Nika so she would fail the drug test and be sent back to Virginia, just to narrow down the list of suspects so it would be even clearer it was me." He paused. "And I didn't want her to feel stuck the same way we did when we were in the army. Failing the drug test would get her out of the NDEB, and she'd never think of it as charity if she didn't know who did it."

"So you really thought that something so cruel would *help?*"

Don't try to tell me you had any good intentions.

He ignored her. "Calvin—" Long pause. "I was trying to get Calvin into trouble, so I told him what I was planning and threatened to kill him if he ever said anything about it to you. That's why he was acting so strangely, and that's how he ended up the primary suspect when the drug mission went wrong. But I didn't realize what was going to happen. I didn't know Vita was going to show up. He never told me he was coming."

So the last thing Calvin said wasn't "you know." It was Yuno. All along, he knew. If he had just told me sooner . . .

But, she realized, he couldn't have—not if he'd been subjected to the same ceaseless surveillance that she had been for the past week. Kira would've known the moment the words left his lips.

Kira straightened up and continued. "The point was to get everyone out of the way so that you'd figure out that it was me. After all, the only thing I wanted was for you to remember. Then I hacked your phone and sent you all those messages to be as obvious as possible. Of course, I wrote the riddles, too."

"And you wanted revenge," said Ari sarcastically. "I know you did. I don't blame you because I would've done the same thing. But don't try to beat around the bush anymore like you did with your stupid riddles."

"I didn't," he denied. "I'm telling the truth. I didn't do this for revenge, although I was bitter, or I would've done it differently. I wanted you to remember; I wanted to drag you out of the dark hole you were stuck in, and I wanted to show you how . . . how awful everything was. That was so I could see if you were sorry at all. I just—" He sighed and buried his face in his hands. "I just wanted things to go back to the way they were before all this happened, and I didn't know a better way to wake you up."

"So that's why you did this?" Ari shrieked. "You killed Yuri and Calvin for this? You almost killed Lucas for *this?* And you're telling me 'oh, it's fine, I just wanted to be friends!'"

"Yuri and Calvin aren't dead."

Ari was stunned into silence.

"Vita paid the hospital staff to say that they were. They're locked up somewhere, but they're going to be released soon."

"You didn't even need them. You just dragged them into your little game for the fun of it. You could've just gone off and lived your own happy life and tried to forget the past, like I did!"

"And look how you ended up!" Kira was finally getting angry. "You would've just let yourself starve if I hadn't done something. Have it your way. There was absolutely no good motive behind any of this, I just wanted to get even with you for being an arrogant traitor." He stood up yet again and resumed pacing. The angrier he got, the bluer his eyes looked, and they were glowing now. "Of course that isn't true, Ari! I wanted it to hurt so you'd actually *try* for once."

Ari was about to reply when the door burst open and Vita entered. He looked back and forth between them with a satisfied smirk. It was easy to read the rage on Kira's face and the bitter guilt on Ari's, and he had probably been listening the whole time.

"You've left out a bunch of the story," he said to Kira. "My role is so insignificant if you tell it like that." Then he turned to Ari. "I'm K, of course. I have no idea why Kira decided to call me that—he might as well have just told you. Anyway, he didn't explain why I gave him the job at the NDEB." He chuckled. "It wasn't out of the goodness of my heart. I did it because I knew he'd hire you. And I knew you two would destroy each other and in the process, destroy the agency you work for." His smile was getting even wider. "Just wait until I send these pictures to the media! A subordinate tied to a chair by a superior, getting threatened and yelled at about a past even the agency didn't know about. I wonder how that's going to sound."

"Do you rely on the media for everything?" asked Ari dimly as his phone's flash lit up her face.

"A wise man uses his assets well," he said, replacing his phone in his pocket.

Kira said nothing.

"Ever since the army days, I've been planning out how I could use you. Of course, I'm responsible for what happened to your division, too. Before all that new funding went to the NDEB, your division was my primary annoyance. But you can hardly complain since you were so involved!" His eyes turned back to Kira. "When are you going to finish your plan?"

No reply.

"Oh, come on! Don't say you're chickening out now!"

Still no reply.

Vita took a gun out of his pocket and handed it to Kira. He accepted it mechanically, his fingers closing tightly around the barrel. "Do it," Vita hissed. "This is the part I was waiting for."

"If I do it, you'll publish my name," said Kira dully. "You'll send me to prison."

"Now why would I do that?" cried Vita. "No, no, no, Kira. You have a lot left to learn about human nature if that's what you think. We're not all binary numbers, now, are we? I'd make you one of my agents. I'll give you everything you could ever ask for if you just kill her now."

"What good would that do you?"

"Plenty! Her death would be all over the news. 'Gross incompetency'—I can see the headlines now, calling your organization a 'murderous franchise,' just like they always do. Its authority would be gone in a matter of hours. Beautiful, isn't it? Pull the trigger!" Vita tiptoed around Kira to his other shoulder. "Do it, like we agreed."

"You planned to kill me this whole time," remarked Ari, her eyes fixed on Kira. "That means you lied when you said you didn't want revenge."

"Things haven't changed," he said, slowly cocking the gun. "I tried to get your attention and change things, but it didn't work. If I let you go now, you'll turn me in."

Ari was silent. It didn't matter if that was true or not. There was no reason for Kira to believe her if she denied it.

Well, this is a pretty easy way to die.

Are you even serious? It's stupid! Pointless! All because of one simple decision.

Ari closed her eyes.

It's not your fault that Kira ended up this way.

Who else can you blame?

"Get it over with," she said shortly.

"What are you talking about?"

Vita watched quietly from the front of the room, a wide smile on his face.

"Just make the voices stop. I don't care what you do."

He raised the gun and pointed it at her head. This time, his hands didn't shake.

"I just want to know one more thing," said Ari. "You could have killed me earlier. Why didn't you?"

"I wanted to give you a chance. And I wanted to see what you would do with that chance."

At least you won't have to worry about solving those riddles anymore.

This is what they mean when they say bad deeds always catch up to you.

Kira pressed the barrel to her forehead. "Anything else you want to say?"

Ari bit her lip.

CHAPTER 18

But the gunshot Ari was expecting never came.

Unable to wait any longer, she opened her eyes and looked up at Kira. He was pulling the magazine out of his gun, shaking the lone bullet out of the chamber. It clinked onto the floor by Ari's shoes.

"I'm done."

Vita's mouth was wide in disbelief. "You dragged me all the way out here for something like this?" he mourned. "This is too boring! I'll have to spice things up a little!"

Kira leaped in front of Ari, apparently thinking that Vita was going to shoot. Ari was so confused by his sudden defection that she couldn't even try to escape. She heard Kira's magazine click back into his gun, and she flinched, wondering if he was going to change his mind again. But he pointed it at Vita.

"I'll shoot. I mean it."

He shrugged. "Shoot me and your whole plan goes to waste."

"No, it doesn't. This was never part of the plan in the first place."

Vita's laughter was explosive, and under any other circumstances, Ari would've wanted to smack him. But she recognized it as a danger signal. He was getting angry.

"You promised me you'd kill her. She's a loose end for both of us."

"I made a mistake. I lost sight of everything I'd planned thanks to you and those six months you put me through."

Ari blinked, astonished. What could he possibly have been thinking about that could've changed his mind so dramatically? One moment, she'd resigned herself to letting him kill her, and the next, he was defending her. Was it possible that he just wanted to take both her and Vita down together? Was he going to change his mind again?

"I guess," Vita mused. "I guess you aren't going to do it. I'm disappointed, but I'm too outnumbered to do anything about it." He spread his hands out in dismissive innocence. "I'm not armed. I know you thought I was, but I really thought you were going to kill her. Do whatever you want. You can have this, too." He threw the phone he'd used to take the pictures with on the ground, and it cracked. "I don't care." Like a sulky child, he left the room without another word.

Kira seemed surprised Vita had given up the phone so easily, but after a moment of puzzled silence, he stomped on it until it shattered.

Then he turned to Ari.

"No offense," he said with the tiniest of smiles. "I don't ever want to be like you. Killing you would make me just as bad." He bent down behind her and cut her ropes. "I only agreed to do it because Vita said he wouldn't help me if I left you alive. I was never going to go through with it."

"And you think I'd turn you in."

"Wouldn't you?" He was still smiling. Ari couldn't believe he really didn't care what her answer was. "I think I would if I was you."

"You didn't turn me in," she said.

"I couldn't have. You didn't do anything wrong."

"Stop with that," she said harshly. "I didn't do anything illegal. But I did something wrong, and we all know it. You could've gotten me in trouble if you really wanted to."

"I did want to. And I did get you in trouble." He spread his arms and looked around the warehouse. "Only I couldn't do it legally, so here we are."

"After all this time, why would you give up so easily?" Ari was still on her guard, and she clutched the severed ropes behind her. In a pinch, they might be an effective weapon. "You were willing to risk people's lives just to get my attention and make me remember. Why stop now? Why not make sure you're safe?"

His face pinched into a frown. "It doesn't matter what you decide to do to me now. I've got nothing left to lose. Maybe somewhere along the line, I did want revenge. But what I really wanted above everything else was to somehow undo everything we went through."

"You keep saying that. But you seriously couldn't think of an easier way?" She was almost laughing, struck by the bizarreness of the situation.

"I thought if I did something this awful, you'd turn me in," he said softly. "I thought that unless I could get you to hate me, you'd feel too guilty to do it. But if you did, then I could tell everything I knew about Vita without getting you in trouble."

"W—what?" Ari stammered. "What do you mean?"

"If I walk into a police station tomorrow and tell them what Vita did to me, they'd just laugh and think I was crazy. But if you turned me in to the NDEB, there'd be interrogations. I could tell them everything I knew. If I accidentally said anything that implicated you, they'd dismiss it as me trying to get back at you. Vita would get what he deserves—which is far worse than the punishment for attempted murder—and you could go on to live your life however you wanted. I *might* get off with a lighter sentence because I was an informant. Everything would work out if you turned me in." He fidgeted with the strings of his hoodie. "You probably know already, I was the man who talked to you in the bar the night before you interviewed with the NDEB. I wanted to see if you'd changed at all. Back then, I said you hadn't. But that wasn't true. I got the feeling if I told you who I really was, you'd run away and I'd never have the chance to get you to turn me in without feeling guilty. You weren't the same person who threw me under the bus without a second thought just to escape the military. You'd been feeling guilty ever since, and it showed."

Ari broke into wild laughter. "Your goal this whole time was to finish off Vita, not me?"

Kira knelt on the floor beside her. "Sort of. Maybe. It was one of my goals. I don't know. All I know is that I want it to be over now."

"There's no way you could have forgiven me that easily. Not after what I put you through."

"Who said it was easy? But I thought . . . " He thought for a moment. "I wasn't perfect either. Neither of us were. I had to find forgiveness, too, and the more I searched, the less I found it. I thought the only way I could be forgiven is if God Himself did it for me, and I couldn't reasonably ask for that if I wouldn't do it."

Hysterical tears streamed down Ari's face, though she couldn't tell whether she was really crying or if she was just laughing too hard.

"We have to find Vita," she said, wiping her eyes with her free hand. "Then maybe I can try to figure out what you mean by that."

"We can let the police find him. You just have to go back to the NDEB with me and tell them what I did. That way, there won't be any difficulties getting a warrant for his arrest."

"You think I'm really going to turn you in right now?" she snapped, standing up and shaking herself free of the cut ropes. "There's a lot we need to talk about before you can go to prison. Don't be in such a hurry. Let's go."

"But—"

Ari's mind was finally clearing. Though she couldn't make heads or tails of Kira's wild confession, she knew there was no point in trying to divide her attention between goals. There would be time after they caught Vita for her to decide what she wanted to do about Kira. For now, they had a chance to catch the man they both hated. Surely, even if Kira had lied, they could work together for at least that long, no matter what happened afterwards.

"He probably left in his car," she said aloud. "We need to call a taxi. Give me my phone."

Kira silently fished in his pocket and handed it to her.

"I'll wait here for the taxi and follow you. Kira, you're a faster runner than me. You go after him on foot. See if he got out of the car anywhere nearby or if you can catch a ride."

"You're just going to let me leave? You don't think I'll run away?"

"If I find Vita, I know I'll find you. I don't think you were lying when you told me what he did to you, so I'm sure you want to catch him as much as I do." Ari stared at him, then reluctantly added, "You've done your best to let me down, but you haven't succeeded yet. I don't think you will this time either."

He nodded, then handed her his gun. "Stay safe," he said, and before she could protest, he was already outside.

Ari followed more slowly, struggling to predict everyone's next move. She was almost certain that Kira wouldn't try to escape until Vita was a prisoner, so she didn't need to worry about where he'd gone. But what would Vita do next?

Her eyes flicked to the phone that he'd dropped, and she pinched herself, trying to keep her thoughts from straying back to Kira's words. *Focus, focus. You need to focus.*

Why would Vita have dropped that phone if it had the proof he needed to finish off the NDEB?

The only possible conclusion was that he had some other proof. Or perhaps, she thought, he was planning to get proof in a different way.

Kira's plan was to have me turn him in so that I wouldn't be a suspect, even if he implicated me when he accused Vita.

That same plan, she realized with shock, could work just as well in reverse.

If Vita turned Kira in, the police wouldn't be likely to listen to his testimony against Vita, especially if he doesn't have much proof besides his own stories of what he experienced. And if I'm not around to back him up and tell what I remember about the army, he won't have a chance of getting Vita convicted.

So Vita's plan . . . would be to kill me and turn Kira in.

How the tables turned. She kicked the folding chair across the room in frustration, then peeked out the front window to see if the taxi had arrived. It hadn't. But from somewhere faraway, she heard a whine, gradually getting louder and higher-pitched. Police sirens. That only confirmed her suspicions.

She took off running down the street, praying that she could somehow find Kira before those sirens did.

CHAPTER 19

At last, she found Kira. It would've been hard to miss him. He was standing in the middle of a four-way intersection, shading his eyes, surrounded by spotlights, police cars, and flashing strobe lights that made his pale face look like it was glowing. Even at a distance, she could tell he was confused. Distracted, perhaps, by chasing Vita, he hadn't stopped to think through what the enemy's counter-move might be. Ari cursed. If he'd known, then maybe he could've helped her come up with a plan.

I shouldn't have told him to leave.

But it was too late for regret. Ari stayed hidden in the shadows of the spotlights, trying to think of what to do. Could she show the policemen her badge and arrest Kira herself? Leave him and continue chasing Vita?

"Drop your weapons," said one of the officers over a megaphone. "Are you Mikael Lesner?"

"Yes," Kira shouted back.

Interesting. Why wouldn't Vita have told the police his real name? The only reason she could think of was that Mikael's name was directly tied to the NDEB, and any bad press from his arrest would reflect poorly on them.

Still, maybe Kira's double identity could come in handy.

"Get down to your knees and put your hands behind your head."

He did as he was told.

"Don't move," ordered the officer, handing the megaphone to someone nearby and walking slowly toward Kira's back.

Ari watched, agonized. Her chances of rescuing him were getting slimmer and slimmer with every step the officer took.

I'll do it. I'll go out there and take Kira into my custody. Then, surely, we can think of something. Anything to make sure Vita gets arrested before he does.

Kira turned to face the officer approaching him. One of the police officers in the crowd moved suddenly, like he was startled. Ari's gaze involuntarily flicked to him. There was an unmistakable expression of fear on his face. He was staring at Kira like a hawk, and his hand was moving to the holster at his hip.

He thinks Kira's going to fight back.

She opened her mouth to scream at him to stop. But before she could make a single sound, she was interrupted by a gunshot.

She squeezed her eyes shut, ears ringing from the echo.

When she opened her eyes, Kira was facedown in the middle of the road. The officer had jumped back into the queue with a curse, and the policeman who'd fired was on his knees, blank horror written all over his face.

Ari didn't bother stopping to think about what she should've done. Ignoring the warning cries everyone was shouting at her, she shoved her way into the circle and knelt beside Kira.

"Open your eyes," she commanded, her voice shaking. "Look at me."

He did, for just a second, in a quick flash of blue. Ari sighed deeply, relieved.

"Go find him," he whispered.

"Who?" Ari hissed. The officers would be in earshot in a moment.

"Vita."

A thin stream of blood trickled from the corner of his mouth, and Ari wiped it away with her sleeve. But no matter how hard she tried, it just kept coming back. He was choking. She tilted his head back to clear his airway, and his gasps turned into a racking cough.

"Don't give up," she hissed. "You're the only one who can testify against Vita. You've got to make it. You have to."

He tried to say something, but Ari put her hand over his mouth. The policemen were too close, and if they realized that Ari wasn't just a worried onlooker—if they realized that she knew Kira and was trying to help him escape—she'd be arrested next.

She planted her hand in his hair and yanked his limp head up to look at her. "They're calling an ambulance. Stay with me until it gets here."

But his eyes were glazed like he was falling asleep. The louder she shouted, the less he seemed to hear her.

She slapped his cheek with increasing desperation. "You're going to be fine," she told him, willing herself to believe it, too. "Just stay with me."

For a moment, she was distracted by the flurry of motion behind her. When she looked back at Kira, he was unconscious.

Someone behind her was pulling on her shoulder. "Miss? We need you to step away, unless you're a medical doctor or law enforcement."

She flashed her badge impatiently. "I'm NDEB," she said. "Get me a first aid kit."

Kira's chest was such a mess of blood and tattered clothing that she couldn't tell if he was at risk for a punctured lung. Everything she touched stained her hands red. *Hollow point bullets, curse that crazy policeman. There won't be enough gauze in the first aid kit to stop the bleeding.* All she could do was sterilize her hands in isopropyl alcohol and press them over where she thought the wound must be, trying to seal it away from the air. His chest rose and fell under her hands, but the rhythm of his breaths was getting steadily slower.

Just before the ambulance arrived, she slipped Kira's phone out of his pocket. If anyone would've known where Vita was, he would—he'd shown her clearly enough that he hadn't forgotten his old hacking skills. She pressed his finger on the sensor and unlocked it, then slipped it in her pocket.

"I'm going to win this for us," she whispered to Kira, giving his hand a squeeze before the paramedics carried him away. "No, for me. I'll worry about you later."

Taking advantage of the confusion surrounding her—the officers yelling at the policeman who'd shot Kira, the echoing ambulance siren, the curious onlookers—Ari slipped away into a back alley and checked Kira's phone. Sure enough, he did have a tracking app. She could see her own location in blue, and there was someone else nearby who was marked in orange. That icon had a V beside it, and it was moving slowly away.

He was so close that Ari guessed he must have been watching when Kira was shot. Perhaps that hadn't been a rookie mistake, after all. Perhaps Vita had planned this out all along. But it hardly mattered now.

There was no time to waste. With a last glance to see where she was going, she took off running. This time, fueled with adrenaline, she didn't want to risk waiting for a taxi. Vita's icon was moving slowly enough that he might be on foot. If so, she had to catch him before he found a car.

About half a mile down the road, she spotted a shadowy figure ducking around a corner. It was moving too fast to be an ordinary pedestrian, and Ari recognized Vita's silhouette. The sight gave her the last spurt of energy she needed to catch up with him.

She waited to pounce until they were close to a dark alley. Then, with the speed of a cat, she covered his mouth with her hand, kicked his knees limp, and dragged him into the darkness.

"You had this all planned out." She held him firmly against the wall with her arm across his throat. If he moved, she was positioned to crush his windpipe. "You thought Kira was your slave to the point where he'd kill me. And that I'm depraved to the point where I'd kill him if he didn't. Well, you thought wrong. Kira and I were friends once. I may have messed up what we had, but I'm not the same person I was back then. Neither is Kira. He wants me to live, and I want us both to live. If he dies—" She choked on her own words. "I'll find you. I'll take your evidence no matter what I have to do. I won't let anyone torment him anymore. You've picked the two worst people to have as enemies."

"Maybe you should just let him die," sputtered Vita, grimacing. "Admit it. You've thought about it. If he dies, you don't have anything to worry about. I won't turn you in—all I wanted was to destroy the NDEB, and I have everything I need to do that. Especially if Kira dies. You'd be safe from him and me, and you could live your life just like you've always wanted to."

His words struck home with Ari, and she shoved him harshly back against the wall.

"I never once thought about letting him die, not after he saved my life."

That was a lie, and she knew it. She'd made her decision in a split second, but in the moment before she ran out to help Kira, she hadn't quite been able to stifle it: *If he dies, you don't have to worry about him going crazy and dragging on this stupid riddle game.*

The thought had been so swift that it barely even registered, but it was there, and the thought alone was enough to revive the old feeling of guilt. She wanted to strangle Vita, wished that the blood on her clothes was his and not Kira's, cursed him aloud for trying to tempt her. But she couldn't hurt him. If she did, she'd be arrested and would never get to know what happened to Kira. She'd become the guilty one, just like her old self had been.

Keeping her eyes fixed on Vita's face, she pulled Kira's phone out of her pocket and dialed 911.

Kill Kira. Kill him. You don't have to worry anymore.

It would be self-defense. It's justified. You can do whatever you want. You won't get punished.

There was no erasing the thought Vita had planted in Ari's mind. All night, fighting with herself, she paced up and down her room. The voices wouldn't be quiet, and her own thoughts were just as overwhelming.

Kill him. You have every right.

Almost involuntarily, she was forming a plan in her mind. She could cut the cord to Kira's life support and make it look like he did it himself. It wasn't very far-fetched to think he'd commit suicide after what he'd been though, and she knew nobody would ever think to question her as a suspect.

But there was a third voice mixed with the two that were the loudest.

Kira's better than you. He stopped himself when he was given the choice to kill you. You haven't really decided what you want to do yet.

The essence of Kira's plan was to sacrifice himself to save you.

If he told the police the whole story of what happened between him and Vita, and if they decided to trust him, you'd go to prison, Ari. For accepting bribes from a superior officer. You'd deserve it. That would be justice.

But he decided not to. He wanted you to turn him in so that the police would think he had a grudge against you, just in case he let anything slip about your involvement. That way, you'd be safe.

She sank down on her bed, legs aching and sore from her run and from the long hours of walking up and down her bedroom floor.

You and Kira are both killers. The only difference between you is that he's no longer a killer. Don't you want to know why?

Her shoulders shook, and she broke down sobbing frustrated, exhausted tears. She cried until her head ached and her mouth was dry, and then she cried some more. And eventually, completely worn out, she collapsed into sleep.

She happened to be carrying a knife the day she heard that Kira was awake and off his ventilator. It felt heavy in her pocket as she walked to the hospital. She was halfway there before she realized she couldn't stand it anymore, and she ran all the way back to her apartment, threw the knife inside, and locked the door behind her.

Forgiveness doesn't work if it's one-sided.

Then she went to visit Kira.

He was a shadow of what he had been before his injury, and his face had gone from stark white to pale gray; but his eyes were bright and alert, and he waved to her as soon as she peeked in the room. His lips were a little less tight than before, and his smile seemed to come a little easier.

Ari closed the door behind her and pulled up a chair beside his bed.

"Have you changed your mind on having yourself arrested?" she asked dryly. "After getting shot by the police."

"It wasn't the best customer service, that's for sure." He chuckled. "I haven't. I'll still do anything to—"

"To have Vita arrested. I know; I know. Well, I have news for you. I caught him myself. He's in prison now, and he's already been interrogated."

"What?" Kira shot up in his bed. "And what has he said about us?"

Ari shrugged. "Nothing. Before he was interrogated, I tried to think of everything he might be likely to say. I don't think he can talk about the military without implicating himself, and he certainly can't mention either of us. We're safe for now."

"What exactly is he in for?"

"Right now, it's manslaughter. Neither Calvin nor Yuri has turned up yet, so there's nobody to say they're still alive."

Kira sighed and dropped back against his pillows. "Everything that happened in the military will be a secret forever, then."

"You wanted it to become public?" Ari's expression softened. "You wanted to show that we weren't the bad guys, like everyone said?"

"Something like that."

They fell into silence. Ari fidgeted with her sleeves.

"You know," she said at last, "can we just say we're even with each other?"

Kira smiled. It was the first time she'd seen Kira smile sincerely, and one of the rare times she'd seen Mikael smile at all.

"Your secret is safe with me," she added. "And I don't have much of a choice besides trusting that mine is safe with you. I don't want to let the past determine where we go in the future."

He solemnly held up his pinkie finger. "Promise."

Ari couldn't hold back her laughter, and Kira watched her with a small smile until she got her breath.

"You know, you're not done yet," he said. "You have to go back to Virginia and get Yuri and Calvin out of trouble. And if you can, tell the NDEB that Nika was framed for taking drugs. That way, she won't have a mark on her record."

"I can't do much without implicating you," said Ari, struggling to think seriously again. "The NDEB will never believe that Nika was framed without solid evidence. And about Yuri and Calvin—I don't even know where they are."

"Feel free to implicate me. I'm not going back with you."

Ari froze. "What? Why not?"

His eyes met hers for a moment, then dropped to the blanket. "There's no other way. The NDEB probably already knows that I was behind the riddles. The case can't just remain unsolved forever. If I ever get caught, I'd have to confess, and that would be the end of it."

"B-but," Ari sputtered, "You didn't commit a crime. Besides, I promised never to tell anyone that it was you. If we keep that a secret, I don't see how anyone could find out."

"Calvin knows. He's clever. I bet he's already found a way to contact the NDEB."

Ari couldn't think of a reply.

"But he doesn't know why I did it," continued Kira, twisting the blanket between his fingers. "Be honest. If you were him, would you ever believe me?"

"We'll convince him," insisted Ari. *We were so close. So close to patching everything up. We can't fail now.* "I'll tell him. I'll—"

"He's paralyzed, Ari. From when Vita shot him. And he knows enough to blame that on me."

He laughed, a choked laugh that turned into a cough. Ari helped him prop himself up against the pillows.

"I'll be fine," he continued. "Once I'm out of here, nobody will find me. I didn't go through all that army training for nothing. Besides, the NDEB doesn't know my real name. I didn't even tell Yuno that."

Ari hesitated.

Finally, she burst out, "I don't want to go back without you. I'm not done talking to you. I don't feel like I ever really got to know you, not when you were Kira and not when you were Mikael. I just want us to be honest with each other for once, and we can't do that if you're not here."

Kira didn't respond.

"Why don't you let me come with you?"

His eyes flicked up in terror. Ari could tell he'd expected her to say that, and he didn't have his excuse prepared.

"I'll go back to Virginia and tie up the loose ends," she hurried. "Then I'll meet you somewhere, and we'll figure out how to live like normal people. If we don't get along, we don't have to stick together. But I'm not ready for you to leave yet."

He shook his head so hard that the bed rattled. "No. You have a whole career ahead of you at the NDEB. I'm not going to let you throw that away."

"I don't recall it being your choice." Ari rested her elbows on the bed, suddenly exhausted. "I want to stop living with a guillotine over my head. I'll never be able to live with what I've learned about myself until I'm certain you've forgiven me. And even then, I'll still have to forgive myself. And I can't do that until you tell me everything that happened. Every detail. Everything you went through. I need to know so I can apologize for everything. To you, to Calvin, to Yuri, to Nika . . . to God, even. There's no other way for me to live in peace. The voices won't shut up if I don't."

Kira's face crinkled in amusement, and Ari was so keyed up that she couldn't stop herself from giggling. There was nothing to laugh at, but a few moments later, they both broke down.

"I'll let you know when I'm discharged," Kira said at last. "I'm not making any promises. I'm only saying that you'll know about it. But meanwhile, go back to Virginia and tie up all your loose ends. Find Yuri and Calvin. Tell them the truth about what happened. Make sure Nika's okay. And make sure—make sure this is what you want to do."

"I'm already sure," Ari assured him, wiping the tears from her eyes. She took a long, deep breath and stood up. With a last wave goodbye, she let herself out into the hallway.

"I'll see you soon."

CHAPTER 20

By the time Ari got back to Virginia, Nika had already been discharged and was working a temporary job at Ari's favorite organic grocery store. Ari watched her from behind a newsstand for a while before she approached. Nika's eyes were dull and lifeless, and it didn't seem like she'd recovered much from her time in the NDEB. But when she spotted Ari, her whole face lit up.

"I'm so glad," she sobbed breathlessly. "When I heard that Mikael had been killed, I was so scared for you. I tried to text you a hundred times, but you never answered your phone. I thought that was it. I thought our whole team had fallen apart."

"Where exactly did you hear that Mikael was dead?" Ari was startled.

"Yuno told everybody."

Clever, Ari realized with astonishment. He and Kira must have had a mutual agreement not to turn each other in, or there was no way he would've covered for Kira so effectively. She'd almost forgotten that their stories were so closely intertwined.

Did Kira know all along that there was a chance I wouldn't turn him in?

She couldn't believe he'd had that much faith in her. Perhaps they had come to trust each other more than she thought over the months they'd worked together at the NDEB.

Nika noticed the smile on her face and asked, "What are you so happy about?"

Instead of explaining, Ari handed her a coffee.

"Long overdue repayment," she said in response to Nika's mystified stare. "You were an amazing teammate, Nika. I'm glad I had the chance to know you."

Her next order of business was to find out what had happened to Yuri and Calvin. If Kira had been working behind the scenes to fake his own death, she reasoned, it was quite possible that he'd already made arrangements for Yuri and Calvin's release. If so, they were probably already back in Virginia.

And sure enough, Ari ran into Yuri the very next morning at a mission debriefing at the NDEB headquarters. She was so excited to see him that she enveloped him in a bear hug before he could escape, ignoring his irritated grumbling.

"Where have you been?" she asked playfully. "Taking vacation while the rest of us worked?"

"Hotel," he said very briefly, sitting down at one of the office chairs.

"You were locked up in a hotel?"

"Yes."

"Why didn't you just call the front desk and ask them to let you out?" If there was one thing she'd learned about Yuri during the short time she'd known him, it was that teasing was the only way to drag details out of him.

He glared at her and tossed his head defiantly. "Obviously, the phone wasn't hooked up, the door was locked, the room was on a high floor, and there were guards in the two rooms beside me. Satisfied?"

"But were you comfortable?"

"Yes," he admitted reluctantly. "It wasn't awful. They had better vodka than I can buy in Russia."

He clammed up after that, recognizing that Ari was baiting him.

Throughout the meeting, she half-expected Calvin to come walking in just like before, holding his official-looking clipboard and fiddling with the projector. But she waited in vain. His name was never even mentioned in the briefing, and Yuri, probably believing that he was dead, didn't bring him up. She'd have to find out what had happened to him for herself.

After the meeting, she slipped upstairs to Yuno's office and knocked on the door.

"Come in."

She let herself inside and closed and locked the door behind her. Then, keeping her face fixed in a friendly smile, she pulled up a chair and sat down across from him.

"I know what you've done," she said. "I'm sure that K—I mean, Mikael—has already agreed to keep your secret in exchange for his freedom. I don't want to mess that up. All I want from you is to tell me where Calvin is. Why is he still listed as deceased on the NDEB's register?"

There was a long pause. Yuno scanned Ari's face, perhaps wondering if she was bluffing, and she waited in patient silence. She knew there was no way he could misinterpret her hatred. Anyone who would take orders from Vita was an enemy to her, and she couldn't hide her feelings for long.

"He's severely injured and still in the hospital," said Yuno, handing Ari a file. "I didn't know whether letting him out would be a breach of the deal I have with Mikael. Right now, he doesn't realize he's a prisoner, though I've told the hospital to make sure he doesn't leave the grounds. But I'm sure Calvin will want his revenge once he figures it out."

"That's for me to worry about." Ari was relieved that he didn't seem to know about Mikael's second identity. If he had known, he wouldn't have suggested that Calvin was a threat.

She took the file and stood up. "Let's keep this conversation between us."

The hospital where Calvin was undergoing rehab was about only a mile from the NDEB. Ari decided to walk, enjoying the cold, spring air blowing on her face. It felt like home, like a fresh beginning, like a chance to make things right.

That's how this should have worked from the beginning. You should have forgiven Kira, the army, everyone. If only you'd started there, none of this would've happened.

She caught sight of Calvin in a wheelchair in the hospital gardens. He was sitting under a willow tree, but instead of looking up at the clear, blue sky, or at the greenery surrounding him, his eyes were fixed on the ground.

Ari approached slowly, feeling almost shy.

"Hello, Calvin."

He didn't look up at her, but she could tell from the way his shoulders tensed that he was surprised she was there.

"At least one of us survived." His voice was barely audible.

She cleared her throat. "Actually, everyone survived. Except for Mikael."

This time, he did look up. "Even Yuri?"

Ari nodded.

He leaned back in his wheelchair, rubbing his eyes. "Thank goodness."

"You knew all along," said Ari, seating herself on the grass beside him. "Mikael told you his whole plan, almost from the start. Why didn't you tell me?"

"You don't think I would've if I could've?" The wind whistled through the tree branches, echoing his bitter laughter. "Mikael said he would kill me if I told you. I tried to tell you when Vita shot me because I figured there wasn't much more Mikael could do then."

"That was brave of you."

"No. I just wanted to stop having to worry about keeping the secret. I felt I was carrying the weight of the whole team on my back. I *was* carrying that weight. If only I'd been braver, maybe things would've turned out differently."

"That's not true," Ari assured him. "It was my fault, my fault from the very beginning. If only I had let go . . . " Her voice trailed off. She couldn't explain what she meant by that.

Calvin didn't press her. "I heard Mikael is dead. Is that true? What happened to him?"

"Yeah." *Well, in some sense, that's not even a lie.* But her excuses didn't make her feel any better. "The NDEB got a tip that he was behind the riddles. It seems he was working with Vita all along, and Vita double-crossed him. He was arrested, but he fought back, and the police shot him." That was the official story she'd heard during the briefing.

"Will you ever be able to walk again?" she asked suddenly, running her fingers along the cold metal of Calvin's wheelchair. "What have the doctors told you?"

"They don't know. I don't know. And frankly, I don't know if I care." Calvin was gloomy again. "I'd much rather know why Mikael did what he did."

Ari bit her lip, wondering how much she could safely tell him. "Before he died," she began slowly, "Mikael told me that he intended for you to be kicked out of the gang. He said that he explained his plans to you just to make you anxious, so that you'd be acting suspiciously."

"Go on."

"But when he saw Vita shoot you, he was the one who saved your life. He risked his own life to patch you up. He even held Vita at gunpoint." The scene was burned in Ari's memory, and she squeezed her eyes shut. "He never meant for you to get hurt. I don't know if that helps."

Calvin had been watching her throughout her story with a half-hearted smile. "It really doesn't," he said. "But thank you anyway, Ari."

"What would it take for you to forgive him?"

He tilted his head back thoughtfully. "A long time. A good motive for everything he did. I don't know."

Ari's throat tightened. *All things he'll never get.*

"I'm sorry," she blurted out. "If I had pressed you harder, maybe you could've told me what Mikael was doing without him finding out. Maybe I could've saved both of you."

"Both of us?" Calvin frowned. "Ari, you're not making sense. You're talking as if you don't have anything against Mikael. How could you let it go so easily?"

"I don't think I have the right to judge him," she answered. "I mean, everything that happened . . . it's too difficult to explain, but solving the riddles showed I was the one at fault all along. I suppose you never got to see the last riddle, but it made that pretty clear. If there's one thing I learned from all this, it's that the past should never dictate the present."

A sudden breeze blew a long strand of willow into her face.

"I think this was all God's judgment," she said, brushing it away. "I deserved it. But you and Nika and Yuri didn't. And for that, I don't know how I'll ever be forgiven."

Calvin laughed, a short, sharp laugh. "By definition of being God, I think He's capable of forgiving if you ask. And you seem sincerely sorry. Seek and you'll find, you know? An often-overlooked Sunday school principle that applies more to adults than it does to the kids who learn it. But it might take me a little longer to forgive you if this really is your fault."

"I wouldn't expect you to, after everything I did. But thank you for saying that. I guess I'll have to find out for myself if it's true. I think I'd feel bad even showing my face in church right now, but if it's the only way . . . "

"The pastor will start off with 'no matter how bad you are . . . '" Calvin seemed to be lost in his own thoughts. "That's what they always do. You'll think nobody as bad as you ever set foot in those walls, and you might even be right. But so what? God's not much of a God if there are limits on how much badness He can stand. Besides, you're hardly the worst person to have ever lived, or you wouldn't be trying to apologize in the first place."

"You don't seem like the religious type, Calvin. Do you really believe that?"

He huffed. "I didn't until I saw how much baggage I had that I don't stand a chance of getting rid of by myself. Now I think I need help. And if there's even the slightest possibility of getting it, I'm going to try."

Ari nodded in silent agreement. It didn't seem fair to come crying to God only when she'd gotten herself in a mess she couldn't untangle when she'd never given God's existence a second thought before. But maybe that was inherent in the idea of judgment. Maybe even judgment was, by itself, a kind of second chance.

"I could get started on that whole forgiveness thing if you told me why Mikael did it." Calvin's voice broke in on her thoughts. "You said it was about your past, so you should know."

She flopped down onto her back, wondering how to condense the story enough to make it understandable, or even believable. She'd told it to herself over and over, but she had never told it without confessing what she'd done so long ago. And poor Calvin, trapped forever in his wheelchair, blaming Mikael for what had happened—he was the last person she could trust with that information, however much she wished she could.

"I can't," she said. "I can only tell you I truly believe that Mikael did the best he could with the hand he was dealt. And I know he never meant to hurt you. And in the end, most of it was my fault, not his. I just didn't let myself see it that way until it was too late."

Silence.

"You understand why that's not enough," said Calvin at last. "That doesn't even make sense."

"And that's why Mikael is dead." Ari smiled at him. "Really and truly. He's never coming back. Neither am I."

"Where are you going?" He raised an eyebrow.

"To come to terms with myself." She stood up, stretching and taking a deep breath of the cool, sweet-scented air. "To try to find God's forgiveness, I guess. I'm sorry, Calvin. I know it doesn't mean anything now. But I'm still sorry. I hope things turn out okay for you. I wish there was more I could do."

"Wait!" he cried, but Ari was already leaving. She didn't want him to see that flooded with remorse and anxiety and frustration, she was on the verge of tears.

Of course it was too much to hope that he could forgive you. You'll have to find your peace elsewhere, Ari.

Only a few minutes later, just as she was rounding the corner next to her apartment building, she received a text from Lia.

Lia: *We're back from Canada!! Can we come see you? We have to say thank you!*

Thanks for what, I wonder? Ari was in no mood for visitors, but she wanted to see Lia.

Ari: *Sure. I'm at home.*

Not even twenty minutes later, Lia and Grey arrived at her doorstep, carrying a huge basket of flowers. Ari set them on her counter, and they overflowed onto the stove, spreading thick, yellow pollen everywhere. The mess would've annoyed her if it didn't seem so gregarious, a happy reminder that some things would never change. Lia—the one person Ari had always relied on, the one who had really solved the riddles in the end—at least if all else failed, Ari could always depend on her to smile.

"Oh, it looks so nice in here!" cried Lia, clasping her hands. "How have you been, Ari?"

"Just fine," she lied.

"How's Nika doing?"

"She's better now that she's out of the NDEB."

"And Yuri? I heard he got back somehow—that's amazing! Calvin, too!"

Ari dropped onto the sofa, too tired to stand. "It is pretty amazing. But I don't think Calvin is doing very well. The doctors have told him that he might not be able to walk again."

"That's better than being dead," observed Grey. Lia slapped him, and Ari didn't respond.

"And Mikael?" Lia asked.

"He's . . . it's complicated," Ari murmured. She took a deep breath and recited the story of his death yet again. "He died in the hospital," she finished. "I'm really just surprised he lasted that long. Of course, nobody was able to get a confession out of him."

"You can't be serious." Lia was suddenly stern. "So many people have died in the hospital, Ari. You expect us to believe that?"

There had never been any point in lying to Lia. Fickle, forgetful, and moody though she was, she was a world-class psychologist. Ari rubbed her forehead. She shouldn't have expected to deceive her.

But Lia didn't seem particularly bothered by the revelation. "Sorry." Her voice relaxed back to its normal pitch. "It was just so obvious that I had to point it out. If Mikael had died in front of you, that would be a different story. I know you'd never lie about that." The pointed glance she gave Ari suggested otherwise. "But at a certain point, coincidences stop being coincidences."

"What's so odd about it?" Grey asked. "Calvin and Yuri didn't die because Vita kidnapped and locked them up somewhere. But Mikael was more seriously injured than either of them, if the reports are accurate, and he *did* go to the hospital—there's a clear-cut record of his admission, and multiple eyewitnesses. Vita's in custody now, and he couldn't have bought them all off. Besides, even if he could have, it doesn't sound like he *would* have, since he was the one to sell Mikael out in the first place. It doesn't seem very far-fetched to assume he really *was* killed."

"And if Mikael wasn't really Mikael?" Lia smiled slyly at Ari. "You don't have to worry. Your secret is safe with me. I trust your judgment on this, Ari."

Ari sat in silence for a moment, wondering what to say. Lia wasn't much of a threat—she'd probably forget the whole story by the time she got home. And even if she did remember, she'd never go back on her word. Grey, however, was different. He'd never forgive anyone who threatened Lia, not even if Ari somehow managed to convince him that Lia was never really in danger.

But then again, how long could she keep the secret bottled up inside?

"Yeah." She relaxed. "Sorry for lying, Lia. I wasn't supposed to tell anyone."

Grey stared back and forth between them, clearly astonished, but he didn't say a word.

Lia stood up, pulling Grey to his feet with her. "We'll leave you alone now," she said with a bright smile. "Just be safe, Ari."

Grey held the front door open for her, and she started to leave. But suddenly she stopped, turned back to Ari, and added in a low voice: "And don't forget that Vita managed to fool the entire U.S. military. Nobody knows what he did, and we'll never be able to tell them. But don't trust the NDEB to keep him in custody for long."

With that, she disappeared.

How did she know about Vita? She couldn't have known that unless she also knew about Kira.

Ari hugged a pillow to her chest, musing.

So she must've figured out the whole thing.

But how?

There was no point in guessing. Ari's secrets might be out in the open, but Lia would never tell hers. Perhaps there really were some things that were better left unsaid.

CHAPTER 21

She stared at the train whizzing by, mesmerized by the blur, struggling to read the number on the cars. It had been so long since she'd taken a train, especially a train in a foreign country, that she'd forgotten where to look. The English-language guide she'd been given was just as confusing as the real thing, and she hoped she wouldn't miss her connection just because she didn't know which car to get into.

As the train slowed to a grinding halt, squealing until she covered her ears, the doors opened, and she saw a familiar face hiding behind the crowd of strangers. She pushed her way through the passengers and stood next to him. He was on his phone, paying no attention to his surroundings. But he looked up when he saw her, and he smiled.

"Are you ready?" he asked.

She enumerated on her fingers. "Passport, check. Résumé, check. Foreign language skills, zero. I'd say I'm as ready as I'll ever be."

"Did you say your goodbyes?"

"I did. But I'm not leaving forever. I owe you a lot, but even you couldn't ask me to do that." She pulled out her phone and searched through her emails, then showed him her screen. "One year. That's how long they allowed me to defer employment."

The train began to move, and they tumbled into their seats. The faded faux velvet sent a cloud of dust up into the air, obscuring the view out the window. She ran her finger along the table that separated them, and it came away dark brown. It reminded her of where she'd come from and where she'd been.

"Consider this a new adventure," she said suddenly. "I'm coming with you because I think we're both the same kind of deranged, and I think we can help pull each other out. The simple fact that we were able to forgive each other must mean that God Himself wants us to succeed because that's not something either of us could've managed on our own. But I don't have any delusions about the future. The story doesn't end here just because we aren't trying to kill each other anymore."

He gazed out the window, distracted, before replying. "You have something specific in mind."

"I do. I don't think we've beaten Vita yet."

They were picking up speed, exiting the dark station. The car was flooded with warm sunlight. Her skin prickled.

"There might come a time," she continued, "when you have to reveal your identity so he can be convicted for the real crimes he committed long before he caught the NDEB's attention. If you had to, would you?"

She knew what his answer should be. If he'd told her the truth about what his plan had been all along, he'd never hesitate, not even for a split second. He would have already decided long ago.

"Of course." His tone was soft and quiet, barely carrying over the sound of the train, but it was sincere. "I would have done it already if I thought it would help."

The other passengers were staring at them, evidently bothered by the fact that they were still talking when the car was supposed to be completely silent. She settled back in her seat and pulled out her journal and pencil, the ones she hadn't touched since she'd left Seattle, and spread them on the table in front of her.

SO SECOND, AND THIRD, AND FOURTH, AND FIFTH CHANCES REALLY DO EXIST. SPILLED MILK CAN BE PUT BACK IN THE BOTTLE. ENEMIES DON'T ALWAYS STAY ENEMIES. WHAT AM I SUPPOSED TO BELIEVE NEXT—THAT EVEN VITA MIGHT SOMEHOW BE REDEEMABLE? NO, I DON'T THINK HE'LL PUT IN THE WORK FOR THAT.

NO MATTER HOW MUCH WE BOTH WANT IT, I DON'T THINK KIRA AND I WILL EVER SEE EACH OTHER AS FRIENDS AGAIN. ALLIES, MAYBE, BUT THAT'S ALL. ONE DAY, WE'LL PROBABLY DRIFT APART. OR IF VITA DOESN'T GET HIS REFORMATION ARC, WE MIGHT BECOME TEAMMATES AGAIN. WHO KNOWS?

FRIENDSHIP WASN'T WHAT SAVED US. IT WAS THE SIMPLE REALIZATION THAT NOT ONLY WERE WE FAILING MISERABLY, BUT WE WERE ALSO DRAGGING EVERYONE ELSE DOWN WITH US THAT PUSHED US TOWARD LETTING GO OF THE PAST. AND I DON'T THINK WE COULD'VE DONE THAT ON OUR OWN NO MATTER HOW MUCH WE WANTED TO.

I CAN'T HELP THINKING THAT AS MUCH AS WE WANTED TO WRITE OUR OWN STORIES, WE WERE NEVER THE AUTHORS. WE WERE PUSHED TOWARD FORGIVENESS AND SAVED BEFORE WE EVEN KNEW WHO TO THANK. BUT I'M DETERMINED TO FIND OUT IF WHAT CALVIN SAID ABOUT FORGIVENESS WAS TRUE BECAUSE IF IT WAS, THERE'S HOPE FOR US YET. IF THERE IS A WAY FOR US TO BE TRULY REDEEMED—NOT JUST IN OUR OWN EYES, BUT IN THE GRAND SCHEME OF THINGS—I WON'T STOP LOOKING UNTIL I FIND IT.

For more information about
Lauren Smyth
and
With Love From the Past
please visit:

www.laurensmythbooks.com

For more information about
AMBASSADOR INTERNATIONAL
please visit:

www.ambassador-international.com

Thank you for reading this book. Please consider leaving us a review on your social media, favorite retailer's website, Goodreads or Bookbub, or our website.

Alisen, a teenage girl, is routinely awakened by the same terrifying dream.

The nightmare gets more detailed and longer every night, but the terror remains the same. She tries to dismiss it as something she ate, or maybe a book she read, but then she meets Kale.

Kale is having the same nightmares.

Believing there must be a deeper meaning, Alisen and Kale delve into politics and biblical prophecy. Together, they discover that everything in their dreams has a counterpart in real life, which leads them to believe that something terrible is coming. Is there any way avoid this catastrophe and save thousands of lives? Or will their worst dreams come true? They must choose whether to turn to God or to each other to save them from the very end of the world.

Stories of the Night combines political intrigue, biblical prophecy, and military adventure into a suspenseful story that leaves the reader with the choice of where to place their ultimate hope.

Barely out of their teens and trained as assassins, Rigel members are taught that the Kalideyes are evil and must be destroyed.

Makise—now named Maru—and her team fight against all odds during their training within the Rigel organization to rid her country of the dreaded and mysterious "people" called Kalideyes. Facing horrors, nightmares, depression, and injuries, how many will survive?

As Maru prepares for her first mission, she realizes that relying on herself in times of crisis isn't enough, but her teammates are as broken as she is. When she is forced to fight for her life, who will be there to save her?

It won't be long before Maru learns the truth behind the enemy and an even bigger truth, but are these enough to lead her to safety?